Battle of Mount Badon

OF

ONCE AND
FUTURE
HEARTS
BOOK 6.0

TRACY
COOPER-POSEY

STORIES RULE
EDMONTON • ALBERTA

Praise for the
Once And Future Hearts
series

Imagine how good is the author in her craft that she is capable of surprising us here readers even though the Arthurian cycle is one of the most rewritten one in western literature.

What a great storyteller! I never thought that anyone could tell an Arthurian tale as well as Mary Stewart, but Tracy Cooper Posey has succeeded. I am just in awe of her ability to meld historical detail with legends and turn out a mesmerizing story.

It takes me back to the magic I felt when reading Mary Stewart's stories of Merlin. Tracy Cooper-Posey has written another winner!

As a long time, self proclaimed Arthurian Legend junkie I couldn't wait to dive into Tracy Cooper Posey's new series. Tracy once again proves to be a master story teller as she weaves the delicate threads of this beloved legend into her own.

Oh my goodness. Of course I was not sure what to expect with this but what I got was a wonderful story set in the time just before King Arthur. Invading Saxons, Romans, Kings, princesses, mysteries, Merlin, and romance? Wonderful beginning to a new series and I cannot wait to read more.

I also love the fact that her female characters are definitely not boring, whiny or TSTL.

Tracy Cooper Posey is brilliant at weaving stories with individuals that are completely believable in their thoughts and dialogue.

Ms Tracy has an amazing way of telling a tale. It's magical :-)

Maps

GREAT
BRITAIN

Segontium
Yr Wyddfa

Ynys Witrin
Camelot

Venta Belgarum

Mount Badon

Tintagel
Dinsule

Who's Who and What's What

Aeron: Guenivere's horse.
Accolon: Accolon of Gaul. Minor son of Gaulish king. Companion to Uther.
Aglovale: Son Pellinore and Alis. See <u>Listenoise</u>
Agravaine: Son of Lot. See <u>Lothian</u>
Alis: Wife to Pelinore (dec.) see <u>Dunoding</u>.
Alun: King of Brocéliande. See <u>Brocéliande</u>
Amaria: Daughter of Mair & Arawn Uther (See Corneus)
Ambrosius Aurelianus: (Welsh: Emrys Wledig). High King of Britain (dec.) See <u>Pendragon</u>.
Anwen Idria: Daughter of Idris & Rhiannon. See <u>Strathclyde</u>
Anwen of Galleva: Heroine, *Pendragon Rises.* See <u>Galleva</u>.
Arawn Uther: Son of Arawn and Ilsa. See <u>Brocéliande</u>. Husband of The Lady of Corneus. See <u>Corneus</u>
Arawn: Hero of *Dragon Kin.* King of Brocéliande. See <u>Brocéliande</u>.
Arthur: Son and heir of Uther Pendragon and Igraine. See <u>Pendragon</u>.
Ban of Benoic: Brother to Bors, and exiled from his own kingdom by Saxon incursions. See <u>Benoic</u>.
Bedivere: Welsh: *Bedwyr.* "Bedwyr of the Perfect Sinews". Oldest son of Bedrawd, Duke of Corneus. See <u>Corneus</u>.
Belenus: Lancelot's horse
Bevan: King of Calleva. See <u>Calleva</u>.
Blavet: Large tidal river, location of Lorient, capital of Brocéliande, Lesser Britain.
Bors the Elder: King of Guanne. See <u>Guanne</u>.

Bors the Younger: King of Guanne. See Guanne.

Brandegoris: Brandegoris of Estangore. See Kernow.

Brandérion: Village in Lesser Britain, the birth place of Ilsa.

Brennus: Idris' horse.

Brigid: Caradoc & Ula's daughter. See Brynaich

Budic: King of Morbihan. See Morbihan.

Cadfael: Hero of *Born of No Man.* See Dunoding.

Cador: Duke of Cornwall. See Cornwall.

Cai: Son of Ector. Companion to Emrys. See Galleva.

Cailleach: Cara's horse

Calleva: Kingdom in the south of Britain, neighbouring Cornwall.
. See Calleva.

Campbon: By the great Briére swamps of Lesser Britain. Capital of Guanne.

Cara: Caradoc & Ula's daughter. See Brynaich. Heroine of *Battle of Mount Badon.*

Caradoc: King of Brynaich. See Brynaich

Carnac: King Budic's summer residence in Lesser Britain, where Ambrosius and Uther prepared to take back Britain from Vortigern. See Morbihan.

Claire of Brandegoris: Mother of Elyan the White by Bors the Younger. See Kernow.

Claudas: Frankish King and conquerer. See Berry.

Coria: Corbridge, in modern parlance.

Cynbel: Athur's horse

Devian: Daughter of Mair & Arawn Uther (See Corneus)

Dinadan: Son of Brunor. Siblings: Breunor, Daniel. See Kernow.

Dindrane: Daughter Pellinore and Alis. See Listenoise.

Dornar: Bastard son of Pellinore. See Listenoise.

Doward: Hill fort where Vortigern perished.

Ector: Count of Galleva. See Galleva.

Elaine of Listenoise: Daughter of Pellinore and Alis. See Listenoise.

Elaine: Ban of Benoic's wife. See Benoic.

Elen: Daughter of Arawn and Ilsa. See Brocéliande. Wife of Cador of Cornwall.

Ellar: Lot's seneschal

Elyan the White: Son of Bors the Younger and Claire of Brandegoris. See Guanne.

Emrys Myrddin: Son of Idris & Rhiannon. See Strathclyde

Evaine: Bors the Elder's Queen. See Guanne.

Forest Sauvage: Where Galleva is located, close by Hadrian's Wall. See Galleva.

Gaheris: Oldest son and heir of Lot. See Lothian.

Gareth: Son of Lot. See Lothian.

Gawain: Son of Lot. See Lothian.

Gorlois: Duke of Cornwall. See Cornwall.

Guanne: Kingdom in Lesser Britain. See Guanne.

Guenivere: Welsh: *Gwenhwyfar*. See Camelard.

Hector de Maris: Half brother to Lancelot du Lac. See Benoic.

Héric: Ban of Benoic's lands, within Guanne, Lesser Britain.

Hoel: Hoel the Great, Hoel of Brittany. King of Morbihan.

Horsa: A Saxon leader

Idris the Slayer: Northern warrior. See Lothian.

Igraine: Daughter of Emlawdd Wledig. Wife to Gorlois of Cornwall. See Cornwall and Pendragon.

Ilsa: Heroine of *Dragon Kin*. See Brocéliande.

Iseult of Ireland: Daughter of Anguish of Ireland and Iseult the Elder.

Kahedin: Son of Hoel. See Morbihan.

Kay the Stalwart: Son of Idris & Rhiannon. See Strathclyde

Keincaled: Gawain's horse.

King of the Magyars: Husband to Julia. Father of Sagramore. See Kernow

Lady of the Lake: A title bestowed upon powerful women who control the Perilous Forrest and the Lake at the heart of Brocéliande. The title is not hereditary. See The Perilous Forest.

Lamorak: Son of Pellinore and Alis. See Listenoise.

Lancelot of the Lake: aka Lancelot du Lac. See Benoic.

Leodegrance: King of Camelarde.

Leolin: Mair's horse

Lot: King of Lothian.

Lowri: Daughter of Cadfael and Lynette. See Dunoding.

Luca: Daughter of Mair & Arawn Uther (See Corneus)

Lucan: Son of Bedrawd, Duke of Corneus.
Lynette the Elder: Heroine of *Born of No Man*. See Dunoding.
Mabon: King of Calleva.
Maela: Daughter of Vortigern. Wife to Mabon. See Calleva.
Mair: Daughter of Bedrawd, Duke of Corneus. Heroine of *High King of Britain.*
Mared: Daughter of Bors the Elder. See Morbihan.
Mark: Brother to Tristan the Elder. See Kernow
Merlin: Myrddin Emrys. See Pendragon.
Morbihan: Kingdom in Lesser Britain. See Morbihan.
Morgan le Fey: Daughter of Gorlois and Igraine. See Rheged.
Morguase: Daughter of Gorlois and Igraine. Wife of Lot.
Morlaix: Kingdom north of Brocéliande, in Lesser Britain.
Nareen & Isolde: Caradoc & Ula's twin daughters. See Brynaich
Newlyn: Caradoc & Ula's son. See Brynaich
Nimue: Lady of the Lake. See The Perilous Forest.
Pellinore: King of Listenoise.
Percival: Son of Pellinore and Alis. See Listenoise.
Perilous Forest: The heart of the Brocéliande forest, where The Lady of the Lake lives.
Rhiannon: Daughter of Anwen and Steffan. Companion to Cai and Emrys. See Galleva
Sagramore: Son of the King of the Magyars and Julia, Princess of Rome. See Kernow.
Scorff: Smaller river that runs into the Blavet by Lorient. Fresh water river.
Steffan of Durnovaria: Hero, *Pendragon Rises*. See Galleva
Tewdwr: Son of Hoel. See Morbihan.
Tielo: Rhiannon's horse
Tintagel: Fortified rocky island connected to mainland Cornwall by narrow natural bridge of rock.
Tor: Bastard son of Pellinore. See Listenoise.
Tristan the Elder: King of Kernow.
Tristan the Younger: Bastard son of Tristan the Elder. See Kernow.
Ula: Caradoc's queen. See Brynaich
Urien: King of Rheged.

Uther: Uther <u>Pendragon</u>. High King of Britain.
Uther Rawn: Son of Mair & Arawn Uther (See Corneus)
Vannes: Principal town of the kingdom of <u>Morbihan</u>.
Vedra River: The Tyne, in modern parlance.
Veris: Son of Mair & Arawn Uther (See Corneus)
Via Statra: Roman road between Vannes and Corseul, Lesser Britain
Vivian of Maridunum: Mother of Merlin.
Vivian: Accolyte of the <u>Perilous Forrest</u>. Lover of Nimue.
Vortigern: High King of Britain. Died at Doward. Succeeded by Ambrosius. Wife: Olwen. Sons: Vortimer, Catigern. Daughters: Maela.
Ynnis Witrin: Avalon.
Yr Wyddfa: Snowden

HOUSES, CLANS AND TRIBES

BENOIC

<u>Ban & Elaine</u>
Ban: King of Benoic
Elaine: (see <u>Brocéliande</u>)
Hector: Ban's son (by Suzanne de Maris)
Lancelot du Lac: Their son

BERRY
Claudas: King
Claudin: His son
Dorin: His son

BROCÉLIANDE

<u>Arawn & Ilsa</u>
Arawn: King of Brocéliande
Ilsa of Brocéliande: Arawn's queen. (See <u>Morbihan</u>)
Elaine: Arawn's sister (see <u>Benoic</u>)
Evaine: Arawn's sister (see <u>Guanne</u>)
Alun: eldest son of Arawn & Ilsa, King of Brocéliande

Arawn Uther: second son of Aran & Ilsa
Elen: Daughter of Arawn & Ilsa (see <u>Cornwall</u>)

BRYNAICH

<u>Caradoc & Ula</u>
Caradoc: King of Brynaich
Ula: Caradoc's queen.
Brigid: Caradoc & Ula's daughter
Cara: Caradoc & Ula's daughter
Nareen & Isolde: Caradoc & Ula's twin daughters
Newlyn: Caradoc & Ula's son

CALLEVA

<u>Mabon & Maela</u>
Mabon: King of Calleva
Maela: Mabon's queen. Daughter of High King Vortigern & Olwen.
Bevan: Mabon & Maela's son. King of Calleva (see below)
Bryn: Mabon & Maela's son. Partner of Druston (see <u>Dunoding</u>)
Lynette The Younger: Mabon & Maela's daughter. (See <u>Dunoding</u>)
<u>Bevan & Lowri</u>
Bevan: Mabon & Maela's son. King of Calleva
Lowri: Bevan's queen. (see <u>Dunoding</u>)
Branwen: Bevan & Lowri's daughter
Eira: Bevan & Lowri's daughter
Martyn & Trevor: Bevan & Lowri's twins ons
Betrys: Bevan & Lowri's daughter
Deryn: Bevan & Lowri's daughter

CAMELARD

<u>Leodegrance & Gwenhwyfach</u>
Leodegrance: King of Camelard
Guenivere: Leodegrance's daughter

CORBENIC

Pedr: King of Corbenic. aka The Fisher King
Elaine: Pedr's daughter

CORNEUS

Bedrawd: Duke of Corneus (serves Kernow)
Bedivere: Bedrawd's son, companion to Arthur
Lucan: Bedrawd's son, companion to Arthur
Mair: Bedrawd's daughter. The Lady of Corneus, after Bedrawd.
Wife of Prince Arawn Uther (see Brocéliande)

Mair & Arawn Uther
Veris: Son of Mair & Arawn Uther
Devian: Daughter of Mair & Arawn Uther
Amaria: Daughter of Mair & Arawn Uther
Uther Rawn: Son of Mair & Arawn Uther
Luca: Daughter of Mair & Arawn Uther

CORNWALL

Gorlois & Mari
Gorlois: Duke of Cornwall
Mari: Gorlois' Duchess.
Cador: Gorlois & Mari's son (see below)
Gorlois & Igraine
Gorlois: Duke of Cornwall
Igraine: Duchess of Cornwall (see Pendragon)
Morguase: Daughter of Gorlois & Igraine (see Lothian)
Morgan: Daughter of Gorlois & Igraine. aka *Morgan le Fey* (See Rheged)
Cador & Elen
Cador: Gorlois & Mari's son. Duke of Cornwall.
Elen: Cador's Duchess. (See Brocéliande)
Constantine: Cador & Elen's son

DUNODING

<u>Cadfael & Lynette</u>
Cadfael: Hero of *Born of No Man*. Vortigern's War Duke.
Lynette: Cadfael's wife
Bricius: Cadfael & Lynette's son (see below)
Alis: Cadfael & Lynette's daughter (see <u>Listenoise</u>)
Lowri: Cadfael & Lynette's daughter (see <u>Calleva</u>)
Drusan: Cadfael & Lynette's son, partner of Bryn (see <u>Calleva</u>)
Eogan: Cadfael & Lynette's son (see below)
<u>Bricius & Maeve</u>
Bricius: Cadfael & Lynette's son
Maeve of Ireland: Bricius' wife
Cadoc: Bricius & Maeve's son
Tegan: Bricius & Maeve's daughter

GALLEVA

<u>Ector & Druscilla</u>
Ector: Count of Galleva
Druscilla: Ector's wife
Cai: Ector & Druscilla's son. Companion to Arthur.
Steffan & Anwen of Galleva
Steffan: Hero of *Pendragon Rises*
Anwen: Heroine of *Pendragon Rises*
Rhiannon: Their Daughter (see <u>Lothian</u>)

GUANNE

<u>Bors & Evaine</u>
Bors The Elder: King of Guanne
Evaine: Bors' queen (see <u>Brocéliande</u>)
Bors The Younger: Bors & Evaine's son (see below)
Lionel: Bors & Evaine's son
Mared: Bors & Evaine's daughter (see <u>Morbihan</u>)
<u>Bors The Younger</u>
Bors The Younger: Bors & Evaine's son. King of Guanne

KERNOW

Tristan the Elder
Tristan The Elder: King of Kernow
Brandegoris: Cousin to Tristan (see below)
Mark: brother to Tristan (see below)
Tristan: Son of Tristan the Elder
Dinadan: Friend of Tristan's.
Brandegoris of Estangore & Julia
Brandegoris: Cousin to Tristan
Julia: Princess of Rome, wife to Brandegoris
Sagramore: Son of Julia and the King of the Magyars
Claire: Daughter of Brandegoris & Julia
Mark of Kernow
Mark: brother to Tristan. King of Kernow

LISTENOISE

Pellinore
Pellinore: King of Listenoise, descendant of Joseph of Arimathea
(see below)
Tor: Pellinore's bastard son and heir
Dornar: Pellinore's bastard son
Pellinore & Alis
Pellinore: King of Listenoise, descendant of Joseph of Arimathea
Alis: Pellinore's queen (see Dunoding)
Percival: Pellinore & Alis' son
Aglovale: Pellinore & Alis' son
Dindrane: Pellinore & Alis' daughter
Lamorak: Pellinore & Alis' son
Elaine: Pellinore & Alis' daughter

LOTHIAN

Lot & Morguase
Lot: King of Lothian & Duke of Orkney
Morguase: Lot's queen. (See Cornwall, and also Pendragon)
Gaheris: Lot & Morguase's son & heir
Gawain: Lot & Morguase's son

Agravain: Lot & Morguase's son
Gareth: Lot & Morguase's son
<u>Idris & Rhiannon</u>
Idris of Lothian: Hero, *War Duke of Britain*
Rhiannon (see <u>Galleva</u>): Heroine, *War Duke of Britain*
Anwen Idria: Their daughter
Emrys Myrddin: Their son
Kay The Stalwart: Their son

MORBIHAN

<u>Budic of Britanny</u>
Budic: King of Morbihan
Isla: Budic's bastard daughter
Hoel: Budic's son & heir (see below)
<u>Hoel & Mared</u>
Hoel: Budic's son & heir. King of Morbihan.
Mared: Hoel's queen. (see <u>Guanne</u>)
Tewdwr: Hoel & Mared's son
Kahedin: Hoel & Mared's son
Isuelt of the White Hands: Hoel & Mared's daughter

PENDRAGON

Ambrosius: High King of Britain (see below).
Uther: Ambrosius' brother & heir (see below)
<u>Ambrosius & Vivian</u>
Ambrosius: High King of Britain (see below).
Vivian: Princess of Dyfed
Merlin: Ambrosius' bastard son by Vivian
<u>Uther & Igraine</u>
Uther: High King of Britain
Igraine: Uther's queen. (see <u>Cornwall</u>)
Arthur: Uther & Igraine's son. War Duke of Britain. (see below)
<u>Arthur & Morguase</u>
Arthur: War Duke of Britain
Morguase: Wife of King Lot (see <u>Lothian</u>)
Mordred: Arthur's bastard son by Morguase

PERILOUS FORREST, The

Nimue: Lady of the Lake
Vivian: Nimue's second in command and partner

RHEGED

<u>Urien & Morgan</u>
Urien: King of Rheged. Cousin to Lot of Lothian.
Morgan: Urien's queen. (See <u>Cornwall</u>)
Owain & Morfydd: Urien & Morgan's twin son & daughter.

STRATHCLYDE

<u>Idris & Rhiannon</u>
Idris: King of Strathclyde.
Rhiannon: Idris' Queen. Foster sister to Arthur.
Anwen Idria: Idris & Rhiannon's daughter
Emrys Myrddin: Idris & Rhiannon's son
Kay the Stalwart: Idris & Rhiannon's son

Chapter One

Venta Belgarum, Britain. Late summer, 496 C.E.

ara had only to step into the narrow street containing the house her family had been assigned to know her simple ambition to bathe in the river through the lagging heat of the afternoon would not be granted. She could hear Brigid's voice raised in harsh protest. Brigid's tone was one she would not dare use at court.

Cara hitched her heavy sword, resettling it on her shoulder, as she quickened her pace toward the little, two-story house jammed between two other almost identical houses. As a rider in the Queen's Cohort, she did not use a scabbard, and she had no belt to thrust the blade through and carry it that way. Leather for belts was scarce and used for armor, instead. Those who walked behind her must simply stay out of the way of the naked blade. She did not have the patience or energy to do aught but let it lie over her shoulder. It had been a hard morning's work on the training field.

As she grew closer, Cara heard Newlyn speaking. Her brother's voice had deepened in the last few years and didn't match his dewy face. The figure of the boy would soon catch up with the voice of the man, though. War had a way of making everyone seem older than they were.

What was the shouting about? What had happened? Why were Brigid and Newlyn arguing? She could hear the clatter of dishes drifting through the open shutters, too.

Cara picked up her pace. The heat kept most people indoors through the sleepy afternoon, although if this noise continued, the families in the surrounding houses would rouse and come to investigate.

She pushed open the unbarred door and closed it behind her. The air in the house was warm and closed in, despite the open shutters. No breeze stirred through the windows. There were no windows on the other side of the house to let the air pass through. The back of the house stood against a house on the next street. Both sides of this house were shared by the houses on either side, too. It was an aspect of living in a city which Cara did not particularly like.

Although there was much about living in a great city like Venta Belgarum which she had learned to suffer with, for the honor of fighting in the Queen's Cohort. Belonging to the Cohort let her hew Saxons, as many as she could.

Cara ignored the still, prickly heat of the little room and took in the activity of her family.

Brigid stood at the rough worktable, folding and stuffing linens into one of the great packs which had traveled on the cart with them from Brynaich, in the north. She looked upset, which was not unusual. There was a great deal about city life Brigid did not enjoy, either. She tolerated it because being here allowed her to mingle at court.

Now, though, her pale red hair was in disarray and she wore no jewelry, not even her precious enamel earrings. Her dress was one of roughest linen, with the chaff still showing in the threads, undyed and wrinkled. Brigid normally took pains with her appearance and fussed over the few ornaments and beauty aids they had obtained.

Newlyn stood in the corner of the room by the front window, his arms crossed, his gauntlets fisted tightly. He scowled, too. He was the one member of the family with her father's black hair. Everyone else had acquired some version of her mother's Saxon white hair, mixed with the black of her father.

The twins were both crying, beside Newlyn. Nareen's cheeks were blotchy with tears, matching her hair. Isolde's almost-white hair stuck out at angles. She sniffed as she took items from the shelf and pushed them into another big pack, to clatter against whatever was already in the pack.

Cara turned to her mother. Ula stood at the end of the table, wrapping loaves and hunks of meat in cloth with quick, practiced movements. She pushed them into another of the packs. Her white, straight hair shifted against her shoulders as she moved. She was a tall woman, with a small waist despite bearing five children.

Inside the pack, Cara could see the last of the precious flour and the three remaining apples she had scrounged from the abandoned orchard on the far side of the keep, three days ago.

"What is happening, mother?" Cara demanded, dropping her sword to the table.

"We are to give up our house!" Brigid cried. "It is so *unfair!* There are six of us, and barely enough room in this house as it is. Now we must make way for someone else!" She rammed the folded linen into the pack, which wasted the effort of folding it in the first place.

Nareen gave a little, breathless sob and sniffled.

"Give up...? Who is demanding we give up the house?" Cara clenched her fists. "Where are we to go? They cannot do this to us!"

"'They' are not doing anything to us," her mother said. Ula's voice was low and musical, even when she was stirred to hot emotion. Cara did not think she was angry now, though. Her mother seemed to be the calmest in the room.

"I don't understand," Cara snapped.

"Mother *gave* them the house," Newlyn said. His tone was harsh.

Cara's mouth dropped open. "Is this true, mother?"

Ula straightened. "I do not like your tone, daughter."

Cara drew in a breath, quashing her disbelief and irritation. It had been many years since her mother disciplined her with more than her voice. Only, Ula had been trained by *her* mother how to fight and use her strength. The note in Ula's voice was a warning that Cara had pushed her tolerance close to the edge with her sharp demand.

"I apologize," Cara said, fighting to keep her voice moderated and pleasant. Brigid had learned the way of it far better than Cara had. "May I know why you gave up the house?"

Ula nodded and went back to wrapping the last of the small loaves on the table. "King Bevan and his queen and their family... and most of Calleva, too—they have been burned out of their homes."

Another kingdom fallen to the Saxon flaming bows. Cara's middle tightened and her heart ached with fury.

"When the messenger King Bevan sent reached Cai, I was there," her mother continued. "I offered this house for Bevan and his kin. There are eight of them just in his immediate family and no large houses left in the city. It is appropriate we give them this one. They will be here by sunset."

The house was not *that* large. No houses outside the King's keep were large. This one barely contained the six of them. Cara couldn't imagine a family of eight squeezing into it, although that was not her concern.

"He gets our house because he's a king," Newlyn growled. His arms were still folded.

"Father was a king, too," Isolde said, beside him.

Ula looked up, frowning. "It has nothing to do with rank. There are more of them than there is of us, that is all. They have just lost their home and everything they possess. They will be upset and the comfort of a roof and a soft bed will be a kindness for them."

"*We* lost everything, too," Brigid said darkly, snapping the strap closed on her pack with a sharp tug.

"Six years ago," Ula replied. "And now, see, there are things we must pack in order to move. We have food and clothes which they do not. Be charitable, Brigid. Selfishness makes your face settle in ugly lines."

Brigid immediately smoothed out her expression.

Cara shrugged and unbuckled her armor, more than happy to take the hot garment off and let the air bathe her torso. "I don't care where we live, as long as I remain with the Cohort." She grew still, the horrid thought only now occurring to her. "We *are* staying in Venta Belgarum, aren't we, Mother?"

Brigid gasped, growing pale, as she lifted her head to stare at their mother with wide eyes. She would not want to give up her tenuous place at court any more than Cara could bear to give up her position in the Cohort.

"I am to meet with Cai this afternoon, to find a house we can use," her mother replied.

Relief touched Cara.

"What if there are no houses we can use?" Nareen asked, her voice rising high. "What if we have to live outside the walls, in a wagon or a tent, or on the ground?" Horror made her damp cheeks grow paler. More and more people had taken to living outside the walls of Venta Belgarum in makeshift shelters, as refugees from across Britain flooded into the city. Most of them were burned out or forced off their lands by Saxon bands who raided, burned and looted wherever they went. The temporary housing outside the walls bore little relationship to the ordered camp Arthur's army had once maintained there. This despite most of the pavilions and shelters the army had used being pressed back into service for the homeless in the city.

Bedivere, the war duke and Arthur's marshall, had spared a little of his attention to arrange patrols of armed soldiers to guard the borders of the outside quarters. Although patrols and guards did not serve as well as a high, stout wall.

"If it comes to it, we will live outside the walls," Ula told Isolde. "While we have food and a cushion upon which to rest our heads, we will be thankful." Her tone was firm.

Cara reached to the shelf which Isolde was slowly clearing and snatched up one of the three wine flasks sitting there. There was little food and most of it was preserves from previous years' harvests, for the Saxons had burned this year's crops. Yet there was always plenty of wine, which could be stored almost forever. This flask was slightly less than half full. She unstopped it and drank deeply. With a pause in between to breathe, she emptied the flask in two big mouthfuls.

Newlyn's smile was admiring. Her mother, though, made an irritated click of her tongue.

Cara waggled the empty flask in her fingers. "Empty. Now there is less to carry."

Newlyn snorted, his arms uncrossing and hanging free for the first time since she had stepped into the house. He resettled the sword on his hip—*he* had been given a belt and a scabbard. "I am on duty soon. I must go."

Brigid rolled her eyes. "*So* serious."

"Newlyn has his role to play, as have we all," Ula chided her.

"He's guarding a *field!*" Brigid pointed out, her tone disparaging.

"The last oat field still standing," Isolde replied. She and Brigid usually took opposite sides of any argument.

Cara reached for the last flask of wine before Isolde could pack it away. "What good do guards do, anyway? How does one stop a flaming arrow out of the dark?"

"Cara," her mother said, her tone chiding.

Cara drank a mouthful of the wine from the new flask. It was sour. With a grimace, she jammed the stopper back in the flask and tossed it back to Isolde, who dropped the pack in her hands in order to catch it.

As Newlyn opened the door and stepped outside, Cara removed the last of her armor and plucked the simple tunic she wore beneath away from her sweaty flesh. "What do you want me to do?"

Ula buckled the straps on her pack and straightened. "I must meet with Cai and learn where we are to stay, now. Direct the last of the packing, Cara. We have yet to deal with the upstairs rooms."

"Mother, I am older than Cara!" Brigid protested. "I can direct the packing."

"Cara has accepted that this move is necessary, unlike you, Brigid. She will ensure that the deed is done by sunset."

Brigid scowled, another unlovely expression she never used at court. "Cai, Bedivere, Percival, Druston...none of the senior officers are giving up their quarters for families." Her tone was sour.

Ula nodded. "They live in the poorest and smallest quarters on the very edge of the city, where they can guard both the walls and the people inside it. No one lives in luxury, Brigid."

"Even King Arthur eats squirrel," Cara added.

Brigid moaned, for she hated squirrel meat with a passion.

Ula patted Cara's shoulder as she stepped past.

"A roof at least, please, mother!" Cara called after her. She could put up with sleeping on dirt, for soldiers were expected to do so all the time, although there was nothing more miserable than being wet through and smelling of damp wood smoke.

"I will see what I can arrange with Cai," Ula replied, her tone serene.

Chapter Two

Rhiannon sailed into the big hall, her red gown fluttering at both sleeve and hem and her dark hair gleaming. Cai was at the big table, muttering over his lists of houses and cottages and scowling. Bedivere took a moment to be glad that finding shelter for the constant influx of people from across Britain was not his job, before turning to greet Rhiannon.

Rhiannon smiled at Bedivere. "I haven't seen Cai wearing that scowl for many years. When we were children, he would always try to make me write out his assignments for him, even though my writing looks nothing like his."

"We have another family and their people on the way," Bedivere explained.

Rhiannon's expression sobered. "Oh, no! Who is it, this time?"

"Calleva."

"Calleva! So close…" Rhiannon shivered. "The fortifications around Calleva were solid. King Bevan has been improving them for years. If Calleva has fallen…" She shivered, then glanced around the almost empty hall and at the big, high chair on the dais. "Arthur is not here."

"He met with the town aldermen today," Bedivere explained. "The meeting has gone on longer than any of us expected. I am waiting here to speak to him, as the senior officers do every evening before supper."

"There is much to discuss, I am sure," Rhiannon murmured. "From finding more food, more water, more weapons, more... well, everything." Her smile was strained. "It is good that Arthur is not here. I wanted to speak to Cai and Merlin..." She looked around.

"I am here," Merlin said, from behind them.

The druid stood at the big doors into the hall, the bright afternoon sun behind him, dazzling everyone.

The page shut the door with a solid thump, cutting off the light and the heat. In the dimmer light, the gray in Merlin's hair showed clearly, although his black eyes were still bright with youth and energy. He nodded at Rhiannon. "You were saying?"

Rhiannon glanced at Bedivere.

"I will leave you—" Bedivere began, for the Queen had not included him among those she sought to speak with.

"You should stay, Bedivere," Merlin said, striding over to the big table where Cai sat. "You need to hear this."

"I do?" Bedivere said, startled.

Rhiannon looked just as surprised. She did not protest, though. She merely raised her brow and moved over to the table.

Merlin pushed aside Cai's lists. "Queen Ula will request this house, Cai. Give it to her." He pointed at the page in front of Cai.

Cai's frown deepened as he checked which house Merlin pointed to. "I cannot give her that one! It's not fit for beasts and besides, there's naught but officers along that street and she's got naught but children around her..."

"There is nowhere else which will satisfy her," Merlin assured him.

Cai blew out a breath and pushed the sheet aside. "Very well, then." He stood and lifted Rhiannon's hand. "Queen Rhiannon."

Rhiannon slapped his shoulder. "Oh, sit down, Cai! Arthur might return at any moment and I *must* speak to you and Merlin before he does."

Bedivere pulled out a stool for her and took a seat on the bench beside Cai. Merlin stood at the end of the table. He wore a simple dark tunic and trews and none of the trappings of office and rank which appeared at court these days.

It baffled Bedivere as to where the men found the brooches and torcs, pins and crowns they wore to distinguish themselves from everyone else. Scavenged from among the wreckage strewn across Britain these days, he guessed. He found it difficult enough to keep his armor, weapons and fighting equipment in good working order, which was essential. It had taken him a month to find a replacement buckle for his belt. He'd scavenged the copper buckle he now wore from among the ashes of another burned-down farmhouse up by Eboracum, in the early summer.

Rhiannon glanced at Merlin, then at Cai. "You can add the house I have been using this summer to your list of empty houses, Cai. I am returning north tomorrow."

Merlin did not look surprised.

Cai rubbed his jaw. "Idris sent for you?" he asked, his voice a deep growl. "He expects you to travel through the gods know how many bands of roving Saxons bent on trouble?"

Rhiannon tilted her head, as if she was silently chiding Cai for his uncharitable thoughts about her husband and king. "Idris demanded I stay right here, in the very heart of Arthur's army. Only, I cannot stay and you know that." She paused. "Merlin knows that."

Cai looked up at Merlin. So did Bedivere.

Merlin remained silent.

Rhiannon sighed. "This summer's campaigns were brutal, Cai.

Bedivere, you are Arthur's war duke. You can confirm this. The last five years have been terrible for Arthur. Last year, the fighting lasted until the solstice. This year, the fighting started earlier than ever—we had alarms from the borders of the Saxon Shore before the first green showed. The northern kingdoms are no better off. Idris does not worry me with details, although I know he is struggling, as all the northern lords are. We are *all* struggling." Her voice was bleak.

Bedivere scratched at the table top with his thumbnail, feeling the rough wood against his flesh. The table was stained and rickety. It, like most of the tables and stools in the hall, had been cobbled together from the remains of other tables.

Everything they lived with, and *in*, these days, was patched and barely holding together.

When Aesc, the Saxon king, was not at the front of his enormous army, leading them into battle against Arthur, he instead directed bands of soldiers out across Britain. The bands moved ever west, deep into territories which had never before seen a day of war. The bands burned crops, houses, villages, roads and whole forests. They killed herds and poisoned wells.

The refugees had begun to stream into Venta Belgarum two years ago. The numbers only subsided to a trickle in the very depths of winter. Cai had taken control of every house in the city, with the aldermen's approval, dispersing refugees and soldiers across Venta Belgarum. Everyone lived cheek-by-jowl and still there was no room. Those who did not wish to be separated from their families and assigned to different houses and beds chose to live outside the city walls, yet still within sprinting distance of the gates.

Cai's next strategy would be to turn out every soldier and officer from their quarters and put them outside the walls. Then he would give those quarters over to the people still sleeping upon the ground.

"Only, I won't do it until I absolutely must," Cai often protested. "The army is all which stands between us and doom at the hands of the Saxons, Bedivere. You tell me—a soldier who is well fed and sleeps upon a bed is far stronger than one who sleeps in the rain with an ear ground into the dirt."

Bedivere had agreed with Cai's priorities and had tried to compensate by posting a heavy rank of guards around the camp beyond the walls. He relied more upon the far-ranging patrols he sent out each day to monitor the lands around the city. An early warning would be more useful than a guard at the gate. It would give everyone time to slip inside the walls before the Saxons arrived.

Aesc's unorthodox tactics ground down the spirit and strength of Arthur's men. The lack of food and clothing and shelter wore away the fortitude of Arthur's people. Rhiannon had merely voiced what Bedivere could see for himself. It was what they could all see. The struggle was being fought everywhere.

While Cai shifted uncomfortably on his bench, Rhiannon said, "In such uncertain times, the kingdom itself *must* be stable. Arthur has no heir…" Her voice faded. Her eyes were troubled. "He must marry, Cai. He must have a son to take his place should… should anything happen to him."

Bedivere also shifted on the bench. The pain in Rhiannon's voice, the knowledge, was discomforting. Why had Merlin insisted he hear this? It was an intimate matter and if it must be spoken of at all, it should be held among those closest to Arthur. Cai and Rhiannon had grown up with Arthur, with Merlin as their tutor.

He glanced up at Merlin, to suggest once more that he should leave. Merlin's gaze was already upon him, in the startling way he had of anticipating what a man would say next.

"Stay and listen," Merlin said softly.

Bedivere swallowed and remained silent.

Rhiannon blinked quickly. "Cai, you can see why I must leave, yes?"

Cai cleared his throat. "I agree he should get himself an heir. It's only right. But—"

"But he will not, as long as I am near at hand," Rhiannon finished, her tone brisk. "Therefore, I must go back to Strathclyde. It can hardly be more dangerous there than anywhere else in Britain these days. I intend to ride with a full complement of northern men around me and my sword strapped to my hip. I will travel as carefully as I can but travel I must."

Cai blew out his breath. Then, with a troubled expression, he nodded. "Aye, it might be best, after all," he breathed.

"And you and Merlin between you must convince Arthur that it is time for him to find a queen," Rhiannon added.

Cai jumped. "Now, wait a minute. It isn't my place to direct Arthur on such a matter. He is my king."

"You're his brother, Cai," Rhiannon said, her voice husky. "He will not listen to anyone else. You and Merlin, though...you two, he will listen to, if you explain it to him properly."

"I suspect the King would rather wait until he has completely defeated the Saxons, once and for all, before worrying about such domestic matters," Bedivere said carefully. It was a reasonable guess, for there were a great many things he had heard Arthur put aside for later.

"Our only concern should be victory over the Saxons," Arthur said frequently in council and around the fire at night. "Everything else can and *must* be put aside in favor of that single ambition. Nothing else will matter if we do not find a way to push the Saxons from our lands and hold the borders closed against them."

Cai nodded, relieved at Bedivere's support. "Yes, yes. Cador's son...what's the lad's name?"

"Constantine," Bedivere supplied.

"Constantine is Arthur's heir until he gets his own. The kingdom will go on whether he marries or not."

Rhiannon shook her head. "Not in the way it must. *Because* the times are so uncertain is the reason he must find a queen. Therefore, I must leave, so that he can. You must convince him of the necessity."

Bedivere thought of Mair, his little sister, who was now Lady of Corneus. She ruled the land in his stead with her husband, Prince Arawn-Uther, supporting her as her war duke. Her leadership left Bedivere free to serve Arthur.

There was a degree of comfort in knowing his lands were in good hands and would be well-managed no matter what happened to him. He could understand Rhiannon's concern, although it was not his place to say so.

He also felt Cai's discomfort as the big man shoved thick fingers through his shorn hair. "Hell's hounds and ravens..." Cai muttered.

"Don't you see?" Rhiannon asked, her voice soft, and endlessly patient. "If I linger here, he will not be able to bring himself to it."

Cai let out a gusty breath. Then, reluctantly, he nodded. He pointed at Merlin. "*You* get to break the news to Arthur. I don't want to be within bowshot of the man when you broach *that* subject."

The corner of Merlin's mouth twitched. "It might help if you sit upon him while I explain it to him, as you did when you were children."

Cai gave a reluctant laugh and Rhiannon smiled, even though the expression did not reach her eyes. Bedivere admired her fortitude and clear thinking. She was putting the High King ahead of her own wishes and risking a dangerous journey north to make sure of it.

The big doors to the hall opened once more with a creak of dry, dusty hinges. The figure silhouetted in the late afternoon sun slipped through the doors and shut them again.

"I thought the hall would be packed with officers," Lancelot said, as he pulled off heavy riding gloves and slapped them against his thigh. "It is as if everyone fell asleep while I was in the north." He moved over to the table, his dark eyes dancing.

"Lancelot!" Cai said, pleased. "You're back!"

Rhiannon patted Cai's hand. "You can give Lancelot my quarters."

Cai rolled his eyes, then got to his feet and thrust his big arm out toward Lancelot. "It is good to have you back."

Bedivere also got to his feet. It would be a great advantage to have Lancelot and his men—and his damn chariots—on the battlefield. As much as he disliked the awkward vehicles, Bedivere was level-headed enough to admit they *were* effective—especially at the beginning of a battle. They broke up the front ranks of the enemy with surprising effectiveness.

In that regard, he disagreed with the older officers—King Mark, Bevan, even Cador and Leodegrance—who all thought the chariots had no place in war. Bedivere *did* agree with them that Lancelot's way of fighting, which seemed to have spread through most of the army, especially among the Queen's Cohort, was an abomination of style and honor.

"No man should need to put two hands on his sword or fight left handed!" King Mark often protested in his gravelly, deep voice. "A third and fourth blade, hidden knives and sharp edges…where is the honor in winning by such means?"

Lancelot's response to such challenges was invariably, "Defeat is defeat. Does it matter how I force the Saxons to submit, as long as they do?" There were few arguments against that logic. Yet roiling in Bedivere's gut was the feeling that Lancelot's way of fighting was simply *wrong*.

He would not hold it against the man, though. Lancelot was a brilliant fighter and useful to have on the field. Bedivere would not discard a weapon because he objected to the curve of the blade. "Are you here to stay, this time?" he asked Lancelot.

"I am here at Arthur's pleasure," Lancelot said, gripping Cai's arm. "Where he sends me, I will go." His eyes danced in merriment. "Although it would be nice if he failed to send me anywhere for a while. The dust of travel stains the bottom of my soul."

"You have spent far too much time in the north," Cai said in agreement. "It feels like years."

"Because it has been," Lancelot assured him. "Five years, on and off—and more on than off. I know every vale and glen on the road north. It would be nice to sleep upon a bed for a while."

"That bed has just been found for you," Rhiannon told him. "Enjoy it while you may, Lancelot."

He bowed his head. "Queen Rhiannon."

Rhiannon glanced at Cai and Merlin. Then her gaze settled upon Bedivere. "Please press Cai and Merlin into doing what I have asked, Bedivere. You are a leader of men. Direct them to the task."

Bedivere cleared his throat. "If I must," he said warily. "Although I suspect that Cai would sit on *me* if I tried."

Cai grinned. "I would jump on you from the top of the tower."

Rhiannon got to her feet. "Well, I will leave you. I hear more of the officers on their way, now. I must pack and prepare for tomorrow." She gave a graceful nod of her head and left.

Lancelot spun to face the table once more. "Is old Pellinore still attending these meetings?"

"I believe he thinks he runs the council," Merlin said, his tone dry.

Bedivere grinned. Pellinore was nearing sixty years of age, yet was still a powerful man in both thought and deed. He had no trouble keeping the younger officers in line. Unlike the other senior officers, Pellinore was a whole-hearted proponent of Lancelot's way of fighting. When Lancelot was not in the city, Pellinore directed the training sessions. The old man would bawl instructions in a powerful voice which carried from the clearing all the way to the city, when the air was still.

"Good," Lancelot said, pleased. "I have a letter for him from Dindrane."

"You were in Listenoise?" Cai asked, startled.

"Carbonec. Dindrane was there. A retreat, she called it. Carbonec is a pious place." Lancelot ran his long fingers through his dark curls, ruffling them. "I don't understand this new-fangled God at all, although Dindrane is devoted to His service. She says it is a family tradition to serve Him."

"Their ancestor was Joseph of Arimathea," Merlin pointed out.

"What were you doing in Carbonec, Lancelot?" Cai asked, his tone suspicious.

Lancelot shrugged. "What else? There was trouble there, just as there is everywhere. I was helping." He glanced around. "Look, Arthur is clearly not about to attend any time soon and I'm parched. There's sure to be a wineskin in the dining hall. Let's go there and wait for him."

"Done," Cai said, sweeping up his rolls.

"Yes, a fine idea," Merlin said. "It sounds as though everyone is there, already." For there was a soft murmur of voices coming from the connecting doorway which gave access to the adjoining dining hall

"It's a hot, thirsty day," Lancelot pointed out, striding over to the doors.

"It is that," Cai agreed, plucking his tunic away from his chest. "It's nearly the equinox. When is this heat going to break, Merlin? Can you See that for us?"

"It will break when it should." Merlin's tone was complacent.

"Says the magician." Cai sounded disgusted.

Lancelot laughed.

The doors shut behind them, leaving Bedivere at the table,

alone.

He could have joined them. It would have been easy enough to walk with them into the dining hall. He knew everyone who might be sitting at and on the long tables in the hall, emptying the wine skins as swiftly as they could.

It was quiet here, though.

Bedivere settled his hip on the corner of the table and studied the closed doors, through which the merriment grew louder. He would know when Arthur arrived, for the noise would abruptly subside. He could join the council then. For now, he would remain here where he could think.

Only, this silent hall was filled with the same worries and concerns which followed him everywhere, these days.

How did one keep an army strong and able to fight when there was no food, few weapons and no means to make more? How did one defeat an enemy who evaded battle on the open field, and instead struck from hidden places, harassing and driving families from their homes and burning their crops?

How did one engage with an enemy who had no honor and would stoop to any means, intent upon slaughtering every last Briton who stood in their way?

Bedivere's heart seemed to creak with the effort of beating beneath the weight of his thoughts. With a thrust of his foot, he rose and hurried across the still room and pushed open the doors.

The false merriment and raucous fellowship enveloped him, muffling the dark voice in his head.

Chapter Three

ara learned only two days later why her mother had accepted the narrow, cramped quarters on the edge of the city.

True, the place had a roof, but that was its only charm. It was a festering box of explosive heat, with the back wall exposed to the sun all day and only a single window. There were no rooms inside, just the open space closed in by the rough timber walls.

They all slept in the same room where they ate. There were no beds. Cara taught everyone the army way of keeping bedding in a tight roll until needed, although in the hot, still nights, they did not need furs or blankets over them.

During the day, they kept the stack of bedrolls in a spare corner, out of the way.

They tripped over each other. Newlyn's tall presence made ablutions and dressing awkward, until their mother nailed a sheet across the corner of the room where they stacked the bed-rolls, for the women to change and bathe behind.

There was no worktable to prepare meals upon and no

stools to sit upon to eat the meals. There was no fireplace to cook the meals over, until Newlyn tore up the plank floor right beneath the window and dug into the earth beneath with his dagger.

"I suppose the officer who had this room must have eaten in the King's hall," Brigid surmised. "I wonder who it was?" Her gaze became dreamy.

Cara rolled her eyes.

The planks Newlyn had ripped up from the floor they placed across four spindly sawn-off willow trunks, to make a worktable. It was inclined to wobble until they pushed it up against a wall and nailed it to the wall with copper nails which Newlyn dug out of the planks themselves.

Cara dealt with the inconveniences and shortcomings by never lingering in the house longer than necessary. She slept there and ate there. Otherwise she spent longer and longer hours training or roaming the woods for nuts and fruit, edible grasses and herbs— anything which could be added to the cooking pot. More could be gathered in these southern woods than could be found in Brynaich. Once Cara learned to identify the edible plants, her pouch grew swiftly full each afternoon.

On the second day, she returned to the house earlier than usual. It was a hot day with thick clouds hanging low over the city, bruised and dark, making the day seem as though it was already turning to twilight. Throughout the afternoon, the clouds rumbled warningly while the air did not stir. Not even the crickets and wasps buzzed in the torrid heat.

Mid-afternoon, though, the air shifted. Cara looked up and around from the base of the oak where she had found tubers. She was not alone in the forest. Dozens of women roamed the trees, always with a heavy contingent of armed soldiers spread out among them to watch their backs while they scraped and plucked and harvested.

The woman crouched by the nearest tree to Cara also looked up and around, startled. Her gaze reached Cara.

Cara watched as the woman's focus shifted to the left side of her face. Then the woman turned away, barely hiding her expression. Cara had seen such faces many times before, though.

The air shifted again. The damp hair at Cara's temples lifted. Brittle leaves stirred in the trees and on the ground.

Everything grew still once more.

The woman returned to digging her own tubers.

Cara blotted her damp brow against the sleeve of her tunic and concentrated on digging out the last root without destroying it in the process. A stout twig was more useful than her knife, which sliced into the roots when she dug.

A breeze washed over her. Cara straightened and turned her sweaty face into the wind. She grimaced. The wind was still stupefying hot and brought no relief.

She stuffed the mangled tuber into her pouch and yanked the pouch closed. She would take the food to the workbench for her mother to find later in the day, then go to the shallow pool, a mile up the river. Swimming in the pool was forbidden, because it was too far from the walls of the city and no soldiers could be spared to guard the swimmers.

Cara did not care. She had reached the end of her fortitude. The hot wind, the heat, the tiny, smelly quarters, was too much. She was used to the open glens and empty lands of Brynaich. There were too many people in the city. There were too many bodies, too close together. Everything was cramped, small and mean.

She was hungry and there would be no meat with tonight's meal. Even if Newlyn caught fresh meat this afternoon, they still could not eat it until it was hung and properly dressed.

Her temper roused by the stack of frustrations, Cara strode through the trees out onto the meadow which spread between the city walls and the tree line. A wide path through the temporary shelters hugging the city walls led directly to the gates. The wind picked up the dirt of the path and flung it up into her face, scouring her skin.

Even the guards at the gate had wound cloth and kerchiefs over their lower faces, to protect their skin. They nodded as Cara passed by. Of course they knew who she was. Her face was far too recognizable.

Once she was inside the walls, the wind was stilted by the houses and roofs. It gusted unevenly along the street with less ability to tear at her skin with its hot fingers.

No one lingered on the streets, either. The wind encouraged them to stay indoors.

Cara turned right directly inside the walls and hurried down the narrow street which ran in front of the huddled-together houses to reach hers. As she approached the house, two men stepped out of the hovel beside hers, both wearing formal tunics and war boots, their swords strapped to their hips.

The taller of the two had dark honey-blonde hair. The other's hair was lighter. They spoke softly together as the shorter one made sure the door of the house was properly shut. None of the doors facing the street had locks...although no one had anything worth stealing, either.

Cara recognized both men because they were together and because of their hair. It was Lord Bedivere and his younger brother, Lucan. From dark blond to lighter blond...and Cara had heard their younger sister, the Lady of Corneus, had pure white hair.

As Cara drew closer, the front door of her house opened and her mother stepped out, wiping her hands on a cloth. The houses were so narrow that simply by stepping through the door, her mother arrived right beside the two officers.

"Oh!" her mother said, startled. "Lord Bedivere...Lord Lu-

40

can. I had no idea this house was yours! I hope my family's activities have not disturbed your rest?"

Cara frowned and moved to her mother's side.

"Queen Ula," Lucan said, bowing his head in a graceful acknowledgement. "We are rarely here for your activities to disturb us."

Bedivere was the quiet one. Cara knew little about either officer, except they were close companions of the King, and highly trusted, skilled soldiers. They were the house of perfect warriors. They dedicated themselves to serving Arthur.

In Cara's private opinion, it made them stuffy and overly dignified. Bedivere in particular spent all his time with the older officers and companions— King Mark and King Pellinore in particular— instead of keeping the company of officers nearer his own age.

Bedivere glanced at Cara briefly, silently acknowledging her presence. Then his gaze returned to her face. Unlike everyone who saw her, he did not tear his gaze away as if he was embarrassed to look upon her. He studied her, without flinching.

Cara dropped her gaze to the pouch on her hip and focused upon the simple act of loosening the ties from around her waist, discomfort plucking her middle.

Brigid emerged from the house, joining the tight circle of people. There were five of them in the street, which nearly filled the full width of it. No one else needed to squeeze by, though.

"My oldest daughter, the Princess Brigid," Ula told the two men.

Cara jerked her head up, suspicion forming quickly. She flicked her gaze over Brigid, from hem to head. Brigid wore the pretty green gown she usually kept aside for when they were asked to attend the King. Her hair had been combed and hung in soft waves down her shoulders. A simple ribbon held her hair back from her temples, instead of the glittering pins she normally wore, although the effect was just as pleasing.

Brigid nodded at Bedivere and Lucan as they both bowed their heads, their hands on the hilts of their swords.

"It is a pleasure to meet you, Princess Brigid," Lucan said, his smile hinting that he spoke nothing but truth. "You are a balm upon weary souls."

Brigid smiled to bring out her dimples. "It is kind of you to say so, Lord…?"

"Lucan," he replied. He waved toward Bedivere. "My older brother, Bedivere of Corneus."

Cara remembered the fuss surrounding the Corneus family in the first few days of *her* family's arrival at Arthur's court. Bedivere had given up his right as the oldest male to rule Corneus as its Duke. Instead, he had arranged for his sister, Mair, to rule in his stead, which allowed him to stay with King Arthur.

Cara couldn't help but admire his dedication and loyalty. Bedivere was a soldier, through and through.

"Oh, Lord Bedivere, I apologize. I did not realize who you were," Brigid said. "You have not been in the great hall when I attend the King."

Lucan laughed. "Bedivere likes to stay out of the way."

Bedivere shifted, as if the topic was uncomfortable, or tedious. "There are already too many officers providing hysterics and drama each evening. I see no need to add to it."

He was just as stuffy as Cara had guessed. Perhaps he was *too* dedicated to being the perfect warrior?

"Now Lancelot is back, the drama will increase tenfold," Lucan added, although he didn't sound upset by it.

"Why would Lancelot's return increase the drama at court?" Ula asked, her tone genuinely curious.

Both men stirred, as if they realized they had been indiscreet.

Cara rolled her eyes. "Because half the court thinks Lancelot's way of fighting is terrible, mother. That's why no one likes him."

Brigid's mouth turned down. She abhorred talk of fighting and battles, for she knew little about either and could not sustain a charming conversation about them.

Bedivere, though, shifted to look at Cara squarely, without flinching. His expression was mild. "You learn to fight with Pellinore and Lancelot, then?"

Cara curled her hand into a fist. She wanted to reach for her sword, only it was propped in the corner of the house behind the bedrolls. "You disapprove." She made her tone flat, for despite his mild tone, she could see something which looked like disappointment in his gaze.

Bedivere raised a hand. "You ride in the Queen's Cohort. You have earned your place among them. I would not dispute your abilities."

"Only you do dispute the wisdom of learning new ways to fight," Cara shot back.

Lucan's eyes widened, as he glanced at his brother.

"Oh, this wind is frightful!" Brigid said in a light voice as the breeze whipped through the narrow street, ruffling everyone's hair and clothes.

Bedivere remained still, as if he did not feel the wind at all. His gaze did not shift from Cara's face. "Why is it necessary to learn new tricks? I slaughter the enemy well enough already."

Her mother stiffened in surprise. Brigid's mouth popped open, as she glanced from Lucan to Bedivere.

Lucan scratched at the back of his head with an awkward expression.

Cara, though, shook her head. "Your ability to slaughter Saxons is undisputed, Lord Bedivere." She paused. "So is mine."

A furrow formed between his brows. For the first time Cara noticed that his eyes were a tawny brown, almost a golden color.

Brigid gave a nervous laugh, trying to disperse the tension.

"Your way, Princess Cara, is not honorable," Bedivere said flatly.

"Your way, Lord Bedivere, will kill us all."

Bedivere's eyes widened.

Brigid gasped.

"Cara!" Ula whispered, her tone a warning one.

Cara shook her head. "Honor is no shield against the Saxons. Was not this summer and the last proof of that?"

Ula gripped Cara's arm. "We will not keep you from your duty, Lord Bedivere. Lord Lucan." She tugged Cara toward the house.

"Thank you, madam. We are expected at the keep," Lucan replied, his tone just as polite as Ula's. He took his brother's arm in a similar manner and turned away, bringing Bedivere with him.

Ula pulled Cara into the house.

Brigid stumbled in after them. "How dare you...you spoiled everything!" Brigid hissed at Cara.

Cara shrugged off her mother's hand and turned to her. "How dare *you!* This is why you made us give up the other house. You wanted us to be here, beside Bedivere and Lucan! You dressed Brigid up like a fowl and thrust her at them! No wonder Bedivere spoke of dishonor!"

Ula did not flinch or grow angry at Cara's remonstrations, which were far beyond what she normally tolerated. Instead her mother just nodded. "Yes, I planned it this way. I didn't know who was in the house beside us. I *did* know this street is filled with officers and sooner or later we would meet them."

"*Why* mother?" Cara cried. "Do you believe either of those men do not know exactly what you were doing out there?"

Ula took the pouch from Cara's hands and tugged at the cord. "Your father died fighting my people, Cara. For his sake, I will *make* these people accept you, for they are all you have. *All* of you. If it takes dishonorable manipulation, then I will do that." She turned to the worktable to shake out the contents of the pouch onto the scoured planks.

Cara's heart thundered unhappily. She remembered Bedivere's steady examination of her face. "We're half-Saxon, mother. They hate us. They will always hate us." She added bitterly, "And they *should*."

Chapter Four

The very beginning of the council meeting was warning enough.

Normally, Arthur would stroll into the hall and mingle with his officers. A grip of a hand, a thump of a shoulder. A jest, a concerned question. Arthur could spread peace and satisfaction the way farmers flung their seeds. Bedivere had often watched Arthur move around the room, and how the officers watched him once he had left their sides.

Bedivere had never seen anyone engender devotion the way Arthur did. Even he was not immune to the power of Arthur's presence. When Arthur spared a moment to speak to Bedivere directly, Bedivere always felt as though his day had grown brighter.

Today, though, Arthur did not quietly stroll into the room and speak to whoever was nearest. Instead, he thrust open the narrow door which led to his private quarters and strode into the room, his fist around the hilt of Excalibur, the knuckles white.

Bedivere straightened on his stool, alerted.

Arthur walked straight to the dais. He curled his hand into a tight fist and hammered on the arm of the big chair.

From the same narrow door, Merlin and Cai emerged. Cai looked deeply unhappy. Merlin, as usual, gave no hint of his thoughts and feelings. He moved to the back of the hall, while Cai walked to the high-backed chair on Arthur's right, at the foot of the dais.

Arthur's hammering silenced the hall. "Sit," Arthur said.

His tone was enough to send everyone to their seats without protest or murmur. They sat and grew silent once more, with none of the usual jokes and comments. The man who settled on Bedivere's left was Bricius. Bricius had been recently made King of Dunoding by Arthur, in honor of his and his family's service to the High King. Dunoding laid west of Snowden. Bedivere remembered the wild, rocky lands from the time when Arthur and his companions had ridden to Segontium to retrieve Excalibur. Those lands had always belonged to Bricius and before him, Cadfael, and on through many generations. Now Bricius was king of that small kingdom. The title was well deserved.

Bricius glanced at Bedivere. He lifted a single brow.

Arthur didn't sit in the high chair as usual, either. He kept his tight fist upon the arm, the other around Excalibur. He quartered the room with his gaze, as if he searched for enemies. In the late afternoon sunlight coming through the high windows, his dark red hair and beard gleamed with fiery highlights. The blue eyes glittered with equal fire.

Bedivere braced himself.

"You should all know that today, I have agreed to be wed." Arthur's voice was hard, with no joy in it.

The soft mutter in response was stilled instantly. Everyone remained upright, their attention upon Arthur. No one dared ask the most obvious question.

Arthur nodded, as if they had. "Leodegrance has accepted terms. After a suitable betrothal, I will marry his daughter,

Guenivere." He looked around the hall, as if he searched for opposition. As if he was braced for it.

No one spoke.

Even Leodegrance, King of Camelard, sitting on his tree stump stool, did not dare look pleased.

Bedivere considered the match as fairly as he could. He'd seen Guenivere only once, several years before. She had been very young but even then, her beauty and poise were remarkable. She had sent a ripple through the army, as soldiers tried to see the great beauty for themselves and perhaps meet her. Leodegrance and Cador, who had fostered her in Tintagel, had wisely kept her cloistered until she returned to Cornwall.

Surely that was not the reason why Arthur had settled upon the girl? Beauty was nothing in the grand scheme of things. Her family, though, was one of the great Roman British families. Leodegrance could trace his ancestors directly back to Rome and the line of Caesars.

Was that her value?

Troubled, Bedivere let the matter lie. It was not his place to question Arthur's decisions.

Arthur said in the same stiff, furious tone, "Travel is too chancy these days. Lancelot, you will take your best men to collect the woman. I put her safety entirely in the hands of my greatest warrior."

Lancelot grew still. Bedivere remembered his yearning wish to remain at court at least for a while. That wish had just been snatched away. Lancelot had been here only two days.

Instead of protesting, Lancelot bowed his head. "As you wish, Arthur." His tone was neutral.

"I do," Arthur said flatly. "Does anyone intend to speak upon this?"

Again, the stifled silence.

Then Gawain cleared his throat. "Would you fling Excalibur at me if I offered my congratulations, Arthur?"

Arthur's jaw flexed. He didn't smile. His gaze shifted around the room again.

It occurred to Bedivere that his expression was that of a hunted man, one who found himself in a corner.

"When might the nuptials be, my Lord?" Druston asked.

Arthur's fingers tightened around Excalibur. "They will take place when I am ready," he said flatly. "Any more questions?" He glared at them all.

No one spoke, this time. No one shifted on their stool.

Arthur nodded. "See to it, Lancelot." He whirled and stalked back to the narrow door, pushed it aside, then shoved it shut behind him.

For several more heartbeats, the silence and stillness held.

Then Dinadan blew out his breath. "That is the first time I've seen a betrothal used as a weapon. He cowed an entire room of men. I must remember it."

A nervous scatter of laughter came in response.

Bedivere let out his own breath, the tension in his middle relaxing. So did other men in the big circle. Abruptly, everyone spoke at once, to their neighbor and across the circle.

Bricius, beside Bedivere, pursed his lips and let out a soft whistle. "It did come from nowhere. Did you know he was even thinking of marriage?"

"I believe he looks only to secure the High King's throne," Bedivere said diplomatically.

Bricius nodded, frowning.

Gawain crossed the floor. "Did you know of this, Bedivere? You didn't look surprised." Before Bedivere could speak, he added, "Camelard! It would be more fitting for him to choose a northern woman, to unite north and south, don't you think?"

Lancelot clapped Gawain on the back, as he joined the group. "Arthur is from the north himself. A southern lady seems appropriate."

"He was born in Tintagel," Bricius pointed out. "It's as south as a man can get. It would be more fitting to honor a house which has been loyal to Arthur from the beginning."

"Which he did," Bedivere inserted. "Leodegrance was among the first to swear fealty."

"So was my father," Bricius said. "My daughter is of the right age to wed, too."

Gawain frowned. "Why a house loyal to him, though? Surely he should use the alliance to stabilize one of the fractious houses?"

"Like yours, Gawain?" Lancelot asked, his tone light.

"We have been loyal to Arthur from the beginning!" Gawain said, his tone heated.

"Clearly, it does not matter which house Arthur picks...there will be one of us at least who objects to that choice," Bedivere said.

Everyone paused to consider, still scowling. The tension eased a little.

King Mark, on the other side of the room, spoke to a tight group of older officers, his deep voice strident. His tone was low. Bedivere could not properly hear was he was saying. Pellinore patted the southern king's shoulder in sympathy.

Pellinore's presence on that side of the room explained why Gawain had crossed to this side. The tension over Pellinore's execution of Gawain's father, Lot, had never fully gone away.

Everyone watched Mark, now.

"Have you read the poem about him?" Lancelot murmured.

Bedivere frowned.

"Poem?" Bricius asked, baffled.

Lancelot smiled. "I had been here a handful of hours when I heard about it...about Mark and..." He glanced around. "The Lady Morgan," he added, his voice low.

"Gossip," Bedivere said, his tone sour.

"Instructive gossip, though," Lancelot replied, his tone thoughtful. "The poem describes Mark as addled and led by...not his mind, shall we say?" He met Bedivere's gaze.

Bedivere sighed. It was common but unspoken knowledge that Mark spent more time in Morgan's bed than his own. He was not the only man to do so. Morgan spread her charms around to reap the benefits of such dalliances. Mark, though, seemed oblivious to her true nature.

Lancelot had spent years fending the woman off, for he precisely understood her nature. His gaze now reminded Bedivere of that.

"Mark will come to his senses soon enough," Bedivere said stoutly. "He is a good man, and wise."

"It's been years already," Lancelot pointed out.

"You are as direct with your mouth as you are with your sword," Bedivere replied, and felt his jaw slacken. He was as surprised at the comment as Lancelot, Gawain and Bricius appeared to be. Where had it come from?

Lancelot, though, didn't take offense. He smiled, instead, his dark eyes dancing. "You insist upon fighting in the old ways, Bedivere, for it serves you. Yet it helps few others. Women, weak and sick men, cannot fight the way you do. Directness serves everyone."

Bedivere thought of the woman he had met today. Cara of Brynaich. She had been utterly direct. Rudely so. Yet every time he came back to that short and provoking conversation, all he felt was a budding sense of admiration. She had been disparaging, yet there was an underlying respect for him and Lucan. She had used the same tone Lancelot used now. It was the chiding, provoking attitude which fellow officers used.

He knew of Cara because Queen Lowri, who led the Cohort, reported daily to Bedivere on the strength of the Cohort. She had spoken of Cara here and there. "The girl is driven by anger," Lowri told him. "Still, anger serves well enough, these days."

Yes, Cara of Brynaich had been angry, beneath her superficial politeness, today. Did the scars have anything to do with that anger? The red markings on her face told a story which Bedivere could easily read. Two slashes across her left eye, running from her blazing red hair—which was darker than Arthur's fiery red—across the socket, and under her cheekbone. The longer scar reached down almost to the corner of her jaw. She had been lucky to not lose the eye. Her high cheekbone and strong forehead had saved her from that.

What Bedivere read from those two sword slashes was that Cara had been facing the Saxon who delivered the blows. Facing him with her chin up...and she had not turned away when he gave her the first cut.

Had she been protecting someone? Her younger siblings?

Perhaps her anger came from being half-Saxon and living in a city filled with people who hated Saxons with a passion which grew with each day of deprivation.

Whatever the source of her fury, her directness was the same as Lancelot's and drove toward the same end; death to Saxons.

Bedivere had to approve of that, no matter what the means or the motive behind it.

As THE PERFUNCTORY MEETING BROKE up with an unsettling feeling of shock, Lancelot moved back to Bedivere's side. "May I speak with you, alone?"

"Outside, then," Bedivere said. "It must be cooler out there by now."

"It will be much cooler later tonight," Lancelot said. "First the sun must set and the rain settle in. Tonight, everyone will sleep well, especially the wounded." He glanced over his shoulder. "If we remain here, we will soon be alone. This table will do."

He pointed to the table where Cai most often muttered his way through his reports and sheets of lists and other vexing administrative matters the big man turned his hand to, when he was not wielding a sword.

Bedivere moved over to the bench Cai used. Lancelot did not follow him. Instead, he strode toward Arthur's high chair, his long legs swinging, and scooped up the flask of wine and the cup which was always laid out for Arthur by the pages.

He grinned as he came back to the table. "Arthur won't mind," he said in response to Bedivere's startled look. "He's probably sitting with his back to a wall, drinking that firewater the northerners make from oats, stewing in his misfortune at having to marry."

He sat and poured the wine into the metal mug, filling it almost to the brim. He pushed the mug carefully toward Bedivere. "That is yours." He raised the flask. "This is mine."

Bedivere smiled and reached for the cup. Lancelot's irreverence matched his directness. In a way, they were both refreshing. Older officers tended to walk stiff-legged around Arthur, treating him with deep reverence while pulling apart his leadership behind his back—all in the name of helping him, of course. The older men had wisdom and experience Arthur did not. He was not fool enough to dismiss their concerns when they voiced them.

"What must you speak with me about?" Bedivere asked, after several sips of the excellent wine. There were cellars full of wine in the bowls of the keep. They might die of hunger, but not of thirst.

"It seems I must take to the road again," Lancelot said.

"My sympathies," Bedivere replied.

Lancelot shrugged. "I do what Arthur asks, always. Yet that

leaves only you behind to protect the city, Bedivere."

Bedivere almost choked over his wine. "There are nearly thirty officers sitting about the room in Council, now. I assure you, I am not the only one who would defend the city, if it comes to that."

Lancelot shook his head. "You are in Arthur's inner circle. There are few of us who are. You, like me, have devoted yourself to his cause, to defeating the Saxons. You might insist upon tradition, although you are an effective fighter, just the same, for those old ways were designed for a man of your strength and height." He waved his hands, dismissing the argument. "Cai has his hands full with the inner turmoil of the city. It is your task to see to its defenses and that is why I must warn you."

Cold, invisible fingers walked up Bedivere's spine. "You consider me not sufficiently braced against Saxon attack?"

"I consider you not sufficiently warned, that is all," Lancelot said. "You have not traveled as I have. You have not seen how it is across Britain." Lancelot lowered his voice. "The Saxons are gaining, Bedivere. If we do not find a way to turn the tide, they will defeat us. Perhaps not this year, but certainly next year. They care not about honor and the forms of battle, not like you do. They are racing across the land like the sea across the summer country— they will drown us all."

The cold fingers turned into a full shudder. Bedivere gripped his cup. He could find nothing to say in response. What did one say when a man predicted the end of all things?

Lancelot drank. "Venta Belgarum is a hard city to defend, Bedivere. It is too big."

"The city has never fallen."

"Because it has never been attacked, not by a foe like this one." Lancelot pushed the flask aside and gripped his hands together. "How can I make you understand? Aesc fights like I do... where do you think I learned it from? He gives no quarter, he will never stand back and let you pick up your sword. He does not care about the rules or honor or how a war is supposed to be fought. He sends men out to burn and plunder and pluck the heart out of us. He slaughters women, children, the sick, the old, the weak, because in his mind, we are *all* his enemies, every last one of us. He does not mean to win a simple war, Bedivere. He means to destroy Britons and remove them from existence. Then he will spread his people out upon the lands he has reduced to ashes and make them his own."

Bedivere swallowed. "They are desperate. They need lands to thrive..." It was the same reasoning Arthur had been using for years, to explain the ruthlessness of the Saxons.

Lancelot shook his head. "They hate us. We need to hate them, if we are to win this." He reached for the flask with a grimace. "When the Saxons reach the city, Bedivere, you must be braced for that hatred." He drank deeply.

"Again, I must ask; you think I am not ready for that?"

Lancelot hissed as his large gulp of wine went down. "I do not know for certain," he said, with a candid tone. "I fight the Saxons because I hate that they are taking our lands and killing our people. Do you know I have not once set foot upon my own lands? They have been denied to me my entire life. I have watched friends fall to the Saxon blades. Now I see homes and villages and whole kingdoms ablaze. I don't just hate the Saxons, Bedivere, I *revile* them. I repudiate their claim to Britain and would happily lay down my life to see them defeated. Only, I would much rather live and see them destroyed. You, though...I do not know why you fight at all. Fury is absent in you. You fight for no reason I can detect."

Bedivere took a sip of the wine. His heart thudded. "I fight to serve Arthur."

"As do we all," Lancelot said dismissively. "You do not approve of my way of fighting, of anything I have said about hate and anger. I know that. No, don't bother to deny it," he added as

Bedivere opened his mouth to speak. "We must disagree on how to slaughter Saxons, even as we work together to ensure they *are* slaughtered. Which is why I warn you now. See to the city's defense, Bedivere. When they come, it will not be the way you expect, the traditional way you think a battle should be joined."

Bedivere drank deeply. Lancelot's words and warning were unsettling, making his gut roil, even as he tried to argue and dismiss Lancelot's concerns. "It is not that I disapprove of you, Lancelot. It is that I do not understand you. Because I do not understand you, I cannot trust you. Do you see?"

Lancelot's gaze was steady, the black eyes holding warmth and a touch of humor. "At last, a direct response." He pushed the flask toward Bedivere. "Here, take the rest of it. I must pack and be on my way. It is cooler to travel in the night and I long to feel the rain on my head." He got to his feet and paused, his long fingers resting on the table. "I am not a complex man, Bedivere. I hate Saxons and I will do whatever I must see them destroyed and peace restored to Britain. That is my only interest in life. Everything I do serves that single purpose."

"Including escorting princesses," Bedivere shot back.

Lancelot threw his head back and laughed. "It will be just my luck the woman is a toad with the conversational skills of a pebble. Ah, well…I serve at the King's pleasure and this he demands of me."

Bedivere sobered. "You were not here when Guenivere first met Arthur. Of course…"

"Why do you say it like that?" Lancelot asked curiously.

Bedivere shook his head. "No, it is nothing. You will learn for yourself soon enough if the princess meets your expectations."

Lancelot gave him a short bow. "Watch the walls, Bedivere!"

"I will," Bedivere assured him.

Lancelot whirled and left.

The hall felt much larger once he had gone.

Chapter Five

It rained all the next day, which made everyone in the city relax. Arguments were forgotten and slights forgiven. Despite the city-wide hunger, people actually smiled as they hurried past each other, their cloaks over their heads as they splashed through muddy puddles.

Cara attended the daily morning training in the big clearing in the forest, a half-mile from the city, taking her place among the ranks of fighters and moving through the drills. The rain pelted them steadily, which she didn't mind, except that it made her hand ache. She was forced to squeeze her sword hilt to offset the slipperiness of the wet leather.

After basic drills, the company broke up into groups to work through practice bouts. After each short bout, the men and women surrounding the pair would discuss each move and counter and alternative moves the opponents might have used, instead.

While the groups worked, Pellinore and his senior officers ranged between the groups, adding more advice and suggestions. Today, Lancelot was once more absent.

Even though Cara enjoyed the training, the ache in her arm

became painful. She moved over to the huge oak on the side of the clearing. Its long branches, thick with dark green leaves, would shield her from the worst of the rain while she rested. She would let her arm recover before returning to her circle.

She ducked under the outer branches and paused. Bedivere sat on one of the big roots lifting out of the dirt. There were no weeds or grasses under the tree, for the canopy was too thick to let sunlight through.

Bedivere lifted his gaze away from the people moving about the clearing to meet hers.

"I didn't know you were here," Cara said.

"Clearly." He paused. "Sit if you wish."

Cara considered finding another tree. Only, that would be too much effort. She did want to rest her arm.

A root thrust up from the ground on the other side of the massive trunk. She settled on it and rested the sword beside her. She put her forearm on her knee. It throbbed. From experience she knew that the more she worked the arm, the less the ache would be on the morrow.

"You need wax."

Cara looked at him. "What did you say?"

"Wax." He lifted his chin, to point at her sword. "When it is wet like this, the leather on the hilt grows slippery. You pour wax on the hilt, then, when the wax is cool but still pliable, you grip the hilt so the wax forms around your fingers. The wax sheds water. You don't have to grip so hard to keep hold of the sword."

"It will ruin the leather," she pointed out.

"Then re-wrap the hilt, once the danger of rain has passed." He shrugged.

"Why are you here?" Cara demanded. "I thought you had no time for Lancelot's way of fighting?"

"I do not."

Cara shrugged and went back kneading her hand and arm,

while watching the training.

Even though Bedivere said nothing, she could still *feel* him sitting there, taking in everything which happened in the clearing. Measuring. Judging.

She turned to him. "You know that honor did not serve us in Rome, do you not?

Bedivere pulled his attention away from the clearing once more. His golden brown eyes settled on her. "Rome?"

She pushed her hair over her shoulder, the rings she used to contain it clicking together. "Yes, in Rome. Hundreds of years ago, we marched upon Rome and confronted their armies. We outnumbered them, but we offered to settle the matter with single combat, to determine the winner."

Bedivere's eyes narrowed. "Let me guess. We won the fight."

Cara nodded. "Only, the Romans turned and crushed us with their armies, anyway! We were retreating, the victory ours. They ignored the honorable conclusion and fought us, anyway."

"Of course they did. They were Romans," Bedivere said, his tone dry.

"They fight just as the Saxons do," Cara added.

"Yes."

His flat answer gave her nothing to respond to. Cara gripped her wrist, digging her thumb into the tendons to relieve the ache.

Bedivere stirred. "Just because our enemies fight without honor, does that mean we must cast ours aside and fight as they do? We should be above such littleness of spirit."

"Even if it means being slaughtered where we stand?"

"I hold my own," Bedivere said. His small smile spoke of his confidence in his strength and skill as a fighter.

"I heard your little sister laid you flat on your back, using Lancelot's way of fighting."

He scowled and stirred. Was he reconsidering sharing his tree with her? Cara said quickly, "Lancelot's way of fighting works for women, who are not as strong as men. It works for the weak and those who cannot fight as you do. The Saxons are indiscriminate about who they fight. They run women and children through with their swords, they sever the heads of anyone they come across with their axes… We can no longer stand on the sidelines while the menfolk fight our battles. We *must* defend ourselves. Lancelot's way of fighting—as dishonorable as it seems to you—lets us win against foe who are bigger and stronger. Why would I *not* use it?"

Bedivere didn't answer. His gaze returned to the people working in the clearing. There was a ring of metal against metal, grunts of effort and sometimes, laughter. Clapping and cheers.

Meanwhile, the leaves at the edge of the canopy dripped tears onto the earth below.

"If that were all which helps you fight, I might agree with you," Bedivere said. "Only, you carry hatred and anger into battle with you."

"*Yes!*" Cara said, her voice hoarse. "Of course I do! I want to kill every Saxon holding a weapon. I want *peace.*"

"Anger skews judgment. It warps your ability to fight." His tone was still cool.

Cara shook her head. "You should let yourself hate them. It would make you stronger than you would ever believe possible."

His eyes widened. He turned to consider her.

The clash of iron came louder. This time, shouts of alarm rose with the clanging.

Cara whirled. "That was behind us!" She lunged and picked up her sword, then peered through the trees. The forest was too dense.

The shout came again. "Saxons! The Saxons are—"

The chopped-off cry sent a shudder through her.

Bedivere stepped out from under the canopy and whistled loudly. Every head in the clearing turned.

He waved. "Saxons!" He pointed.

Cara didn't wait any longer. She plunged into the trees, gripping the damp leather hilt, her heart thundering.

THE WOMAN WAS FAR AHEAD of him when Bedivere ran through the trees toward the sound of battle. He caught a glimpse of her red hair streaming down her back and the blue tunic which peeped beneath her armor.

She was fast. Her long legs gave her speed.

Bedivere let her judge the direction of the fight and find it, while he concentrated on catching up with her.

Behind him, he heard the thud of many other feet, as the people training in the clearing followed him into the trees. He signaled they should spread out.

Pellinore separated the armed warriors in three groups. He gestured that they should circle around and come in behind the clashing fight.

It was a risky move, Bedivere decided. If an entire army of Saxons waited ahead of them, the fighters would run into the body of them and be swallowed whole.

On the other hand, if it was only a small scouting party spying on the city, they could contain them. It would prevent them from passing on to Aesc any knowledge they had gleaned about the city and Arthur's defenses.

Cara brought her sword up over her head, in the typical position Lancelot's fighters used, exposing her belly. She leapt through the trees, screaming.

Bedivere launched himself through the same gap, his sword up in front of him. He was in time to see her bring the big sword—which was larger and longer than most women could control—down upon the shoulder of the nearest Saxon. The Saxon had his back to her and his axe up, ready to bring it down upon the face of a British boy. The boy was one of the young sentries who patrolled around the far borders of the city for just this reason.

The Saxon fell, blood spurting.

Bedivere sized up the tiny clearing in a sweeping glance. A dozen Saxon, one already dead, the second at Cara's feet. The remaining Saxons had the sentries surrounded. The boys milled, their swords half-raised, fear on their faces.

He selected the nearest Saxons and engaged him. Suddenly, he was busy fighting with no more time to think.

The fight did not last long. Pellinore's people rushed in from the other side of the clearing, picked a man each and dealt with him in swift, hard chopping strokes.

Bedivere defeated his man and spun to find another. He was in time to see Cara bring down a second Saxon with hard blows, slashing at his neck and shoulder. She swept his axe out of the way of her belly with a great arc of her sword. Then she swung it high and brought it down in a massive blow which forced the air from her in a harsh, guttural grunt.

The Saxon fell, twitching, and did not try to rise again.

Bedivere moved to where Pellinore stood leaning on his sword, his breath bellowing.

"Everyone, spread out," Bedivere directed, lifting his voice. "Move in pairs. Two miles at least and around the entire city. Scout the land. Make sure there are no other Saxons in the area. As far out as you can and return by sundown. Go!"

Everyone whirled and spread out, slid through the trees and disappeared.

Bedivere gripped Pellinore's arm, which was still mighty despite his faded hair and wrinkled brow. "You must return to the city. Warn them. Get the people inside the gates and shut them, until we know what this is."

"Aesc spying on us, or the overture to battle?" Pellinore nodded, straightening.

Bedivere turned again. The woman, Cara, stood rubbing her arm again. There was no one else in the little clearing who still breathed. Even the young sentries had split up and slipped away. He would remember to praise their stalwart spirit tonight—in front of Arthur, if he could manage it.

"You must come with me, then," Bedivere told Cara.

Her smile was rueful. "I took down two. You took one."

"I noticed."

"Tell me again why anger does not serve me?"

Bedivere put his sword away. "Maybe that is why I came here today." He turned and plunged into the trees, heading south in a big circle which would bring them to the east side of the city.

Cara followed.

Chapter Six

The Kingdom of Camelard centered upon a well-founded fort in the southwest corner of Leodegrance's domain. It could be approached only via a narrow spit of solid ground. Deep bogs defended either side, indistinguishable from the dry land. Lancelot would never have found a way through, if Leodegrance had not insisted upon one of his men accompanying him to show the way.

"There is a reason my lands have not yet succumbed to the Saxons," Leodegrance warned him before he left Venta Belgarum. "I'd rather not see you rot in a bog just yet, so take my man."

Lancelot now appreciated why the Summer Country was named as it was. Everything was boggy or wet with dank, still water. Only in the late summer of the driest years did the land dry and become solid. All of it was a danger to men, horses and wagons, unless one knew the way through it. The hills of land were islands among the deceptively green countryside.

Far to the east, a solitary high peak rose above the horizon, gray with distance. It stayed to Lancelot's sword arm side for the entire last day of their travel. "And that hill, there—whose is that?" Lancelot asked the guide.

"That be Ynnis Witrin, my Lord. The spirits own that place."

Lancelot rolled his eyes. "How far is Camelard from here?"

"Not far, my Lord. If we go too far, we end up in Corneus, which means we've overshot the mark." He laughed mightily at his own joke.

Not long after, the guide pointed. "That's Camelard."

The fort commanded one of the solitary hills which dotted this country, with strong palisades and ditches in concentric rings around the broad, flat top. Smoke rose lazily into the warm morning air.

As they grew closer, Lancelot could see houses built inside the fort. None of them were Roman in style. "I thought the family was Roman?" he murmured.

"Oh, aye, they are, my Lord," the guide said easily. "This here is the fortress they use in troubled times, which is now, isn't it?"

Lancelot grimaced.

"There's a palace, aways beyond, alongside the river and in among willows. It's a grand place, built when the Romans were here. It's terrible to defend. Camelard, though, has never been breached."

"I can see why," Lancelot said, eyeing the narrow, steep track winding up to the massive gates. "That track is scalable only on foot, I judge."

"Right you are, my Lord. We'll be bellowing our breath by the time we reach the top. Brings a warrior to his knees before ever he gets a blow in, it does."

When they reached the gates, Lancelot was ready to agree with the man. He was fit, yet he breathed deeply and his calves ached from the unaccustomed climbing.

A cry went up from the gatekeepers. The gates were unbarred and hauled open.

Lancelot moved back to pat Belenus' neck, for his stallion

bellowed as heavily as he.

The gates swung open, revealing a large paved square, filled with armed men. On the edges of the square were low buildings. In front of them, all manner of activities took place. At least one smithy rang with the sound of a hammer upon iron. Carts unloaded sacks of grain, women carded, spun and wove cloth, enjoying the sunshine and chatting together. More women washed or sewed. Some were making bread upon temporary plank tables.

The sound of industry and peace told Lancelot more readily than any guide's assertion that this place had never been broached. The people behind the walls were too complacent.

He wondered how long it would take the Saxons to teach them the meaning of fear.

Then he shook off the bitter mood and walked into the square. His attitude served no one, least of all him. He reminded himself that he was here on a most joyous duty, utterly unconnected with war.

Except he, Lancelot, was the man charged with the duty because he was Arthur's strongest fighter and commander. If peace held the land, Leodegrance might have escorted his daughter to the High King's side with a full company of courtiers and companions, banners and horns, cushions and color. Instead, Lancelot would hurry the poor woman through Saxon-infested land more treacherous than the bogs they had just passed through, with a contingent of armed men and not a cushion in sight.

Annoyed at the direction of his thoughts, Lancelot frowned and reached for the arm of the nearest boy and gave him a shake. "Here, lad, take my horse. And point me toward where I will find the Lady Guenivere."

The boy glanced down at Lancelot's hand. His face was covered in dirt and sweat. He had been bending over an outdoor oven made of mud, stoking the fire at the bottom with twigs and rubbish. On the shelf above, three round loaves were baking, giving off an aroma of warm, soft bread which made Lancelot's belly clench. He had not eaten or drunk since rising from his bedroll this morning.

The boy wiped his face with his other sleeve—which was also as dirty as his trews and boots. From the smell rising from his clothes, Lancelot guessed he had been tramping about in the bogs at the foot of the fortress. The boy removed the cap he wore, revealing pitch-black hair which gleamed in the sun with a blue hue.

"You must find another boy to take care of your horse, as you have found the Lady Guenivere already. And you are?" Her tone was rich with amusement, low and musical.

Lancelot flexed his fingers, hastily releasing her arm. Only now did he notice the fine line of her chin and nose and the fullness of her lips, which were just as dirty as the rest of her.

He stepped back and bowed his head. "Lancelot of Benoic, at your service, Lady Guenivere." He straightened. "You are not what I expected."

She laughed, showing even, white teeth. "Lancelot du Lac, King Arthur's companion and greatest warrior...you, I did not expect at all." She paused and glanced down at herself. "Clearly," she added, her tone dry.

His laugh caught him by surprise. Lancelot patted Belenus' neck, as he snorted at the sound of merriment. "We'd best start again, shall we? I will find a place with a roof, oats and water for my horse. You might wish to...change," he added diplomatically.

"There is news?" Guenivere stepped closer, her voice lowering.

She expected bad news, Lancelot realized. She was more aware of the true state of Britain than anyone else in this busy square seemed to be. He gave her a small smile. "Good news," he assured her. "The type of news I am sure you do not wish to receive out here, for everyone to learn at the same time."

Guenivere glanced around the square. "I see." She considered, then pointed with a long, slender and graceful finger toward a house with a roof and no walls, across the square. "You will find both water and oats in the shed. When you are ready, you will find me there." She swung her arm to point to one of the more robust houses on the square, one with two stories and strong shutters over the windows, and a thatch roof. It had square Roman-like walls, unlike the other round huts spreading across the top of the hill.

Lancelot bowed his head once more. "Thank you. I will return as soon as I can."

He waved to his men, who waited a discreet twenty paces away. They turned and followed him across the square to the shed Guenivere had pointed out. Beneath the solid roof were stalls for horses and an area in the middle with hitching rails and posts, bags of oats and barrels of water. The place was well-founded. When Lancelot reached the shed, a boy ran out and held out his hand for the reins. Lancelot handed them over. So did his men.

Their horses were led farther into the shed where a dozen boys and young men scurried to tend to the travel-weary beasts. Their competent air reassured Lancelot that Belenus would be cared for properly.

His men gathered around him, their expressions curious or amused.

"That was the Lady Guenivere?" Belmaris asked, in his usual sour tone. "She isn't anything like all the poetry they gushed about her, in the city."

"Dirty washes off," Dyson replied, his tone complacent. "As long as she can bear a child, who cares?"

"At least she won't fuss about sleeping on the ground on the way back," Belmaris added.

That was a point in her favor, Lancelot admitted. He'd had visions of a delicate princess barely able to stay in her saddle, with a preference for a panier, and surrounded by companions and ladies who tsk'd and fussed over every male behavior.

"She's healthy and strong," he told his men. "The rest, as Dyson said, holds no bearing upon anything. I advise you to find food and rest. We leave again tomorrow at dawn."

The men scattered. It seemed likely they would eat well today. The aromas of sizzling meat and baking bread were strong and enticing. A cup of wine and some aged cheese would make the meal richer than any they'd enjoyed for days now.

Lancelot begged a half a loaf of bread from a matron bending over an oven similar to the one Guenivere had been tending. He tore the loaf apart, his mouth watering at the scent of fresh, soft and still-warm bread. A spit turned over another nearby fire, with a deer haunch dropping juices into the flames. The attendant let Lancelot hack off the outer, cooked meat in ragged slices, which he put on top of the bread and covered with the other piece of the loaf.

He wolfed the meal down, regardless of the heat, then licked his fingers. He looked for a wine skin or flasks without success and shrugged it off. He would ask Guenivere for a cup, later.

He threaded his way through the square, heading for the big house.

There were two armed guards standing on either side of the stout door. He nodded at them. "The Lady Guenivere is expecting me."

A guard knocked on the door. "Lancelot, my Lady?" he called through it.

"Enter!" came the call from the other side. It was not Guenivere's musical voice.

The guard shoved the door open and stood back. The swinging door revealed a large matron. Her veil did not fully disguise the gray in her hair. Her mantle fell nearly to the floor in the Roman fashion. She bowed her head to Lancelot. "Prince Lancelot. I am Braneen, companion to the Lady Guenivere. Please come in."

Lancelot took in the bright, flawless white of the companion's gown, the neatness of her appointments and her fragile slippers, as he ducked and stepped through the door. He straightened the pin at his shoulder, holding his furled cloak in place, abruptly aware of the state of his own appearance. The black trews and tunic hid the stains of travel, but not the strain of it. They were both dusty and wrinkled. He had traveled as he always did, with regard only for speed and, in this case, concealment from the Saxons.

The room beyond held exactly the excess of cushions and perfumed swathes he had expected to find. It was unmistakably the abode of a woman—one of high rank, at that.

Candles burned, enhancing the light shed by the open windows. Beyond, the industry in the square made a subdued background murmur.

At the other end of the room was a single high-backed chair. Lancelot guessed by the carvings, the weight of the thing and the iron decorations, that this was Leodegrance's great chair. While Leodegrance lingered in service to Arthur in the city, Guenivere had remade the general audience chamber into one which suited her better.

Arrayed on either side of the chair were five ladies, all of them as neat and well turned out as the matron who greeted him at the door. They all appeared to be as old as Braneen, too.

Behind them, the plain wall was hidden behind pretty cloth. Furs and soft rugs covered the floor.

Guenivere sat upon the high chair, waiting to receive him. Nothing of the dirty, trews-clad woman he had spoken to in the square remained. In the few minutes he had taken to have his horses tended to and find food for himself, Guenivere had transformed herself as thoroughly as she had this room.

Her gaze was steady, revealing blue eyes so light they were

almost colorless, which gave her gaze a hypnotic quality. He had not noticed that quality about them, out in the square.

The deep, midnight black of her hair and smoothly arching brows and thick lashes was the only dark note about her. The remaining details added to a melody of light. Her gown was made of a strange fabric which shimmered silver...or perhaps it was the same blue as her eyes. There was plenty of it, for it trailed the floor at her feet in elegant folds and drapes, revealing only the toe of one slipper, which matched in color.

The gown was held in at her waist by a jeweled belt—the stones on the belt were of the same light, glimmering quality. She wore no mantle over it in the Roman way, the way her ladies did. Instead, she wore a torc made of polished silver, with runes and script which, even from the other end of the room, Lancelot could tell was very old.

An heirloom, then, and of incalculable value, preserved since before the Romans had come to Britain.

Delicate earrings swung from her ears and a single white stone rested on her forehead, just above her brows, held by a fine chain.

Her hair rippled down her back and over both shoulders, free of pins, combs and the elaborate twisting and braiding Roman women preferred.

As he approached the high seat and the lady upon it, Lancelot could not help but approve of the complete absence of anything Roman about the woman. It was as if she had repudiated her Roman ancestry and instead embraced the more ancient roots of the family—those of the tribal Britons.

She was utterly beautiful.

Now Lancelot understood the gossip about her. The raised brows of men and their rueful and lecherous smiles and winks.

Deep in his bones, shattering his calm forever, he felt the impact of her beauty. His step faltered.

Lancelot hid his confusion and recovered his pace. He moved to stand before the chair and gave her a deep bow. As the highest-ranking person in Camelard, she was entitled to the acknowledgement.

He straightened. "I bring greetings from your father, Lady Guenivere, and a message."

She gripped the arm of the chair, the long fingers whitening. "I am to marry the High King," she breathed.

Surprise touched him. "Word reached you ahead of me..." he surmised.

Guenivere gave him a tight, small smile. "You are the first messenger from the city in weeks," she assured him. "That *you* are the messenger, Prince Lancelot, accompanied by thirty armed men, speaks silently of the weight of your message. I am not unaware of my value as a woman."

"And also not unaware of your father's campaign to convince Arthur of your value, either, I would guess," Lancelot added.

Her smile was pure mischief. "That, too," she said in agreement, her eyes dancing. Her flesh glowed pink and soft.

Lancelot's heart creaked. He cleared his throat. "Then, as the content of my message has already been guessed, all that remains is to urge you to as great a speed as you can manage. We are to leave tomorrow at dawn, my Lady, and we will travel swiftly and lightly. I have been tasked with bringing you safely to Venta Belgarum. I have never failed to deliver any wish Arthur has asked of me."

For the first time, Guenivere looked anything but sure of herself. "My women, my...my things..."

"You must travel with as little as possible," Lancelot replied. "If your women cannot ride well and hard, they should remain here. They will merely slow us down. You understand how riddled with Saxons the land is these days, my Lady?"

She gnawed at one corner of her lip. The sign of doubt was

oddly endearing. Only now did Lancelot remember how young she was.

"In truth, I have been somewhat sheltered here," she said, with a confiding note. "News arrives seldom, for we are tucked away, out of the main affairs. That is a blessing, if the land is as chancy as you say."

"It is," Lancelot assured her. He relented a little. "Your ladies and your possessions may be conveyed to you at a later time. For now, your safe arrival in the city is the only matter which concerns me."

Guenivere swallowed. He watched the movement beneath her smooth, fine throat. A pulse beat there, at the base, beneath the creamy skin.

Then she nodded. "Tomorrow at dawn, I will be ready to travel with you, Prince Lancelot. I am glad it is you who is to accompany me. I would feel unsafe with anyone else."

He grew aware of the building tension in him with a touch of uneasiness. She was lovely. She was brave and sensible.

And she was not his.

"Do you require any further information, my Lady?" he asked stiffly.

A tiny frown marred her forehead, as her brows came together. Had his rough tone offended her? It would be best if she *was* offended.

"I believe I understand the arrangements adequately," she replied, her tone just as stiff and formal as his.

"Then I will leave you to prepare," Lancelot said. "Good night, Lady Guenivere."

"Prince Lancelot."

He gave a final bow, whirled and stalked from the room, his heart racing as if he had run here from the city.

Lancelot spent the night in a bed of hay under the shed roof, among the horses. It was warm there. His men were good at guessing when he wanted to be alone and steered away from him. They drank and diced with the locals at the long tables in the square, by the light of braziers.

Instead, he unfurled and wrapped his cloak around him and burrowed deeper into the hay. He tried to think. Despite the heat of the day, which lingered into the night, he was cold.

What was this madness which gripped him?

Yes, she was a beautiful woman. He had met a great many beautiful women. Morgan, Arthur's sister, was reckoned to be more glorious than the sun itself, yet she did not move Lancelot the way Guenivere did.

He had felt…inadequate, standing before her in his travel-stained clothes. He was a dark smudge upon a room which she made ethereal.

Lancelot gripped his temples with forefinger and thumb and squeezed. He could not afford to dabble in petty concerns. He had work to do, in the service of Arthur and Britain. Gawain, with his constant love affairs and heartbreaks; Tristan, with his sure hand with the ladies; even Lucan, who quietly wooed far more women while other men bragged of their conquests. All of them spent energy upon matters which took their attention away from the peril they all faced.

He, Lancelot, had sworn never to be so distracted. To let himself be caught up in such matters took away from his strength as a fighter and leader.

It weakened him.

With a snarl, Lancelot turned onto his other side and closed his eyes. He would pluck her from his thoughts. He would do his duty, deliver her to Arthur, then forget the power of her gaze and the way she glowed.

GUENIVERE ROSE STIFF AND UNRESTED, the next morning. She donned the traveling clothes which Braneen had argued strenuously were unfit for a lady to wear when riding to her wedding with the High King of the land.

Guenivere's night had been sleepless, beset with worries and doubts, plans and concerns. A boy had delivered her a note from her father which Lancelot had failed to give her. Leodegrance had been guarded in his letter.

...an alliance through marriage will solidify Britain, as will the results of that union...

Children.

Because she knew her father well and knew how he thought, Guenivere understood what he had not spoken of in the note. There was opposition to her marrying Arthur. Other houses had daughters of greater lineage. She was well aware of the heritage which the great houses of Britain would afford the crown. So was her father. They had examined each and every remotely suitable candidate for the throne.

What had her father promised to secure Arthur's agreement to marry her? Guenivere thought it unlikely that the daughter of a tiny kingdom in the southern corner of Britain, with little arable land to recommend it, would hold any appeal to Merlin. She knew Merlin was behind Arthur's decision. He was the only man Arthur truly listened to. Her father had pointed out many times that Merlin was the only man who could change Arthur's mind.

What had Merlin seen in the future which convinced him to support Arthur's marriage to a daughter of Camelard?

It was not the only question which plagued her, the long night past.

Wearily, she dressed, braided her hair and tucked the long tail beneath her cloak, where it would not be immediately noticeable. Although Lancelot had not said so, she knew he wanted to travel with as few women in the company as possible. Women needed to be guarded. Protected, if there was trouble, taking the men away from defending themselves.

Trouble, it seemed, was likely, for Arthur had sent Lancelot du Lac. His strongest warrior, who should by rights be defending Arthur and Britain, not ferrying a single woman about the land.

She had heard stories about Lancelot in her brief visit to Venta Belgarum, many years ago. That had been the year when Duke Cador had handed her back to her father, his duties as her guardian completed.

She still missed the rough, solid walls of Tintagel and the smell of the sea, and the constant crash of the waves.

Her thoughts returned to Lancelot, who was to take her to Venta Belgarum. He had not been in the city when she was there. He had been in the north, defending the northern kingdoms against the Saxons who tried to strike through their defenses and reach into the heart of Britain via that path.

That he had succeeded, so far away from Arthur's direction and with only the men of divided kingdoms who regarded each other with suspicion, if not outright hatred, was telling. Lancelot had solidified his reputation that year as Arthur's greatest fighter.

Yet the stories told about him back in the city had been far from complimentary. There had been stories about all the senior officers and Arthur's companions. Cai, who was a mighty fighter, but a slow thinker when not on the battlefield. Bedivere, the perfect warrior with no time for anything but the business of war. Pellinore, who embraced life with gusto—*all* of it, including war and the joys of love, as his extended family attested.

The stories about Lancelot, though, were different. They were not sarcastic observations made with wry amusement. There was a tinge of awe and a note of sourness in the stories about Lancelot.

The gossips spoke of his devotion to war, to the killing of Saxons. They said he was a cold man, who made no friends at court because he considered everyone beneath him, except Arthur. Arthur and he were firm friends, which puzzled everyone. Lancelot was outspoken, to the point of rudeness. Yet Arthur put up with frankness from Lancelot which would have any other man banished.

There was laughter about Lancelot's precious chariots—or there had been the year Guenivere visited the city. Later, she learned the chariots had smashed the Saxon front lines wide apart and allowed Arthur's army to pour into their midst and defeat them within a few hours. The rout had solidified respect for the chariots. The respect had not been extended toward Lancelot, who had insisted upon re-introducing them to war.

Yet there were also whispers that Lancelot often visited the surgery late at night, to sit with the wounded. That, possibly, he talked them back to health. It was said he was such an implacable enemy of the Saxons, that he refused to let the wounded die and give them the satisfaction of one more fallen warrior.

Most of the gossip, after that point, descended into wild speculation about mysterious powers and his strange upbringing in the heart of the Perilous Forest. He had been raised by the Lady of the Lake who lived there, which is where he got his second name.

All the tales left her with the impression of a man who preferred to be alone, who cared for nothing but defeating Saxons, and who had dedicated his life to that task. To that end he had turned himself into an efficient war machine, with no room for any of the normal concerns of men.

Even his plain, dusty clothing, with not a skerrick of decoration or pleasing lines about it, pointed to the pursuit of efficiency and greater effectiveness in battle.

The only odd note about the man had been the thick black curls on his head—a riotous note above an unsmiling pair of black eyes and the firmly trimmed and controlled beard outlining the sharp angles of his jaw and chin.

This was the man who was to escort her to her wedding. If it had been any other man—even Cai, who was good-natured and tended toward kindness—she might have dared to ask the questions which had kept her awake last night.

Was Arthur a good man? Was he kind, behind the gruff exterior?

Was his temper as hot as his red hair hinted at?

Would he be a good husband?

They were personal questions and should be the least of her concerns. Yet, as a woman, she did worry about such things. She would like to learn the answers before she was wed to the man, so she might brace herself.

She recalled Lancelot's harsh tones yesterday, as she carried her pack out to the square where the men were assembling in the pre-dawn light, their horses stamping and blowing in the early morning chill. Lancelot was not a man of whom she could ask such petty questions. He would be irritated by them, for they were beneath his concerns.

Dap stood holding the reins of Guenivere's stallion. She smiled at him and handed him the heavy pack. It contained all which she simply could not travel without, including a gown she could wear for her wedding.

As she stood waiting for Dap to add the pack to the stallion, Lancelot moved through the assembled men, with a quiet word to some of them, a pat on a shoulder or arm for others.

The pages and stable boys held flaming torches to light their preparations and as Lancelot moved into the light of one of them, Guenivere caught her breath.

Sometime during the night, possibly only a short time ago, he had bathed and shaved. He had washed away all signs of heavy, rough travel, leaving only fine, tanned flesh and the black line of beard around his jaw and mouth. His clothes were fit for a king's court—yet still black. The tunic was stitched with gold thread, and a slim torc wrapped the base of his throat. The cloak was made of good wool, dyed evenly, and clipped with a gold pin with the Benoic bear symbol picked out in red.

His trews were slim and his boots clean. Gold armguards flashed at his wrists beneath the cloak. The bronze and gold hilt of his sword was the most utilitarian note about him.

He stopped in front of her.

Guenivere gripped her cloak, suddenly self-conscious. "I thought a gown would be too impractical." She realized she was apologizing.

"One does not escort a future queen wearing rags." He indicated her stallion. "Can I help you up?"

"I can manage," Guenivere said swiftly. She gripped Aeron's mane and hoisted herself up. She moved too quickly and nearly overbalanced.

Lancelot caught her elbow and steadied her.

Guenivere could feel her cheeks heating.

"I'd not have you slide off into another bog. Not today," he said softly, looking up at her.

He'd seen—or perhaps smelled—the mud of the bog on her clothes, yesterday. She had been hunting for cresses and other herbs.

Her cheeks burned even harder.

Then she saw something in his eyes...could it be amusement?

"Are you...laughing at me?" she breathed.

"No," he said quickly. Then, "Perhaps a little. You are full of contrasts, my lady. I remind myself of the lowliest version I have spotted in you to offset the dazzle of the others."

Dazzle?

She searched his face, to see if he was still laughing at her. Yet all amusement had faded from his eyes. His expression had sobered. Instead, his gaze held...

Something shifted in the base of her belly and rolled over.

Her throat closed in, stealing her breath.

Her tunic was abruptly too coarse and uncomfortable. It chaffed her flesh, which prickled and heated.

It did not occur to her to shift her gaze away from his, even though she had long known that to stare openly at a man tended to convey the wrong impression and invite attention she didn't want.

His gaze did not release hers, either.

Dap cleared his throat.

Only then did Guenivere realize she had let her gaze linger for far too long. It still took her a dozen heartbeats to look away from Lancelot. She fumbled for the reins, focusing fiercely upon the task, her heart pattering unhappily.

She heard Lancelot move away. Heading for his own horse, presumably.

Fool! She railed at herself. Now was not the time to become infatuated with a man, the way the giggling girls in Tintagel and here in Camelard did every other month. She had managed to avoid that demeaning fever, herself.

She was on her way to be married and must work to hold herself apart from the everyday concerns of a young maiden. She was a political asset now and must guard her every word and deed.

Chapter Seven

edivere returned to the city drained from the long, slow work of circling the city. They had made a great circuit, a mile out from the walls. It had required keeping all senses fully extended without cease. His hand spent the day hovering to snatch at his sword, if needed.

The woman, Cara, had moved silently beside him, an unvarying ten paces away, her own sword resting on her shoulder. The arm which had bothered her stayed in place on the hilt and he had not seen her rub her arm once while they patrolled.

Neither had she spoken. They could not speak freely, or they might alert any lingering Saxons. Even when he gave directions, though, she merely nodded and moved to do what he said, be it kicking in a stable door to check inside, her sword up and ready, or to move around the edge of a clearing to meet him on the other side, to flush out anyone who might be lying in wait for more gullible travelers to step into the full daylight in the center of the clearing and announce themselves that way.

They came across the other fighters here and there. Even then, she remained silent, while Bedivere exchanged quick snatches of information.

By mid-afternoon he relaxed. They had covered a big enough area to be almost certain the band of Saxons they'd dealt with that morning were the only ones in the area. There was not a Saxon host lying in wait somewhere nearby, ready to leap upon the city if they let down their guard.

The sun was down at the treetops when Bedivere turned toward the city. If they followed a straight line back, they would reach the gates just as the sun set, just as what he had instructed everyone else to do. He could linger at the gates and speak to each pair as they returned for a last report from each.

Cara moved up alongside him. The sword was on her left shoulder and held with her left hand, now. The injured right arm hung by her side, the fingers flexing and curling.

"Just a patrol, then?" It was a question only by the uplifted note at the end. Bedivere suspected she had made it so in deference to his rank.

"It would seem so," he replied

"Still, this close to the city… They're growing bold."

"They have been growing bold for two years. They sense victory." The word came out harsher than he meant it to.

Cara's gaze slid to him, then back to the path ahead. Even though she walked beside him, carried her sword in her left hand and dared speak aloud, she still scanned each side of the path.

Had she put herself on his left to hide the scars on her face? Or was it more of Pellinore's and Lancelot's training? Their fighters had uncommon good sense. He found himself marveling all over again on the way they had split up into pairs and disappeared, to do what he bid without excessive questions, that morning.

Cara had stayed silent all day, a trustworthy left hand who obeyed him instantly. She had not grown impatient, the way Gawain might have. Gawain's tolerance for boredom was low. She

82

had not complained about lack of food or water, the way Cai would have, even though it had been warm despite the rain. She had not complained about being wet through, or that her arm hurt.

And now she scanned the way ahead, still not completely relaxed.

"You did well today," he told her.

"To not do well would be to invite disaster. I have no intention of dying at the hand of a Saxon." Her voice was mellow, yet there was a ringing note of conviction in it which made the small hairs on the back of his neck try to stand up.

"Are you not half-Saxon, yourself?"

She turned her chin, so her face was fully revealed. Her hand lifted toward the scars but did not reach all the way up to them. "Not since I received these."

She returned to monitoring their path.

How many others were tied to Arthur because of the same deep hatred of Saxons? After the last two summers of war, there were far more. Bedivere suspected that everyone who clamored for shelter, for whom Cai struggled to find a bed, also felt the same way.

"Do you really think they will win?" Her question was spoken with a casual air which did not fool him. No one would ask that question if they were indifferent to the answer. No one who fought for Arthur was indifferent.

Bedivere sighed. "I think that way only when I am tired. You must pretend I did not speak so thoughtlessly."

"Would that also require pretending that the Saxons will never defeat us?"

It was a fair question, one he had no immediate answer to.

"Should we not be braced for the possibility?" Cara added. She turned her chin once more and her hand lifted. This time, it did not have to come close to the scars for Bedivere to know what she gestured to. "Saxons spare no one."

"No," he said in heavy agreement. "Yet if everyone lets the thought that defeat is a possibility settle into their minds, then it will *become* defeat, even before we raise our swords."

She nodded, her gaze ahead once more. "Better to fight with fire in the belly, then."

Bedivere laughed as he saw the trap she had laid for him. "Anger does many things to enhance a man in battle," he told her. "What it also does is blinker your sight and ruin your judgment. You should not rely upon it. It will be your undoing."

"If not for my anger, I would not be able to step upon the field of battle," she said, her voice the same low, mellow tone. "I would be too afraid, without it."

"We all face that fear," he assured.

"No!" She halted and turned to look at him, making Bedivere turn back to face her. "I do not believe it. You? Afraid?"

He grimaced. "Fear is in the heart of every fighter—not just the weakest of us. Well, perhaps the very stupid have no fear. The rest of us...of course we are afraid."

She put her hands on her hips. "Then how do you do it? If you do not let anger drive you, what makes you stay there and fight?"

Bedivere opened his mouth to answer...and could not. He tried again. "Duty...I suppose."

Her mouth turned down. She walked on.

He didn't blame her. It was a weak answer. He followed her down the trail, reaching for a better response.

He couldn't find one, not until they were within reach of the city itself and were crossing the open field where those without houses camped. They would not be camped there tonight. Tonight, they would sleep in the streets and the halls of the keep, with armed guards awake and patrolling among them.

They approached the gates when Bedivere caught up with Cara. "All I know is that if we did not stay and fight, then the Saxons would wash over us like winter floods and all would be lost."

She glanced at him. "I should not be afraid to fight, because I am afraid of what would happen if I did not?"

Bedivere scowled and shut up. The damn woman was asking questions no one had dared ask him before. It was easier to not answer.

The speculative glance the guard gave him, and the glide of his eyes over toward Cara, irritated Bedivere even more. "Pay attention!" he snapped.

The guard straightened with a jerk.

Dispensing discipline did not alleviate the stinging prod of her questions. Long after the tall woman had gone in search of her family and the squalid house they crammed into, her questions continued to circle in Bedivere's mind. Especially that night, when he laid upon the narrow, uncomfortable bed in the house beside hers, the questions returned.

Why *did* he fight? For the honor and glory of Britain, yes, yes. For Arthur, of course. What *made* him want that, though? What made him want to defeat the Saxons, apart from being afraid of what they would do if he did not?

He had become a warrior because...well, because every man did. There was no choice in the matter.

Except Merlin refused to pick up a sword. He found other ways to defeat Saxons.

What did it say that Arthur's war duke and marshal of his army did not know why he did what he did?

The blank sensation the questions engendered kept him awake long into the night.

LANCELOT MANAGED TO AVOID SPEAKING to Guenivere for two

days. On the third morning, though, he was forced to it. He approached her bedroll, where she stretched and twisted to remove the kinks which sleeping on the ground always induced. He said, "You should know that we will arrive in the city late this afternoon. I am sending a rider ahead to warn them, so they will expect us... you."

Guenivere froze. "So fast..." She straightened. "Thank you for the warning."

"If you wish to change into something more..." And words failed him. She had only the single pack, which she used as a pillow. What else could she possibly have in there that would equal the silvered blue gown?

Or the slim trews and tunic she wore now?

When had he begun to think of the simple garments as becoming? On her they were delightful. They outlined her long legs and slim hips, which the short tunic failed to hide. She kept the cloak furled around her shoulders, for the days were hot and still as only late summer could be. It further enhanced the effect of the belted tunic and high boots.

And never, not to a single soul, would he breathe of his private delight when he caught a glimpse of her when she was turned away from him.

His pulse had not withstood this journey well at all, despite him staying as far away from her as the small company and tight quarters around the campfire at night allowed.

He had found himself watching her more than he should and fought to hide it from the men. They were quick to spot such things and quicker to judge, especially him, for he chided all of them for letting the ways of the flesh interfere with their work.

Because of his observations he knew she had little in the pack which would match the silver blue dress.

Guenivere tugged at the bottom of her tunic. "I must enter the city as I traveled to it. In such times as these, the people will un-

86

derstand. Perhaps they will even approve of my parsimony."

"I am quite sure they will adore you," Lancelot said. His voice came out harsh with control.

Her limpid eyes widened.

He moved away, irritated. Less than a day to go, then he would be rid of her and his heart could cease its churn.

They had been underway for two hours, when Guenivere nudged her stallion up alongside him from her place two lengths behind, where the guards could surround her. The guards hid her smaller figure from anyone they passed, so that rumor would not run ahead of them.

She gave Lancelot a smile which was possibly intended to be friendly but fell short. The tension in her eyes and the tightness of her jaw betrayed her. "May I ask a question, Prince Lancelot?"

"No one calls me that," he said gruffly.

"Lancelot?"

"Prince. I am a prince without lands. The Saxons took them before I was born. If I had possession of those lands, I would be a king by now. When I have those lands back, I will use the title once more."

She swallowed. "I'm sorry. I should not have bothered you." She picked up the reins, to slow her mount so she could fall back.

Lancelot relented. "Ask your question." He could not seem to control the harshness of his voice!

"It is a trivial thing…"

"I have no objection to being distracted," he growled. In fact, he welcomed it.

Still, she hesitated. He saw the corner of her lip dent, as she gnawed at it again. It drew his attention to the curve of the bottom lip. And the top one. The bow in the middle.

Then she glanced over her shoulder and nudged her stallion so close, their knees were almost brushing. His leg tingled.

"Lancelot… I wanted to ask…I was wondering…is Arthur a

nice man?"

Lancelot's back snapped straight in surprise. He could feel his jaw loosen with it.

With that one reticent, simple question, Guenivere tore aside a veil which had been hiding her inner nature.

He saw the doubts and fears of a young woman...he saw *her*, Guenivere. She rode to a wedding with a man she didn't know, as so many women had done before her. She wanted to know what her future held.

She was about to become the most powerful woman in Britain, yet she was as helpless to pull against the tide as any shellfish half-buried in sand.

A hard, crimping band tightened about his chest. Lancelot found himself using the gentlest tone he could. "Have you not yet met him?"

"Once," she said, her voice small. "I was presented to him when I was fourteen. He was rushed. There had just been a battle. There was blood everywhere, including on him and he was distracted by...by everything, I suppose. All I remember is a tall man with red hair and fierce blue eyes."

"That is Arthur," Lancelot confirmed.

"He seemed angry."

"He frequently is. With Saxons, that is. Saxons and their ways, but not his friends."

She chewed at her lip. He could almost feel the doubt tearing at her. It came to him with a jolt of surprise: Arthur was many things which could be unpleasant, especially when facing the Saxons. His fury and ruthlessness was greater than Lancelot's. His determination to win peace for Britain never failed. One might say he was obsessive in that determination. He was a strong leader and gave no quarter. He demanded loyalty from his men and absolute obedience. Yet he leavened the demand with empathy and understanding for their human frailties. Arthur never forgot his upbringing as the bastard orphan of unknown parentage, in one of the poorest families of a broken country.

Arthur would not like it that a woman was afraid of him, *especially* the woman he was to marry.

Lancelot found himself saying, without forethought or measurement, "Arthur is a *good* man. The best man I have ever met. He is my friend and in this I can speak the utter truth. He will treat you well. You have no need to fear him."

Guenivere's shoulders straightened. Her chin lifted. "I am not afraid."

"Of course not," Lancelot said swiftly. "I merely explain that you do not need to be."

She fussed with her reins, rearranging them. "Well...I thought...thank you for your frankness, Lancelot." She tugged on the reins, so her stallion would fall back, leaving Lancelot alone with his thoughts once more.

Now his thoughts raged like a storm, the restraints torn away. Now he faced the harsh truth.

Guenivere was to be the wife of his king, the man he counted his friend, the first true friend he'd ever had. The temptation which had plagued him for three days was not only treason, it was disloyal to his friend. They were both heinous flaws, yet he counted the latter as the more important of the two.

The stirring of his soul must remain hidden inside, never to be spoken of, or hinted at in any way. He must divert it and let it dissipate. He was a fighter, a warrior. He must concentrate on that.

This moment of insanity would remain secret forever.

Chapter Eight

I t would have been easy to blame the lagging heat of the day for what happened, only Bedivere knew the roots of the problem wound back into the past.

Six years ago, Pellinore had executed King Lot upon the field of battle a moment before the Saxons Lot invited upon his lands swept across the northern kingdoms. Lancelot and the other lords, including the new King of Strathclyde, Idris, spent the next few years pushing the Saxons back to the eastern shores and onto their boats. From there, the Saxons sailed south to join the bands already living upon the crowded shores of Britain.

Lot was found guilty of treason. Pellinore's actions were named just and appropriate.

The gods knew, though, Lot's four sons held no great love for the man. Gaheris, Lot's heir, and Gawain, the second eldest son, both declared their loyalty to Arthur years before Lot's execution. Agravaine and Gareth, the two younger men, followed their brothers' leads.

Yet their father's death impacted all four. Gaheris was thrust into kingship over contended lands far north of where his heart truly laid. Gawain seemed the least upset about his father's demise. "A trial would have been cleaner, but what is passed is over and done with." Then he'd swung the nearest maid into his arms and pressed wine upon her.

That had been six years ago, and everyone thought the matter was closed. Yet Agravaine, who was the most like his father in nature, could not let the matter lie.

It began with snide comments across the campfires. Later, the council hall. Then in more public places, including the dining hall when Arthur was still present.

Pellinore shrugged off the insults and cruel prods with indifference. "We fought. He died. It happens in war," he'd said more than once.

Gareth, who was gentle by nature, unless his temper was roused, was the most easily led of the brothers. Agravaine whispered of injustice and wrong-doing to his younger brother.

A year ago, Gareth challenged Pellinore during a council session. Gareth's face was red and flustered. "It is well known you held contempt and dislike for my father, that you considered him responsible for the death of your sons. You have wished him dead and you made it so. It was not execution of a traitor, but the murder of an innocent man."

It was a claim Pellinore could not ignore. Nor could many other men, who lost sons and brothers, fathers and cousins to the Saxon hoards.

Merlin stepped in at that point, soothing the tempers and upset, with clear ringing speech about justice and truth and simple facts. Bedivere watched with deep interest as the druid wove a story with his voice, painting for everyone those days when Lot schemed against Arthur and the tragic results of his actions... including his own death.

The evening, which started on such a bitter note, ended with most men drinking themselves into a stupor—the wine flowed with suspicious ease that night. Even Gaheris and Gawain drunk themselves to a standstill—and only Cai could ever out-drink those two.

Agravaine, though, slipped away sometime earlier in the night. Bedivere wasn't certain when, for it had been a rare night of indulgence for him, too. He remembered Merlin filling his cup at least twice, yet he did not remember the end of the night.

The grumbles about Pellinore's perfidy subsided and Bedivere had forgotten about them until tonight.

He arrived at the hall shortly before the council meeting was to start. Years ago, the council sessions had always taken place after supper, while men sat around the campfire drinking and discussing matters of war.

Now the council sessions were held before supper, so that supper could proceed as a formal meal, with ladies and servants and tables. In council, they still discussed war and strategies to defeat the Saxons. Now, though, just as much other business was brought to Arthur's attention. Food shortages, housing shortages. Water shortages. Metal shortages—they resolved that by borrowing from the Saxons their method of digging in bogs for what they called "bog iron" until a new mine could be developed. Bog iron did not make good weapons, although it was good enough for nails, hinges, buckles and other implements.

There were also matters of justice, both high and low. The council heard all matters requiring judicial decision, while Arthur was the final arbiter. Whoever he requested was required to dispense the justice.

Which was why Bedivere relaxed over the matter of Lot's death. Arthur had made his decision. It was done, now.

Only, it wasn't.

He arrived at the hall, his belly rumbling. He had failed to find food at the noon hour. His last meal had been a poor breakfast of musty eggs and a handful of stale bread sopped in wine, which had not lasted. Hopefully, there would be meat served tonight, and he could sleep with a full stomach.

The four Lothian men were together on a long stool, with a large jug of wine before them. From their eyes and their lax postures, Bedivere guessed they had been there for some hours. It was one way to deal with hunger pangs, he supposed.

Bedivere halted in the middle of the narrow area between the tables, where the officers passed to reach their customary benches. Pellinore patted Bedivere's shoulder as the older man slipped by him.

Bedivere stirred and moved on to the table close by the High King's chair where he usually sat. It was within reach of Arthur, if Arthur should need to speak to him as war duke.

"There he is! The pissant who murdered my father in cold blood!"

Bedivere froze once more. So did most of the men in the hall. Later, Bedivere would be thankful that the full retinue of officers had not yet made their way to the hall. Only a dozen people waited in the big room. The high chair at the end was empty.

Agravaine tried to rise from the bench. His face was flushed a deep red which matched his hair. His eyes were blood shot and his words slurred. His hand shook as he pointed at Pellinore.

Pellinore stood on the other side of the hall. His thin features were grave as he watched Gareth and Gaheris try to pull Agravaine back onto the bench, with shushing sounds. Agravaine's fury was running as thick as the wine in his veins.

"Your father challenged me, boy," Pellinore shot back.

"After you baited him into it!" Agravaine thumped the table with his fist. "Justice *will* be done, Pellinore! I swear, your time will come!"

"*Silence!*" The roar came from the high chair.

Bedivere spun, startled. He had not seen Arthur enter the room. The man stood with one hand on the back of the chair, his face working in a way which dismayed Bedivere. Arthur was angry.

The room fell silent.

Agravaine dropped onto the bench, which scraped with a high squeal across the stone floor, making everyone wince.

Gawain shot to his feet. "My apologies, Arthur. I'll put the man to bed and be right back...with your permission?"

Arthur nodded. A short movement of his head.

"Gareth, get on yer feet, man, and help me," Gawain muttered. Bedivere suspected Gawain's whisper was meant for Gareth alone, but as the room was eerily silent, everyone heard it.

Gareth got unsteadily to his feet. His own good-natured face was troubled and flushed. The two of them manhandled Agravaine off the bench and force-marched him to the door.

Bedivere turned back to Arthur. "You're earlier than usual, Arthur. Do you want to start the meeting now?"

Arthur's gaze shifted to Bedivere. "These are your men. Your officers." His tone was cold. "You are my war duke. Control them as you should. I will not tolerate outbursts of this kind in my hall. Is that clear?"

It was as if he had been dumped in ice. Bedivere shivered. He found his voice. "Yes, my lord. I apologize. It will not happen again."

No one else spoke. No one cleared their throat or shifted their feet. They did not dare.

Arthur held up a crumpled message roll in his hand. "You will all be pleased to know that Guenivere of Camelard will be here by nightfall. Council is dismissed. The halls will be prepared for a formal dinner to begin when she arrives."

Bedivere's heart gave a hard knock. What could the new queen be served? There was little food to be had. No wonder Cai was not here as he normally was, scratching away at his lists on the table closest to Arthur.

Arthur squeezed the message in his fingers, making the

parchment crackle. "Why are you all still standing here? Go. Prepare."

Bedivere shifted. What could he do to prepare, except to bathe his face, which he had already done?

"*Move!*" Arthur growled.

Everyone streamed toward the door and halted again, when a high clear horn sounded, trumpeting a stream of notes Bedivere recognized. They floated through the open windows.

"The gate!" Merlin cried, his voice carrying even better than Arthur's fury-filled battle shout. "Guenivere is here early! Move it, you dogs! Your smartest clothes and comb your hair. Now! Now!"

Bedivere ran.

THE EARLY ARRIVAL OF GUENIVERE and the resulting scramble was a sour note at the end of a long day. Those inclined to believe portents and signs murmured uneasily as everyone returned to the main hall in dribs and drabs, still adjusting clothing and pins and torcs, and winding cloaks of office about their shoulders.

Heads glistened where hasty buckets of water had been dumped and hair combed into place.

The women fussed over mantles and jewelry and veils as they hurried into the hall and took their places beside their men, for they had also been called to the hall for this momentous occasion.

Only, it did not feel magnificent. Bedivere took his place at the high table, still buckling his armor, which was the most formal and presentable outfit he possessed. The tunics he wore beneath were all threadbare and he had not arranged the making of more, for cloth was as hard to obtain as wheat.

He pushed his hair back with a rough comb of his fingers, as

Pellinore tugged his long tunic into place and resettled his cloak. Pellinore rolled his eyes at Bedivere. "This is *not* a fortuitous start." He murmured the comment.

Pellinore was a superstitious man, Bedivere reminded himself.

"She comes," Pellinore added, nodding toward the door. Beyond the door, Bedivere could hear the murmur of many footsteps, moving along the cloister to the hall doors.

Arthur stepped onto the dais and moved over to the high chair, still arranging his own cloak and pin and belt. Excalibur was not strapped to his side, as usual. He was not smiling.

Another tall chair was hastily added to the table on the dais and stood at an angle to his. The discordant angles were a jarring note.

We're all caught flat-footed by this, Bedivere thought. There were still people hurrying into the hall from the other minor doors, rushing to find their places at the long tables. The Lothian table was empty except for Gawain, Bedivere noted. Did that mean Gaheris remained behind to control his younger brothers, while Gawain represented the family? The two of them had cooler heads than either Agravaine or Gareth. It seemed likely to Bedivere for it was what he would have done.

The fuss outside the door rose to a higher note, warning everyone in the hall that the new arrivals were upon them. Silence fell over the hall.

Cai, as seneschal, stepped inside the doors. He wore a thick tunic which was too tight at the neck and his face was flushed as red as Agravaine's, earlier. The preparations for the feast fell upon Cai's shoulders more than any other officer in the keep, and he had been given no warning.

"The Princess Guenivere of Camelard!" he announced.

Leodegrance stood just inside the door, in his best tunic and a thick torc about his neck. He smiled as the doors were thrown open.

Guenivere came through, her hand on Lancelot's arm.

Bedivere remembered her from the first and only time she had come to the city, several years before. She had still been Cador's ward at that time. She had returned to Camelard after her visit, to help her father with the running of his lands, as he was expected to support Arthur. As the Saxon raids and battles increased, so did the time all the senior officers spent away from their homelands.

Bedivere remembered a slender girl with clear skin, thick black hair and a direct way of looking at the world, with her pointed chin lifted into the air.

That had not changed, except that Guenivere was now most definitely a woman, with full curves. It was possible she was taller. Her head was well above Lancelot's shoulder and he was not a short man.

In this hall of torcs and pins, shields and mantles, armor and swords, Guenivere had made no attempt to outshine the glittering finery. She wore a simple dress of light blue, which swept to her feet and trailed behind her. The belt around her hips was plain leather. Her hair rippled down her back, to below her hips.

She wore no torc or crown or any device to indicate rank. Instead, around her head she wore a wreath of golden, ripe wheat, woven with flowers and leaves.

Bedivere let out a soft sigh. The symbol of bounty. How fitting. Had that been her idea?

He could hear murmurs of approval around the hall, as others noted the symbolism of her headdress and commented upon it.

Her face was pale. Perhaps it was always so.

Lancelot picked up her hand from his arm and held it out toward Leodegrance and bowed to him.

Leodegrance inclined his head in thanks, his smile warm and small.

Lancelot did not smile. He did not murmur to Guenivere or

Leodegrance. Instead, he bowed to Arthur, who nodded his thanks, then whirled on one heel, his cloak snapping with the speed of the movement, and stalked from the hall.

No one else noticed his departure, Bedivere was sure. If they noticed Lancelot beside the new queen at all, then they would have thought nothing was wrong.

Only, everyone watched Guenivere as she walked the length of the hall toward the high table, her hand now on Leodegrance's arm.

The older officers, those who were slighted by Arthur's failure to ally with their houses, stood with gruff expressions, their gazes running over Guenivere, measuring and judging.

The women in the hall swayed and bent around those in front of them for a glimpse of the woman who would be their queen. They murmured softly to each other.

Guenivere did not smile. She gave no sign that she was aware of the frank scrutiny. She came to a halt in front of Arthur's chair, where he stood beside it. Bedivere's usual seat at the closest table put him only a half dozen paces from her. This close, he could see the girl trembled.

She was not indifferent to the contention swirling around her, then.

Leodegrance cleared his throat. "My lord Arthur, I present to you my daughter, the Princess Guenivere, your betrothed."

For a frozen moment, Arthur did not move. Bedivere's heart beat and squeezed as he willed the King to move, or risk offending Leodegrance and his daughter.

Then Arthur held out his hand toward her. "Guenivere, you are welcome in my hall."

Guenivere put her hand in his. "I am pleased to be here, King Arthur. The hall is much grander than the campfire I remember from my last visit to your court."

Arthur's mouth quirked upward. "And the pavilion which

leaked when it rained, yes."

Guenivere gave him a small, effortful smile. "We are all struggling to find shelter which does not leak, these days. It would please me to help you with that."

Bedivere's admiration nudged a little higher. Young, she might be, but she was an intelligent woman and knew every word she spoke would be shredded later and searched for meaning within meaning. She had given them that buried meaning.

A soft sigh seemed to move around the room.

Arthur drew in a breath and let it out. "I am pleased to hear you say so. The feast to celebrate your arrival is the best we can do for now."

"If it is not oat cakes and honey, it will be ambrosial to me," Guenivere said with a light tone.

Arthur relaxed. "I believe we can do a little better than that. Come, sit beside me and eat. You must be tired with the three days of travel and look forward to a meal upon a table."

"I look forward to a seat which does not move beneath me," Guenivere replied as Arthur drew her toward the table that was his.

He glanced around the hall. "Let us begin."

Cai signaled beyond the doors and a stream of kitchen staff sailed into the room, bearing the pitchers and pots and trays with the hastily put together feast.

Conversation leapt around the hall as everyone settled on benches and seats, and sometimes, sawn logs. They reached for the pitchers already upon the tables. The feast had begun.

While Bedivere waited for the trays of meat to reach him, his stomach cramping with rampant hunger, he saw a flash of light green on the other side of the room. That side was where the northern lords tended to linger, including Lothian. At Gawaine's table, Queen Ula took a seat beside him, while her children ranged around the table with him. Cara was among them.

On this night she could not choose to eat elsewhere. No one could.

The green dress was hers. Like Guenivere, she had let out her hair. The red river flowed down her back, rich and thick. The silver rings which twined and kept it tidy shone in the lamp light.

Her brother and sisters were chatting amiably with Gawaine, including the oldest girl, whose name Bedivere could not now recall.

The only one at the table who did not speak was Cara. She sipped at her cup, her gaze on the tabletop. Then she lifted her chin and her gaze met Bedivere's, direct and unwavering.

His heart lurched. Had she known he was looking at her?

As the steaming kettle reached him, Bedivere thankfully tore his gaze away from her and picked up his spoon.

Chapter Nine

It was not possible to sit on the other side of the table and thereby put her back to the room. Cara suffered through the sparse meal. She kept her head down, waiting for the meal to be over so she could leave the hall without insult to the guest of honor. She let conversations flow around her and over her, not participating.

There was far too little meat in the stew and not enough vegetables. It was thickened with oat flour, too. The bread was oily flax bread, although it was fresh. It was a poor meal, yet it was the largest she'd eaten this day.

While she ate and stared at the grain of the wood on the tabletop, Cara stole glances at the man on the other side of the hall. The table he sat at was small, with space for only two. The other man was Lucan, Bedivere's brother.

Why was Bedivere constantly in her thoughts? He was a southerner and one of the most senior officers in Arthur's army. Arthur's war duke.

She had spent nearly a whole day by his side, two days ago, and learned something unexpected; he liked silence.

It wasn't simply because they were quartering land where Saxons may lie in wait and must exercise caution—although that was part of it. There had been many times when silence was not needed, though. He had not rushed to fill the silence with questions or chatter.

Any other man might have spent those moments asking her questions about her family and her life in the north, always sliding closer to the fact that her mother was a Saxon and how did a half-breed Saxons come to be fighting for Arthur?

Yet Bedivere said nothing.

Cara liked silence and solitude. She had never thought to find that quality in another…and certainly not in Arthur's war duke. Such a man, she presumed, would be all bellows and commands.

He was a superior fighter and hunter, though. She had watched him slide through trees and scout the land with uncommon agility. He did not speak, nor did his feet give away his presence.

He had cast the fighters across the land in an effective net which would flush out any Saxons. It proved he was a quick thinker, too.

Yet she always came back to his silence. They walked and said nothing and it was not been the awkward emptiness which others created. He did not rush to fill the silence with useless chatter. They simply walked. When he had a question, he asked it. When he needed to speak, he did. Then he stopped once more.

Yet all the while, his mind worked. She saw the thoughts flickering through his eyes.

What were those thoughts?

Was that why she now stole glimpses of him as she ate? Because he was a riddle she had not unraveled?

Most men were easy to read and even easier to understand. Bedivere was not. Everything she knew about him conflicted with everything else she knew about him.

Wondering so occupied her mind until she reached the bottom of her bowl with a start of surprise. She wiped up the last of the gravy with the last of her hunk of bread, as the toasts were made.

There was no shortage of wine. Everyone held a cupful to raise in salute to Guenivere, to Arthur, and—with a thunderous shout of approval—to the defeat of the Saxons.

Cara drained her cup for that one, thumped the cup back upon the table and got to her feet, as many others were doing. The toasts signaled the end of the formalities and they were free to leave the hall.

There was a general rush for the privies. A smaller stream of people moved along the cloister to the gates which gave access to the keep. Cara moved along the covered verandah with them. She marveled as she always did whenever she came here that the keep was more Roman than British in design. There were square walls and sharp corners, tiles and stonework. Walls were everywhere, including the double walls which protected the keep, with their ramparts. The design had been borrowed from the design of Roman *castrums*, with their palisades and wall-walks and high sentry posts.

It gave the keep an air of permanency, which British forts lacked. The excess of stone ensured the keep would never be burned to the ground the way a British fort could be.

Was that why Uther had adopted the keep as his headquarters?

Cara slowed when she neared the big gates, for she spotted a shadow by one of the thick columns holding up the verandah roof. She recognized the shape.

Bedivere.

She went up to him. "Are you following me?"

"As I was here first, clearly not." He stood with his shoulder against the column and appeared to be studying the well in the middle of the cloister.

She considered the direction of his gaze. No well was that interesting. "Are you brooding?"

His gaze shifted to her. He seemed startled. "Are you leaving the feast already?"

"Yes, and you are changing subjects."

"If you were a less direct woman, you would let me change the subject without challenge."

She lifted her brow and waited. The implied disapproval did not bother her. She had left such concerns behind six years ago. Two slashes of a Saxon sword had removed them as neatly as a surgeon's knife.

Bedivere did not answer her silent challenge. Somehow, it seemed appropriate.

Cara moved around the column and leaned her shoulder against the rough stone. Through the fine linen of the dress, she felt every scrape and dig of the stonework. She didn't shift her arm. With the column between them, it meant he could not see her face.

Behind them, the last of the people hurrying from the keep passed by. This end of the cloister fell silent. At the far end where the doors to the main hall were located, light spilled. Shadows crossed it as people moved in and out of the hall. More lingered by the columns at that end, just as they did here. Those people talked in low voices. Laughter sounded, just as soft.

Cara scanned the fourth side of the cloister, on the right. It was empty.

Almost empty.

The dark shadow was as silent as they. She peered, trying to spot details and learn who lingered there. No lamp light fell upon them. It was a full moon, yet the face of the moon was hidden by clouds right now, leaving the stars to give light.

The shadow shifted and stirred. Cara glimpsed thick, dark

curls.

Lancelot. In black as usual, which explained why he lingered undiscovered on the far side of the cloister.

Now she saw him, she recalled he had not been at the feast when every officer and their families was required to attend. Even his mother, Elaine, had attended, sitting happily beside her husband, Bricius, the new-made King of Dunoding, even though she had all but retired from public affairs.

"Lancelot!" The feminine voice called from farther along the verandah Lancelot stood upon.

Cara frowned. She knew that melodious voice, but could not put a name to it, yet. She watched.

The woman glided along the verandah to where Lancelot stood, a fold of her gown in one hand to lift it at the front. Morgan, Arthur's sister. She wore flaming red, which went well with her dark hair, Cara admitted. It was not a color Cara would ever wear, for it would pull too much attention upon her.

"Morgan…" Bedivere breathed a mountain's worth of meaning into that single word, which Cara could not unravel. Disgust colored his voice. Resignation. Amusement, even.

Morgan le Fey turned Lancelot to face her, with a hand on his elbow. She made it seem gentle and perhaps he allowed the manipulation.

He bent his head. "Queen Morgan." His voice came softly but clearly across the cloister.

"It is good to see you back in the city once more, Lancelot." Morgan's voice was nearly a purr of pleasure. Her hand still lingered on his arm. In the dim light, her white flesh stood out against Lancelot's black garments. "Will you be visiting the surgery as you did before? The patients always appreciate your presence. It soothes them."

It confirmed the rumors about Lancelot's middle-of-the-night activities. Cara nodded to herself.

Lancelot gave a small shrug. "I do what I can." His tone was formally polite. "If you will excuse me—"

"I would share a cup of wine with you, Lancelot," Morgan replied. "To mark your return. You have been missed." Her hand drifted higher up his arm.

Bedivere let out a breath which might have been a sigh.

Lancelot shook his head. "I am not in the mood for celebrations or drinking." For the first time, his tone was not perfectly polite.

"A mere sip, then." Her voice dropped, became intimate. Musical. "Your company alone is enough."

On the opposite verandah, yet another shadow shifted in reaction to Morgan's coaxing tone, drawing Cara's gaze. She recognized the light blue cloak of the man clutching the column there, agony in his face.

King Mark.

He stared at Morgan and Lancelot, his expression stricken, as if he had been run through with a sword. If the rumors were true about Morgan and Mark, then perhaps he really did feel such agony.

"King Mark watches them…" Cara whispered.

Bedivere stirred. "Only now he sees her for what she is, the poor bastard." His voice was just as low.

Morgan's entreaties and charming words dropped to a volume which Cara was unable to hear from this end of the cloister. The dark-haired woman's hand stroked Lancelot's shoulder, the fingers almost brushing his neck.

Lancelot shook her off, straightening and stepping away from her. "I bid you a good evening, my lady." His tone was stiff and without emotion. He bowed and spun away. He strode a dozen paces down the verandah, then turned into a set of doors there. Lancelot was one of Arthur's closest companions. He had quarters in the keep itself.

Morgan did not seem upset by Lancelot's cold dismissal. She even smiled to herself as she picked up her hem once more and glided along the verandah in the opposite direction, clearly heading back to the hall. As she walked, the clouds swallowed up the moon completely, plunging the night into even thicker blackness.

Cara shifted her gaze to King Mark. He was gone.

She sighed and leaned heavily against the column. Her heart worked hard. It was not pleasant to watch the agony of others. "The poor man..." she breathed.

"Mark is not poor," Bedivere replied, his voice as soft as hers. They had both been able to hear Morgan and Lancelot without effort and it was a warning to keep their own voices low. "Nor is he a man who easily accepts pity."

"I did not mean—"

Bedivere leaned forward, to look at her around the column. "He will recover from this and find new strength. Mark has an uncanny ability to adapt. You will see."

"You know him well."

"Well enough."

"You do that—spend your time with the older officers. Mark and Bevan and Bricius, even Pellinore."

"The older men have wisdom and experience," Bedivere replied. "You would be surprised by what they remember and how useful it can be."

"The older men are set in their ways."

"They adhere to tradition and honor, but they are not inflexible."

"Is that why you enjoy their company?"

He didn't answer. Instead, he shifted back once more. She could no longer see his face. She thought he would ignore the question as he had ignored her question about his brooding. Yet after a few moments passed he said, "Last winter was bad."

Cara recalled the ice on the river and the water barrels, and the depth of the snow, which had been extraordinary. And how she could not find a place anywhere in the city which was truly warm. She and Brigid slept together for warmth and even then, they shivered through most of the night. "Yes, it was bad."

"Everyone thinks it was a sign. A portent."

"I did not," Cara replied.

"Almost everyone," Bedivere corrected smoothly. "Only, I have heard the older men speak about winters in the past. Last winter was not the worst they remember. There were four bad winters, twenty years ago. People died. In the north, cattle froze where they stood, even in shelters. Ice covered everything, so it was not safe to walk about outside unless you thrust your sword ahead of you, to stop yourself from sliding."

"That was the year I was born," Cara said. "I have never heard this before."

"Because you do not speak to older people," Bedivere replied.

"I do not see the value in knowing what winter was like, twenty years ago."

"Because those same men who remember the four bad winters recognized the pattern of winters we have had, lately. They told me that as bad as the last winter was, there will be one more winter, far worse. *This* winter."

Cara shuddered. "No! *Worse?* How can we possibly survive…" She realized she had moved around the column to look at him, only when she saw his face. In the dim light, his eyes were hidden by shadow. "Truly, we are to have another winter like the last?"

"Worse than the last," he said, his voice low. He hesitated. "And now, there is little food to tide us over. The stores are depleted." He glanced around, to see who listened. There was no one at this end of the cloister. The noise from the main hall was building, as the wine flowed and tongues loosened. Soon, someone would pick up a pipe or a drum and the music would begin.

Dancing, too.

Cara was pleased to be removed from it all. Only, now she was faced with this far more unsettling thought. "We should collect firewood, more and more of it..."

Bedivere simply looked at her.

With a jolt, Cara recalled that most days when the patrols said it was safe, Cai and a handful of adults took dozens of older children and a big cart into the woods. They returned in the late afternoon with a cart loaded with wood, from splinters and kindling to full trees neatly sawn into logs.

"All this time, I thought Cai was teaching the children their letters," Cara breathed. "Out in the woods, the same way Lancelot and Pellinore teach the fighters..."

"The adults with him teach the children, as they work," Bedivere said. "It is the public reason for the ventures into the woods. If the real reason were known..."

Cara shivered again. "People would feel as ill as I now do. Why did you tell me this?"

The corner of his mouth lifted. "To explain the wisdom of speaking with older people."

"You enjoy not being able to sleep at night?" she asked wryly.

Bedivere laughed.

Cara realized she was smiling at the sound. It pleased her to hear it. A man who spent his time worrying about such matters as terrible winters and dark times to come could surely find little to laugh about.

Was this why Bedivere always seemed so...sober?

His amusement faded. He said, "I *was* brooding."

Startled, she said, "You brood well. As well as you do everything else."

His lips parted in surprise.

"Was the lady's rejection worthy of brooding upon?" Cara asked.

Bedivere's mouth twisted. Then he said, "Arthur criticized something I did…failed to do."

"You made an error? You are the perfect warrior…"

He sighed. "I *strive* to be perfect. Errors are how one learns."

Excitement strummed in her. "*Yes!*" she breathed. "Yes, that is it, exactly! That is what we spend our days learning, out in the forest. To watch and learn what the enemy does and to adjust for it. To be more effective with the next stroke…"

As she spoke, the cloud covering the moon shifted and the blazing white face was revealed. The misty light bathed the cloister. For the first time, Cara saw the details of Bedivere's face. His golden brown eyes, only a shade lighter than his hair, and the red and gold details on his armor, outlining the Corneus shield.

The curve of his mouth, as he gave her a smile full of tolerance for her enthusiasm for Lancelot's way of fighting.

"You should do that more often," Cara told him.

"Do what?"

"Smile."

Abruptly, his smile faded once more. It was like watching the clouds cover the moon. Yet the after-effect of the warmth in his face lingered, heating her middle.

His gaze, she realized, was not on her eyes. It had drifted lower.

To her mouth.

This time, her shiver was generated by something altogether different. Dismay also touched her. How could she feel anything for him? He was sober and serious. He was a senior officer and Arthur's right-hand man. She was a Saxon half-breed, wanted by no one.

His gaze shifted to her eyes once more. His attention was sharp. His body tense.

At least one man wanted her, she realized, her horror building. "Don't," she whispered.

He did not pretend to misunderstand or ask her what she meant. "You think that mark on your face makes you unworthy?"

"And my Saxon blood. My father's northern realm. You have too many worries already, Bedivere."

"A kiss is a worry?"

"Kissing me would add to your worries," she assured him.

Silence.

This time, she rushed to fill it. She could not stay silent. Not now. "You are the perfect warrior. Everyone says so. I would ruin that."

And the light failed as the moon was once more covered by cloud. It plunged the cloister into thicker night.

Bedivere inclined his head. A short bow. "I will accede to your wisdom, my lady." His voice was as stiffly polite as Lancelot's had been. He turned away and moved along the cloister toward the hall.

Cara drew in a shaky breath, listening to the merriment in the hall and the first sour notes of a pipe. When her heart was once more calm, she turned and left the cloister through the main gates. She wished she had stepped through them long minutes ago, instead of pausing to speak to the man.

It would never happen again. She could learn from the past, just as he could.

Chapter Ten

The city braced itself for a royal wedding which did not happen.

Everyone expected that with Guenivere's arrival, the wedding would be put into place as soon as possible. The gossips reminded them that once Arthur had resigned himself to it, he had made his coronation happen within three days. Why would he not rush the wedding, too?

Yet Guenivere took up residence in her father's house and ate beside the King every night, while not a murmur of a single arrangement, not even a date, came forth from the royal apartment in the heart of the keep.

Not even Merlin deigned to answer any of the wary questions about Arthur's plans.

Bedivere dismissed his own speculations. The wedding would take place eventually. Whether Arthur was married or not would not stop the Saxons from their late summer raids. While Cai looked increasingly more stressed as he managed the city's preparations for the coming winter, Bedivere grimly increased the patrols, sending the more experienced warriors out on two- and three-day journeys to hunt down any rumors of Saxon bands.

Last year, the Saxons had not ceased their raids until snow was deep upon the ground and a man's iron sword hilt stuck to his skin when he gripped it.

"It isn't simply war, anymore," Arthur pointed out, on one occasion when Bedivere had been invited to step into his private quarters and share a cup of wine. "It is survival which faces us now. The Saxons smell blood. Aesc has dispensed with any rules he might have once followed."

Bedivere fully expected the Saxons would continue to raid and burn for as long as they could this year, too. They had already ruined most of the summer harvest. If they continued to harass the farms and villages across Britain, the coming winter would finish the task Aesc had set himself.

The only defense was patrols and more patrols. The earlier the warning they received of Saxon incursions, the better they could deal with them.

"The problem is," Cai complained as he shoved his sheets around impatiently, "there is no defense against fire. One can't hew at flames. Even the cold does not stop it. Snow, either. Only water—and there's little enough of that after the summer we've had."

The first frost had once been a signal that fighting was over for the year. This year, Bedivere increased the patrols yet again until *everyone* complained about duty shifts and make-work.

Bedivere assigned those who complained to cleaning and repairing weapons, buffing and repairing armor, war boots, helmets and shields. He held inspections of his men's' fighting gear and disciplined those men who neglected their equipment and weapons. He visited the smith shops daily, exhorting the smithies to keep up their production of blades, spears, shield bosses and other weapons. He argued with bow-makers and the two cart-wrights in the city who knew how to make and repair chariots.

"You are an unexpected ally in this matter," Lancelot told Bedivere.

"I do not do it to support your fighting," Bedivere growled.

"Yet support it, you do." Lancelot smiled—a rare expression for him, these days.

"Leave him alone, Lancelot," Cai growled, not raising his head from his pages. "He's fighting to turn the tide against human instinct. Everyone is relaxing now that winter is nearly here and they shouldn't."

"This year they shouldn't," Bedivere said in agreement. "I can't make the smiths understand that production of weapons must continue. Every time I turn my back, they return to forging plow shares and kettles, as they've always done at this time of the year."

The days grew colder and shorter, although for now, no snow fell. This far south, it was unusual for any snow to fall at all— usually only in the depths of winter. Last year, though, the snow had been calf-deep and had lingered for weeks.

Bedivere expected that even more snow would fall this year. No one else seemed braced for it, though. "Am I the only one who sees it coming, Merlin?" he asked the druid one night when Merlin shared his and Lucan's table for the evening meal.

"No," Merlin murmured. "Although, you and Cai are the men who must ensure we are prepared for it, whether or not we see it."

"I wish everyone could See the future the way you do," Bedivere breathed.

Merlin's expression darkened. "That is not a wish, Bedivere. That is a curse."

Disciplining men and handing out punishment, plus arguing with townsfolk and the aldermen, became a daily chore. Bedivere knew he was unpopular, that the fighting men spat on his boot prints once he was out of ear shot and cursed when his name was mentioned.

He could put up with all of it, as long as they did what he ordered. He no longer tried to explain or make them understand. He gave orders and dealt with those who failed to obey. If he had to pull the army into a state of readiness by its collective forelock, while they kicked and screamed in protest, then he would do so.

Arthur's cold observation often repeated itself in his mind.

You are my war duke. Control them as you should.

News about the Saxon bands faltered, then stopped altogether. The patrols returned with nothing to report, day after day.

"A second winter of fighting is too much for Aesc to stomach, I wager," Pellinore said gleefully, warming his hands at a brazier.

Bedivere shook his head. "We cannot afford to relax. Not yet."

"They're hugging their firepits, as we should all be," King Mark growled, wrapping his cloak around him.

"No," Bedivere said.

Mark lifted a brow, the one without the scar running through it. "You'll have the lads rebelling if you keep this up."

Bedivere didn't respond to that. He didn't know how to. How much longer could he maintain this relentless pressure upon the army?

Deep in the long, cold nights, the thought he could suppress during the busy days would surface. *What if he was wrong?*

Lucan provided the only glimmer of hope against that worry. "If you are wrong, then we'll have spent a winter in battle-readiness. That is all. Next summer, we won't have to blow dust off our shields." He shrugged.

The weight of enmity and disapproval laid heavily upon Bedivere's mind, though.

What spare time he had, he spent sitting at Cai's table by the fire, drinking. Cai remained silent because he had his own worries. It was possible the townsfolk hated Cai as much as the army hated Bedivere.

Arthur found them there, one dim afternoon. The King crossed the hall to stand at the table. He pulled his fur cloak in around him. "The chill bites at one, this time of year."

"My lord…" Bedivere got to his feet.

Arthur rested his hand on Bedivere's shoulder. "Relax. You deserve to."

"I don't believe any of us should relax," Bedivere said shortly.

Arthur's fingers gripped tighter. His gaze was steady. "My deepest wish is for you to be utterly wrong." His gaze shifted and grew unfocused. "Alas, my wishes count for naught, these days." He gave a glimmer of a smile. "Stay true to your course, Bedivere."

Bedivere's chest ached. "I will."

Arthur patted his shoulder, turned and left.

Bedivere sank onto the bench, shaking.

Cai shook his head, watching Arthur leave. "He's in one of his black moods," he said, his voice low. "I've seen them last a season."

Bedivere pulled his cup closer and gripped it. "He's not wrong. Neither am I."

"Aye," Cai said in agreement. "They'll remember, after."

"It requires surviving the before," Bedivere said bleakly and drank.

"At least the army understands discipline," Cai replied. "I can't whip a shopkeeper for failing to store flour. I'm braced for something to give, any day now."

He proved to be prophetic, even though he did not have a shred of the Sight. Only, it was not a shopkeeper who broke, but Guenivere.

GUENIVERE MADE A FUNDAMENTAL MISTAKE at the very beginning, which she didn't recognize until later.

When Queen Morgan failed to arrive at her father's house in response to her summons, Guenivere seethed. She did not tell her father about the implied insult, for he was weighed down by concerns about the contingent of Camelard warriors housed in the city. Arthur would not give them or her father leave to return home. Meanwhile, Bedivere, the war duke, insisted upon useless patrols which sent the men out of the city for days at a time.

Bedivere was universally disliked and complaints about how he was overworking the army were rife. Her father dealt with complaints and tried to leaven the burden of duties and patrols and perpetual battle-readiness, when everyone wanted to shut the door upon the winter and crouch by the fire.

Instead of bothering her father, Guenivere attempted to deal with Morgan on her own. One day, she *would* have to deal with such matters without assistance.

When Guenivere saw Morgan sitting at the Lothian table that night—a rare occurrence—she crossed the hall to confront her.

"Queen Morgan, I would speak with you," Guenivere told her. "If you will but step this way...?"

Morgan turned on the bench and looked up at Guenivere with a polite smile on her clear and unlined face. People whispered that Morgan maintained her appearance with spells and magic. Certainly, she possessed a youthful vigor which defied her true age. Her figure was that of a young maiden's, lithe and slender. She wore gowns which displayed that bounty. All of them were without stain or rent or patches, at a time when every woman stitched together old shirts and sheets to make barely presentable tunics.

Morgan leaned back against the table, as Gawain and Gaheris broke off their conversation to watch the pair of them.

"Guenivere," Morgan said, her voice sultry.

Guenivere did not fail to notice the lack of a title, but let it slide.

"As my future sister-in-law, I welcome you to Arthur's court," Morgan added.

Guenivere squashed her first impulsive response, which was to point out that Arthur had already welcomed her to his court. Instead, she said, "We have not spoken together, you and I. Circumstances have brought me to this. If you will come with me?"

Morgan smiled. "I am comfortable here."

"I assure you, what I want to say to you is best spoken in private."

"You can speak freely in front of my nephews," Morgan replied.

Guenivere's cheeks heated. Only now did she recognize her strategic mistake. She should have sent a page to fetch Morgan to her side at Arthur's table. Instead, she was in the position of supplicant.

Morgan would know that, too. It was why she looked so complacent.

Determination solidified Guenivere's middle, dispelling her nerves. She straightened her spine. "Very well, as you insist. I wanted to speak to you about your..." She paused to pick delicate words.

Morgan's eyes were dancing with amusement. She was enjoying herself.

Guenivere dismissed all considerations of diplomacy. She said, instead, "Your proclivities in the bedchamber are disrupting the court and setting a bad example for the young women who I am expected to train and prepare for court life. This cannot continue."

A soft, indrawn breath came from the next table. Too late, Guenivere realized it was not just Morgan's nephews who had paused to listen them. Everyone within earshot was witness to the conversation, which should have been held in private—and *would* have been, if Morgan had obeyed Guenivere's original request to attend her in the privacy of her father's house.

The discomfort their audience created prodded Guenivere. "I must insist you comport yourself in a way which befits your station," she added.

"My station as the High King's sister, you mean." Morgan ran her gaze over Guenivere, from top to toe. The implication was clear. Guenivere was merely the daughter of a petty king. She was not Arthur's queen, yet. "I am entitled to relax in whatever way I deem fit, in the privacy of my...bedchamber," Morgan added.

"If you kept your activities to the bedchamber as a decent woman would, we would not be having this conversation," Guenivere snapped.

"If you had activities to confine you to the bedchamber, you would not think to have this conversation in the first place," Morgan replied. She paused. "Are you jealous, perhaps, my child?"

The second collective gasp stirred Guenivere's irritation more than Morgan's insult did.

Suddenly, she was tired of it all—of *everything*. The poor meals, the complaints and the endless side-glances sent her way while everyone speculated about why a wedding had not been announced. She knew very well that everyone blamed her for Arthur's lack of haste to marry her. Thanks to the weather, she had been cold for weeks. She was well aware that her blue gown showed signs of wear, while Morgan looked glorious. No wonder Arthur could not bring himself to marry her! She was ragged and unkempt. She had been forced to ask Cai to find a comb for her, as she did not have even the basic items to make herself presentable. They were all back in Camelard.

Enough was enough. Guenivere straightened her shoulders. "Do not bandy with me. You embarrass yourself every time you drape yourself upon another man. You think men actually admire your ways?"

Morgan's smile slipped. Guenivere had struck home.

Guenivere added quickly, "You will behave in a manner appropriate for a matron and queen from now on, Morgan. Do I make myself clear?"

A fine line appeared between Morgan's brow. "I think you have forgotten who it is you speak to." Her voice was low.

"I have not," Guenivere said crisply. "You are only Arthur's half-sister, Morgan, and I would not trade upon that relationship more than it can withstand."

Morgan's scowl increased. "I am Arthur's chief surgeon, girl. You would deprive him of his best physician, for the sake of your overblown sense of morality?"

The entire hall had grown quiet.

Guenivere trembled. She had forgotten that Morgan ran the surgery. Abruptly, she realized she was cornered. Her only way forward was to insist her demands be met. She *must* see this through or be proved toothless and powerless in this court of kings and lords.

Only, if she did insist, she would weaken Arthur's army—they could ill afford to be deprived of a good surgeon. Yet if she held to her position, Morgan would make good her implied threat and leave the court.

From the corner of her eye, Guenivere saw the movement of something black, and refocused, dismay touching her. She watched Lancelot leave the hall, pushing his way through the people who gathered in front of the door, held there by the drama playing out in front of them.

Guenivere pulled her attention back to Morgan, her dismay complete.

Morgan's scowl cleared. She knew she had won. She smiled.

That was when long fingers gripped Guenivere's elbow from behind. "Oh, I would not call you the *best* surgeon, Morgan,"

Merlin said, his tone casual, almost indifferent. "You have skills with a knife, to be sure, although they are teachable skills."

Guenivere held her breath. It was a veiled counter threat. Merlin implied he could always teach another surgeon the same skills.

Morgan pushed herself to her feet, her fury stealing any prettiness from her face. Now she looked her age. She pulled her gown in around her feet and picked up the trailing hem. "You pollute Arthur's court with your useless Christian ways," she hissed and moved toward the hall doors, her head up.

"Let her go," Merlin murmured.

"I will see you to your seat, my lady," another calm voice said loudly, on her other side. Guenivere looked around.

Bedivere stood politely to one side. He inclined his head in acknowledgement and held out his arm.

"I will find wine for your cup," Merlin said, just as loudly as Bedivere. Neither of them needed to shout, for the silence still gripped the hall.

Guenivere was glad of Bedivere's arm, as he led her to the small table Arthur used. Her trembling had increased, now the confrontation had ended. Yet now was the time when she must appear to be completely contained.

She sank onto the chair which had become hers with deep gratitude. She made herself look up at Bedivere. "Thank you." Her voice shook.

Bedivere pulled out the short bench which usually went unused on the other side of the table. "I will sit with you until Arthur arrives," he told her.

Merlin reached over her shoulder and picked up the copper cup which was hers and filled it with thin wine. Then he shocked her by settling upon Arthur's chair beside her.

"Are you a Christian, my lady?" he asked, his voice low. He pushed the cup toward her. "Drink," he added.

She gripped the cup, sipped and almost gagged. Her throat was too tightly bound to swallow. "I am not a Christian," she made herself say. Her voice was still shaking. "Although there is a monastery not far from Camelard, so I am familiar with their tenets. Christianity is spreading, Merlin, and they have strong convictions. If Arthur's reign is to unite all of Britain, then we must pay homage to all beliefs, including theirs."

Merlin did not look shocked, or even amused. He simply nodded. "A sensible position to take, my lady, although you chose the least suitable person in the court to try to bend to your will in this matter. Morgan is far too strong-minded and used to her freedom."

"I see that only now," Guenivere replied ruefully. "Only, this was not an exercise in power—"

Both men chuckled, startling her.

"It was *not*," she insisted. "Morgan is upsetting too many people with her ways. King Mark appears to be wasting away—have you not noticed? And Lancelot..." She swallowed. "Lancelot refuses to be in the same room with Morgan."

Or with her. Only, Guenivere could never say that aloud.

"Good evening, Guenivere," Arthur said. He rested his hand on Merlin's shoulder, not at all upset that the man was sitting in *his* chair.

Merlin rose to his feet. So did Bedivere.

"You missed a moment, Arthur," Merlin said. "I will explain, later."

"I have already caught wind of it," Arthur said, his tone complacent. "Morgan is flexing her influence once more."

Guenivere's heart thudded unhappily.

"This time, Guenivere was involved," Bedivere said softly.

Arthur shrugged and sat down. "Guenivere is still present, in this hall and sitting at my table, while Morgan is nowhere to be seen. I have no need of more details." He picked up the flask of wine with Merlin had placed on the table. "More wine, Guenivere?" His tone was warm.

Guenivere drew in a shaking breath and met his gaze. Warmth and humor showed in his eyes, which provided yet another shock.

Even though she had taken only a few sips, she nodded. "A little more, yes, thank you."

"Enjoy your meal," Merlin bid them, as he and Bedivere moved over to the table where Cai, Pellinore and King Mark sat.

Arthur's mouth turned up in a small smile. "I believe I will," he said softly, his gaze not shifting from Guenivere's face.

Chapter Eleven

Cara found the golden eagle the day of the first frost.

Each morning she followed the same routine as everyone in the army did. Before she was permitted to break her fast, she was first to see to her horse's needs, then tend to her weapons and equipment.

Even the deepening cold of the coming winter did not take away the pleasure she felt in those early hours of each morning. Other fighters complained about the officers' insistence upon the routine discipline. Cara, though, found a pleasant solace in walking through the empty and silent streets to the tiny square where Cailleach was stabled. She would spend time with her horse, feeding him, seeing to his water and brushing his coat, while murmuring to him.

Cailleach would nudge her with his nose, silently asking for carrots or turnips. These days, she could give him neither and she would commiserate with him, rubbing the velvety nose and talking quietly.

On the day of the first frost, her boots crunched on the dirt of the streets, echoing flatly. She was not the only fighter making their way to where their horse was stabled, although she was the only one who kept her horse in the tiny stable off the little square.

When she reached the square, though, she paused at the entrance, for sitting in the corner where the sun would first strike was a huge bird with a curved beak. His sharp brown eyes watched her warily. It was an eagle.

She had never been so close to one before. The size of the creature shocked her. His head would be at least as high as her waist. The sharp talons curved and hooked into the stones lining the square, as he shifted and raised his wings to launch himself into the air.

Only one wing moved freely. She saw, then, why he had found his way into the square. His left wing was injured, It lifted only part-way up. Blood as red as hers marred the top of the wing.

"Oh, you poor, poor magnificent thing!" she breathed and took a step closer.

The eagle reared, the good wing rising, ready to drive downward and lift him into the air. Without the other wing, though, he could not fly.

Cara froze, to remove the threat he felt.

Cailleach, in his stable, gave a quiet snicker. He was hungry.

"Food!" Cara breathed. "You cannot fly, so you cannot hunt." She edged around the square, staying as far away from the eagle as the dimensions of the square would allow.

She reached the rain barrel and bent to pluck the small bucket which was used to bail the water. She plunged it into the water, breaking the thin layer of ice on the top, and ladled the water into Cailleach's trough. Then she plunged the bucket once more. This time, she crept closer to the eagle, as it hissed and tried to lift away from her.

When she was close enough, she crouched and leaned far forward to put the bucket on the ground. She nudged it closer with the tip of her fingers.

Then she stepped back until her back was to the wall, as far away from the bird as she could get. Obeying an instinct she did not fully understand, she crouched once more.

The eagle watched her warily and did not drink.

Cara could understand its caution. She moved around the edge of the square and into the stable, where Cailleach stomped impatiently and hurriedly fed him. She gave him a cursory pat. "I will come back," she promised and moved out of the stable once more.

The eagle was still where she had found him. He watched her movements. His black beak was wet.

He had taken a drink.

Thrilled, Cara held up her hand toward him. "Wait there. I will return with something for you to eat, even if I must bribe the cook for it. Although the gods know what I could use for a bribe. I will pay for it with my house pin, if I must. You just wait, yes?"

The eagle didn't move.

Cara took that as a positive answer. She ran through the streets to the back entrance of the keep, beside the old, abandoned orchard. The large kitchen door stood open and steam issued from inside. The cooks were already preparing bread for the first meal of the day, which would be shortly served in the main hall.

Cara's belly rumbled and cramped. She ignored it. She was used to ignoring the pangs until her first duties of the day were done. She spoke to a cook, shouting in the woman's ear over the noise of the kitchen. Women pounded grain on the table, kneaded dough and feeding the fires of the ovens.

Cara could also smell oats cooking. Oat cakes. Her mouth watered, although there had been no honey to go with the cakes for weeks.

The cook jerked her chin over her shoulder at Cara's request.

"Speak to the boy."

The boy was a lad of six or so, who tended one of the oven fires. He had ash on his cheeks and in his hair, and a bright look about his eyes.

"On the heap outside," he said. "Lots of it."

"Can you put the meat aside, tonight?" she asked him.

He scratched his head. "Gnawed and cold?"

"Gnawed and cold," she assured him. "A bowl, or a kettle. Whatever can be spared to hold it. I will be by tomorrow morning at this time to pick it up."

"Got yerself a cat to feed?" he asked, puzzled.

There had been no cats in the city for a year or more. "Of a sort," Cara told him. She picked up a dirty bowl from the shelf beside the oven. "I will return this." She hurried outside again, feeling an unusual energy. It had been too long since she had something interesting to do.

The last interesting thing had been the night Guenivere had arrived. Her mind sheered away from that thought and she focused instead on picking out the meat scraps from the rubbish heap in the corner of the old orchard. The stench rising from the heap made her gag. If the boy would not cooperate, she *would* bribe him with whatever she possessed, to avoid this task in the future.

Her bowl full, she hurried through the streets. She did not run, for the sound of running footsteps would alarm people.

Relief trickled through her when she stepped back into the square and saw the eagle was still there.

Calming her rapid breath, she again inched closer, a slow step at a time, until she was close enough to once more crouch and slide the bowl toward the bird.

This time, the eagle glanced at the bowl immediately, instead of keeping its gaze upon her. Perhaps the scent caught his attention. Eagles had a better sense of smell than she did. Their eyes were keener, too.

Cara backed away, until the cold wall was against her back. She waited and watched.

When the bird did not move, she slid back into the stable and quietly groomed Cailleach, then petted and fussed over him as usual.

She checked the halter and strapping and saddle blanket impatiently, forcing herself to move through the routine even though she wanted to abandon it and go outside once more.

Her duties completed to a degree which would pass any inspection Queen Lowri might abruptly hold, Cara stepped out of the stable once more.

The eagle appeared to have not moved an inch. The bowl, though, was half-empty.

Pleased, Cara smiled at him. It was a *him*, she decided firmly. "I will be back tomorrow with more, so eat it all if you want." She had no idea how much meat an eagle needed every day. She hoped a bowlful would be enough.

The eagle stayed in the corner of the yard for another three weeks. Every morning Cara arrived with the bucket of scraps the boy, Ban, had put aside for her, she was happy to see the bird there. After a few days, he would let her approach without rearing back and trying to use the damaged wing. Instead, he let her put the bucket in front of him.

After caring for Cailleach, she would scoop another bucket of water and leave that in front of him, too.

Three days later, the eagle did not wait for her to step away before leaning forward and pecking at the meat with a hungry, soft squawk. His beak knocked against the side of the bucket. He seemed cautious about dipping his head right inside the high sides of the bucket. His hunger was huge, though. He pecked quickly, snatching gobbets of meat and swallowing them quickly.

An idea occurred to Cara. When she returned home that day,

she dug out the thick riding gauntlets her father had once used. They were made of well-cured leather and fit no one in the family, not even Newlyn's hands.

The oversized and heavy leather would serve her now.

The next morning when she stepped outside the house, she paused, astonished. A thin blanket of snow covered everything. Flakes still drifted down, a few here and there.

Cara shivered and pulled her cloak in around her and held it closed. The usual early morning sounds of the city were muffled beneath the snow.

"It isn't even the equinox yet!" she whispered.

Bedivere had been right, after all. This winter would be harsh and long, and worse than last year.

Cara shivered and hurried to the keep kitchen, to get the bucket of meat for the eagle, then back to the square to care for both creatures. The meat steamed gently. Even though it was the remains of last night's supper, it was still warmer than the air outside the kitchen.

When she reached the square, Cara drew the long gauntlet from under her cloak and put it on her dominant hand. The eagle cocked his head, watching her. He gave a little squawking sound she thought might mean he was pleased to see her—and his breakfast.

She moved toward him with the bucket, then crouched to bring her down to his level. Instead of putting the bucket in front of him, she put it to one side. Grimacing with distaste, she picked out the cold scraps and curled her gloved hand into a fist and pushed the meat into the space between her thumb and fingers.

Then, with slow movements that wouldn't startle the bird, she held her fist toward him.

He cocked his head the other way, studying her hand. With a delicate movement, he bent. His big hooked beak hovered over her fist. With a darting movement, he snatched the morsel from her hand and straightened, swallowing it.

Pleased, Cara inserted another piece of meat and held out her hand. This time, the eagle didn't hesitate. He tore the meat from her fist and gobbled it.

Cara realized she was smiling. She laughed at her own foolishness as she gripped yet another piece of meat, then another and another.

The bucket was half-empty when the eagle stepped onto her wrist and gripped it through the leather with his mighty talons. It didn't hurt, although his grip was ferocious. Cara resisted the need to jerk away from him or startle him. He flapped his wings, resetting his balance. He moved the injured wing far more freely than when she had first found him here, yet it still did not lift as high or as freely as the other one.

This close, she could measure the full wingspan and was amazed. His wings would spread far wider than she was tall, she suspected.

He bent and plucked at the meat in her fist, his talons gripping tightly.

Cara hurriedly placed another piece in her fist, which he plucked with more neatness than he had when standing upon the ground. She understood, then, that his balance was better when his feet could curl *around* a perch, than when they were spread out upon flat ground.

His primary talon was as big as her palm. What would it do to her wrist, if she was not wearing the gauntlet?

Silently, she added more pieces of meat to her fist as swiftly as the bird could eat them. The level in the bucket dropped.

"So, this is the answer to the riddle," Bedivere said, behind her.

Cara whirled, startled, then tried to abort the movement as the eagle flapped and protested in a high squawk.

Cailleach stomped, in his stable.

Cara turned as carefully as she could. She didn't think the bird would let her put him on the ground, not when there was still meat in the bucket.

"What are you doing here?" she demanded of Bedivere, controlling both her tone and her volume. She didn't want to startle the eagle and she didn't want to disturb anyone sleeping in the adjoining houses. It was still very early.

Bedivere wore a long, thick, dark brown cloak and heavy boots. The cloak was pinned over one shoulder, keeping it wrapped around him to hold in the warmth. "I'm here because you are." He moved forward, his gaze on the eagle. "Cai told me the boys in the kitchen were putting aside meat scraps for a woman they described as the red-headed Saxon. I thought I would find out why you wanted meat no one else cared for in quantities large enough to require a bucket. And lo, I have my answer."

"Don't come too close, you'll scare him," Cara said quickly.

"Not if I move slowly enough. You've accustomed him to humans."

She realized he was keeping his voice down, just as she was.

He drew slowly closer.

The eagle pecked at her arm, a short imperious demand for more.

She crouched once more, her attention returning to the bird. She plucked another piece of meat.

"He's young," Bedivere said softly.

"How do you know that?"

"He still has white feathers in his tail."

She glanced at him, surprised.

"The hawk master in my father's stable used to like to tell tales to a boy who liked to listen." Bedivere rose to his feet once more.

Cara stood, too, bringing the eagle with her. He seemed content to stay on her arm, although he was heavy. "Are you here to tell me I cannot have the meat no one else wants?"

In the cold dawn light, Bedivere's eyes seemed more golden than usual. "It is of no concern to me what you do with the meat. Feed him or do not. He will eventually leave."

Her heart gave a small thud. She had deliberately not considered that day which still laid ahead.

"You are aware, are you not," Bedivere continued, "that eagles eat the same food we do? By helping him live, you are depriving us of what he eats?"

Cara rounded on him. "That is *not* true!" she cried, alarm leaping in her chest.

"Or that he would himself make a meal fit for a king?"

"Do not *dare* try to touch him," Cara growled, reaching for her knife with her left hand. It was an awkward reach. The eagle cried and squeezed her wrist, panicked by her quick movements.

Bedivere's hand came down on her left arm, halting her movement. He shook his head. "You're frightening the bird. Stay still."

She swore. "You're frightening *me!*"

Bedivere gave a click of his tongue. "I am teasing, Cara. I jest." He gave her a small smile. "Eagles are *terrible* meat. Hawks are far better."

Cara's heart thudded as she stared at him. "*Now* I know something you cannot do perfectly. You cannot jest. At all."

He moved closer. "No, I am not good at it." His voice was low.

She swayed backward.

"Stay still," he murmured, as the eagle flapped his good wing.

It was almost impossible to stand still. Bedivere stood far too close to her. Close enough that she could feel the heat of his body.

"What are you doing?" she breathed.

He brought his hand up to her face. With one finger, he gently traced the longer scar on her face. Then the other. "So fierce…"

"Bedivere…" Her voice was weak. She felt as though she begged, although she did not know for what. For him to leave? To not leave? Confusion gripped her.

"I am the most reviled man in the city, these days," he told her, his voice low. "I am no longer the man you must refuse because of who you are. I have brought about worries and ruin all by myself."

"No, you have not—" she protested quickly, but could not finish for his lips met hers, smothering anything else she might say.

She had been kissed before, but not like this. The few kisses she had experienced in the past were weak, fumbling gestures, devoid of meaning or feeling.

This was a real kiss. It was heady, stealing her breath and her thoughts. The only sensations she noticed were his mouth upon hers and his body against hers. Heat glowed between them. His tongue swept into her mouth, stroking and tasting and she sighed at the pure delight it invoked.

Then Cailleach kicked at the back of his stall and gave a soft neigh of protest, making Cara jump, which made the eagle flex his wings and hiss.

Bedivere released her mouth but his hands held her face. His thumb stroked, making her scarred cheek tingle.

"I must feed Cailleach," she said breathlessly.

"Yes." He made no move to let her go. His breath was as swift as hers. His eyes, she saw, were darker than before. Heated with male intent.

"It is my duty," she added.

"Yes." He touched his lips to hers once more, then released her. "Do your duty. I would not have you disciplined because of me. Here." He plucked the other gauntlet from her belt and worked it onto his wrist. "Give him to me." He picked out one of the last pieces of meat from the bucket and pushed it between his fingers, then held out his arm, parallel to hers.

The eagle spotted the meat, yet hesitated.

Slowly, Bedivere drew his arm—and the meat—away from the bird. In response, the eagle hopped onto his arm and bent to eat.

Cara stripped off the grease-smeared gauntlet, her heart pattering and her mind whirling with questions. She hurried into the stable to feed Cailleach before his protests woke people. She skipped brushing him, checked the bridle and saddle quickly and moved back outside.

The eagle perched upon the edge of the water barrel. Bedivere had gone.

Chapter Twelve

wo days after Bedivere's inextricable, unexplained kiss, one of his senior officers, Miles of Laundes, failed to return from a routine patrol. Neither he, nor his horse were found by the hastily put-together search party.

The whisper spread through the city at the same speed as the cold winter wind which whipped at everyone's flesh and made being outside uncomfortable. The snow had not departed or turned to slush. It added to the chill.

For three days, the city waited for news which did not come. By the third day, Cara could tell by everyone's mood that they had presumed the worst; that Miles would not return.

On the same day, Cara's mother announced they would attend the main hall. "Put on your best dresses," she told Brigid, Cara and the twins. "Brigid, you may use my silk ribbons."

Startled, Cara studied her mother. "Why are we attending the hall? Have we been summoned?"

"In the middle of the afternoon?" Ula shook her head.

"What are you planning, mother?"

"If we are to live with these people, we must mingle with

them," her mother said archly, as she smoothed out the pink ribbons with her fingers.

"Then you have no need for me to come with you," Cara replied. "I have mingled with the only people I care to, this day." She had only just returned from training in the forest, which continued despite the weather. The snow merely added to the uncertainty of one's footing, which was good training, Lancelot had assured them, for battles when the ground turned slippery underfoot.

Lancelot had become a harsh task master since he had brought Guenivere to the city, although Cara liked the discipline. She could feel the difference in her strength and agility.

Pellinore had not led the training this morning and everyone knew why, although no one spoke of it. Miles of Laundes was the lover of his daughter, Elaine, and had been for years, even though no formal arrangement had been declared between them.

There were many such informal arrangements these days, both openly acknowledged and not-so-secretly maintained. Cara wondered, as she moved through the training drills, if Bedivere's kiss had been an overture for a similar understanding.

He had not sought her out since then and she avoided the main hall. Even so, her heart hurried every time she visited the stable and the little yard in front, until she saw it was empty of anyone but the eagle, who impatiently waited for his breakfast.

Cara had no intention of stepping into the hall when she was not directed to do so by Queen Lowri or Cai, or Arthur himself.

"You will attend the hall with your sisters," Cara's mother replied to her declaration. "I have spoken." Her tone was cold.

Cara hesitated. She knew that tone. She might wheedle her mother into a softer frame of mind, while a direct refusal to obey would incense her.

"Fine." Cara moved over to the rickety table and reached for the flask of wine sitting upon the temporary shelf, unstopped it and drank.

"You will put your gown on, too," Ula added, for Cara still wore her armor and trews.

Cara lowered the flask. "No."

Ula's jaw flexed.

"If you want me to come to the hall," Cara added, "I will come as I am, as a member of the Queen's Cohort, or I will not come at all."

Ula scowled, but said nothing more. Instead, she pulled Brigid closer and helped her comb her hair and wind the ribbons into it.

Cara thought the pink ribbons clashed with Brigid's red-gold hair. She said nothing.

The five women set out for the keep, their cloaks held tightly around them. Newlyn was on patrol, which made Cara nervous, given Miles' disappearance. Miles was a seasoned fighter. Newlyn had yet to blood his blade.

The entire city was hushed. Even the keep itself, which was normally a noisy place, today held a subdued air. People spoke in whispers and lingered in tight groups, their heads together, when normally they flittered from group to group, crossing the hall like busy bees.

Ula did not linger in the main hall, which was the only public room in the keep that Cara had ever seen. Instead, her mother crossed the hall, leading her daughters, with Cara at the rear, heading for one of the connecting doorways on the other side. As they moved, Cara saw heads turn to watch their progress.

She kept her gaze straight ahead, her resentment settling deeper into her bones. Already she was jumpy and checking every tall man she spotted. Would Bedivere be here, somewhere? Surely, he was busy with his own affairs? The few people in the main hall seemed to be women and some kitchen staff cleaning tabletops in preparation for the evening's meal.

They passed through the wide doorway into the room beyond. It was another hall. This one was smaller, with windows ranging down the side, with their shutters throw open. Low winter light made the room brighter than the main hall, which had no windows at all. The chill in the air was offset by a large fireplace at the end of the room, in which a fire crackled and leapt.

A tall chair sat close to the fire, with a footstool before it. Guenivere sat in the chair with sewing resting on her knee. She murmured to three women, who sat upon stools ranged about the chair.

Cara mentally chided her mother. This was why Ula had insisted they come here. She had heard Guenivere would be in the smaller hall this afternoon and sought to take advantage of her presence.

Irritation slowed Cara's steps, so she arrived at the fireplace after her mother had begun speaking, while Guenivere looked at Ula with a polite expression.

"…daughters, who I recommend to you as ladies of good character. I bid you not hold my heritage against them. Their father was Caradoc of Brynaich."

"King Caradoc, yes, of course," Guenivere said. Her voice was musical and pretty. "And may I meet your daughters?"

The other three woman watched with interest. One of them, with golden blonde hair, was known to Cara. Tegan was the daughter of Bricius. She fought in the Queen's Cohort, in the other wing.

Tegan nodded at Cara.

Cara was secretly pleased to see that Tegan wore her trews and the tunic she wore for training, although she had put aside her armor. Her hair was combed, too.

Ula pushed Brigid forward. "My eldest daughter, Brigid, my Lady. And my youngest, Nareen and Isolde, both eighteen, now."

The twins both giggled self-consciously.

Guenivere raised her hand toward the three women on the stools. "I am sure you all know each other. Branwen and Eira, both daughters of King Bevan. And Tegan, princess of Dunoding."

The three nodded politely. Branwen and Eira were known to Cara, although she had never spoken to them directly. They were Queen Lowri's daughters, although neither of them fought in the cohort. Branwen had blonde hair which fell well below her hips and was held back by a silver clip. Eira had dark hair, which was almost as long, yet was braided the way Cara's mother tied her hair for sleeping at night. All three women appeared to be around the same age as Brigid and Cara.

The youth of the women surrounding Guenivere was highly suggestive.

"If you are in need of companions, my Lady," Ula said, "then I recommend my daughters. There are few ladies of your age at court..." Ula smiled at the three other women. "In fact, I believe you may have all of them around you already."

Cara rolled her eyes.

Guenivere leaned to peer around Ula. "And the other lady, behind you?" she asked. Her gaze settled on Cara. It shifted to the left side of her face, where the scars ran. Then Guenivere gave her a small smile.

Cara studied Guenivere's eyes. They were oddly colored. Almost without color, in fact, which was attractive.

Cara had heard about the public confrontation between Guenivere and Morgan le Fey, the King's sister. She had even heard that Bedivere had become involved at the end. Although the gossips lingered over the novelty of seeing the young and apparently timid future Queen standing her ground while Morgan snapped and hissed in fury before stalking from the hall.

Cara noticed the fine line between Guenivere's brows and the sharp, uplifted chin. Also, the square, straight line of her shoulders. She judged the gossips had not exaggerated the story.

Ula shifted on her feet, so that Cara was fully revealed to Guenivere. "My second eldest daughter, Cara."

Cara grimaced.

"You do not wish to be here, Lady Cara?" Guenivere asked. Her tone was polite, yet there was a note in her voice which made Cara cautious.

"I welcome the chance to meet you, Lady Guenivere," she said truthfully. "You are not what I expected."

"Oh?" Guenivere's brow lifted. "What did you expect, may I ask?"

Wariness gripped Cara. This was the future High Queen of Britain.

Before Cara could formulate a polite answer which gave no offense, Merlin swept past her, his robes swishing. He bent and murmured in Guenivere's ear.

Guenivere's lips parted and shocked wrote itself upon her face. Then she stood and dropped the linen she had been stitching upon the chair. "I am afraid we must abandon this meeting, ladies," she said shortly. "There is grave news."

Merlin had already moved away.

"What news? What has happened?" Branwen asked, getting to her feet, too.

Guenivere's face took on a sorrow-filled expression. "Elaine, Pellinore's daughter...Elaine's body has just been found. I must go to Pellinore and see what I can do to help. Please excuse me."

Tightness gripped Cara's throat. Pain squeezed her heart. She hissed softly.

Guenivere turned to face her. "Excuse me?"

Cara threw out her hand. "I should be out there, not here by the fire! Tegan, too! We might have helped. We might have... have prevented this."

Tegan's jaw was set hard. She did not move when Guenivere

glanced at her.

Guenivere gave a little nod. "In that case, I believe it best you leave and do what you feel you must to help. Good day, Cara of Brynaich." Her tone was cool.

She didn't wait for Cara to reply but turned and moved over to the little door at the back of the room. She stepped into the private apartments and shut the door.

Ula shook Cara's arm. "How *dare* you!" she whispered furiously. "That is the *Queen*!"

Brigid also looked angry. Her face was flushed as she glared at Cara. The other women stared at Cara with bewildered expressions.

"She is not the Queen yet," Cara told her mother, her tone as cold as Guenivere's. "And I spoke nothing but the truth."

Tegan's nod was tiny, yet it was there.

Cara whirled and strode to the door into the main hall. When she reached the gates of the keep, she determined that she would never step foot in the halls again...not unless she was forced to it.

NEWS OF ELAINE'S DEATH BY her own hand rushed through the city. Even sitting with her back in the corner of the tiny house, the wine flask in hand, Cara could hear distant sobs and the murmur of people meeting on the narrow street and passing the news along.

From the house beside theirs on the opposite side from the house which Bedivere and Lucan used, Cara could hear two men—soldiers, she presumed—speak of omens.

"It's a sign, I tell you," one growled. "Last winter was bad. This winter will be far worse. Miles won't be the first to disappear, you'll see."

"Omen, portent, I care not," came the reply. "Someone should be asking *why* he disappeared."

"Gone over to the Saxons? Not Miles."

"Or taken by 'em," said the second. "How close does that put 'em to the city, then?"

Cara shuddered and drank more wine.

Surely Bedivere had thought to ask such questions…and perhaps he was working to find them, even while she sat in this dark corner and drank.

The sun was setting when Newlyn arrived back at the house. His sword clattered as he hung it on the hook he had driven into the wall.

"How does it go?" Cara asked.

Newlyn shook his head. "We rode for miles and miles. There was nothing. No sign, no one we spoke to remembered seeing Miles three days ago."

"What about Saxons?" Cara asked. "Have they seen them?"

"If they had, they wouldn't be in their huts for us to speak to, would they?" Newlyn said, his tone reasonable.

Cara didn't reply. She wasn't sure what she *could* say. Newlyn would simply roll his eyes at her if she said his answer didn't reassure her at all. There was something *wrong* with it, with everything to do with Miles' disappearance, although she didn't know what it was.

It was fully dark when Ula and Cara's three sisters returned to the house. Brigid glowed with happiness. "Branwen and Eira and Tegan are such nice ladies! They asked me to sit with them tomorrow. Guenivere might return tomorrow, too."

"I am happy for you," Cara told her politely.

"It was such a lovely afternoon!" Brigid added.

"No thanks to you," Cara's mother murmured as she reached onto the shelf and pulled down the basket which held their food.

She put it on the rickety table, pulled aside the cloth and peered in.

Cara's chest ached. She knew how little food was in it. The last of the summer vegetables and yams. There had been no meat for a week.

"We will dine in the main hall with the rest of the court, tomorrow," Ula declared, as she laid out the shriveled tomatoes.

Cara's heart sank. She could not protest this time, as she had forcibly argued in the past, that they should eat in their own house, for there would be more food in the hall.

A soft sound knocked upon the roof of the house. Everyone looked up, puzzled.

Cara put the flask aside, her heart racing, for she recognized the sound. Surely, though, she had heard wrong?

More of the soft thudding sounded, accompanied by a whispering note, this time through the wall Cara's back was against.

"What on earth was that?" Brigid said, sounding annoyed.

Newlyn's hand hovered by his sword as he frowned, peering at the wall.

Far away, deeper into the city, someone screamed.

Cara scrambled to her feet and reached for her sword.

At the same time, a heavy whizzing noise came. Out in the narrow street came a heavy thud and a roar. A second thud came. This time it slammed against the front of the house.

Crackling.

Fire!

The flames leapt up, visible through the chinks in the shutter over the window.

"Gods in their heavens!" Ula cried, pulling the twins against her. "It's at the door!"

More screaming and shouting, still too far away for Cara to determine what they were saying.

Another thud came against the house. This time, the wall behind Cara shivered. She leapt away from the wall.

The wall behind Newlyn, the one which they shared with Bedivere and Lucan's house, shuddered beneath pummeling fists.

"The roof! Get to the roof!" someone cried through the wall.

Cara dropped her sword. "Newlyn! The table! Quickly! Help me!" She grabbed the end of the table. Newlyn leapt to the other end and lifted it. They shifted it into the middle of the room.

Now the roar of flames was distinct, making Cara's heart thunder. She knew what the flames and the thudding sounds meant. She even recognized the soft chuffing slaps against the roof and the walls.

The Saxons were attacking the city. They were pouring thousands of burning arrows upon them. Thin tree roots twisted into balls and stuffed with pitch, then launched with giant slings—she had heard the stories from those who had barely escaped the burning of their own villages and towns and houses.

She did not dare let her thoughts linger upon what the sounds meant, or let herself properly hear the screaming and shouting, which was increasing.

She and Newlyn dropped the table and it shook alarmingly without a wall to prop it up.

"You go first," she shouted at Newlyn as the other three girls cried and clung to their mother. "You must smash open the roof." She glanced at the door and window at the front of the house. There was no way through either. The flames crackled and the wood of the walls glowed on the inside. Flames licked in the tiny chinks between door and frame, window and sill.

Newlyn scrambled onto the table without argument and stood upon it as it swayed. He found his balance, while he wrapped the corner of his cloak around the blade of his sword. Then he used the hilt like a hammer, to smash at the timbers over the roof, then ram them aside with a squeal of nails and a shriek of distressed wood.

Smoke filled the house, thick and black. It rolled over the floor in great clouds.

Newlyn leapt for the edge of the hole he had made in the roof and pulled himself up.

"Nareen, Isolde, quickly. On the table," Cara told them. "Newlyn will lift you out. Up, up!"

"Go on. girls," her mother said. Her tone was calm now. Controlled. She and Cara pushed the girls onto the table. They clung together, looking frightened.

Newlyn hung over the edge of the hole. He was lying on the roof. He thrust both arms through the hole. "Quickly!"

Nareen raised her arms and gripped Newlyn's forearms. He pulled her up with a grunt of effort and she kicked and rolled out of the way. Then Isolde was lifted up.

The screaming and shouting came from all directions, now, and muffled by the roar of the fire.

"Brigid," Cara said.

"I'm the oldest," Brigid said stiffly.

"Get yourself up there, or I'll drag you up by your hair," Cara shot back.

"Brigid," Ula snapped.

Brigid scowled and scrambled inelegantly onto the table. She looked up, her arms raised for Newlyn.

Newlyn pushed one arm through the hole. Cara could hear the twins tramping on the roof, now, too.

Then Bedivere's head and shoulders appeared in the hole. "No time!" he shouted. "All of you. Now!"

Cara pushed at her mother's shoulder, as Newlyn snagged Brigid's hands and pulled her through. Ula jumped on the table and threw up her hands. Both Bedivere and Newlyn raised her up.

Cara leapt onto the table, which swayed wildly. The joints creaked and it wobbled. She could feel it sagging to one side.

"Jump!" Bedivere shouted.

Cara didn't pause to look up first. She knew there was no time. She threw herself into the air in a mighty leap, flailing with her hands for any grip, anything she might grab onto.

Bedivere's hand slapped around her wrist, his fingers iron bands. "Your other hand." He held out his right hand.

Cara took a breath and threw her left side upward, to extend her reach. Her fingers felt metal. An armguard. She curled her fingers around it and hung on.

Bedivere pulled, raising her through the hole. Newlyn whipped his arm around her waist and lifted her the rest of the way out.

She rolled onto the roof, which was hot. Now she could see why.

The long row of houses on their narrow little street burned from one end to the other. They were not the only people to escape through the roof, although now they were there, she could see there was no way down. Both sides of the row of houses burned furiously, the flames leaping up higher than the roof, creating two walls no one could pass through. Soon the flames would creep over the edge and the roofs would all burn, too.

For now, the air was clear of smoke, which rose directly up from the flames. It also poured out of the hole in the roof she had just been pulled through. There was no wind to drive the smoke sideways.

"This way," Bedivere said, pointing. He had to shout to be heard over the fire.

Four houses down, a break showed in the wall of flames, on the side of the houses facing the town wall. Lucan stood there with the twins and Brigid. He had a coil of rope wound upon his arm.

"Step carefully," Bedivere told them. "Not all the timbers are sound."

They hurried as fast as they could manage across the hot timbers to where Lucan stood.

Lucan tossed the coil of rope down to the ground between the houses and the town wall.

Lucan and Bedivere kicked and stomped on the roof, until two holes appeared on either side of a support strut. They quickly tied the end of the rope around it and tested the knot.

"Newlyn, you first," Bedivere said. "Have you a knife?"

"Yes."

"Keep it out, once you're on the ground. Go." He slapped Newlyn's shoulder. "Lucan, guard the ground with him."

Newlyn slithered down the rope hand over hand, then Lucan threw himself over the edge and walked down the side of the building.

Cara eyed the flames on either side. They were moving closer at an alarming rate.

"Queen Ula, you next. Are you armed?" Bedivere asked.

"No."

Bedivere reached under his cloak and pulled out his belt knife.

Ula wore no belt. She took the knife with a nod and clenched it between her teeth, then moved over to the rope, laid on the roof and rolled over the edge, her hands on the rope.

"As mother did, so must you," Cara told the twins, pushing them toward the roof. "It's not very far down." Although it seemed to be a *long* drop, to her eyes.

The twins were too scared to protest or fuss. They rolled on-to the edge of the roof as their mother had done, gripped the rope and lowered themselves over. Brigid followed them down, for once not complaining about anything.

"Now you," Bedivere said, pushing Cara toward the rope.

Cara eyed the flames. "I will jump."

"You will turn an ankle if you do. We have a long night of fighting ahead. Down the rope. Quickly, the flames are scorching my feet through the roof. Can you not feel it?"

Cara only then registered the heat baking her soles. Alarmed, she leapt for the edge of the roof and grabbed the rope. She threw herself over the edge and slammed up against timbers which smoked. Behind them, she could hear the roar of a fire gone wild.

She barely hung on to the rope, dizzy.

The roaring grew louder and louder, then become a deafening explosion. The roof where she had been standing erupted. Burning timbers, sparks, smoke and a billow of flames climbed into the night sky.

"Bedivere!" Cara screamed.

He threw himself off the burning roof, a loop of the rope around his hand, to swing out and back up against the wall. The impact drove the breath out of him. His body only barely missed Cara's.

Then he bellowed in pain, his free hand reaching for the one caught in the loop of rope.

The rope was on fire.

"Cut it! Cut the rope!" Bedivere shouted.

Beneath them, Cara could hear the girls screaming and Lucan and Newlyn shouting instructions.

"I don't have a knife!" Cara cried.

Bedivere groaned, his hand scrabbling at his trapped wrist. "My boot!"

Cara let herself slither down a handful of the rope. She spotted the knife hilt tucked in his boot. She pulled out the blade and clenched it between her teeth as her mother had done, then hauled herself up the rope once more. In that moment, she was thankful for Lancelot's harsh training. Her strength was enough to pull herself up the rope, which many women were incapable of doing.

Bedivere groaned softly. His eyes were closed and now Cara

could smell burning flesh. Her belly rolled. She pulled herself up high enough to saw at the rope and hesitated. "I can't cut it without hurting you!" she cried.

"Cut it," Bedivere said, his voice hoarse. "I order you to cut it."

Cara closed her mind to what she must do. She ignored the heat of the flames licking closer, the ferocious heat of the burning wall against her body and Bedivere himself.

It is a log I must release, she told herself and sawed at the rope. The rope was one of the thick ones they used to haul whole trees, nearly the width of her hand in thickness. Even though it burned, she still must cut through the core of it.

She hacked and sawed, moving fast.

Bedivere cried out as the rope groaned and unraveled. They both dropped a little way, then dangled.

The rope was not cut through, yet, although now she was too low to reach the cut.

Cara put the knife between her teeth once more, threw her left hand up to grip higher than her right. She took the knife with her right hand, then lunged upward and slashed at the few fibers of rope which held them there.

The rope snapped. Bedivere and she fell. There was no time to brace herself, for the fall was too short. They landed heavily. Her elbows and lower arms grew instantly numb and she could taste blood in her mouth. She had bitten her tongue. Her head thudded and her neck throbbed. Her hip was on fire.

Bedivere laid still, while Lucan beat at the burning rope around his hand.

Cara crawled over to Bedivere and shook him.

Bedivere groaned. His eyes opened, held in slits against the pain. "Protect the city. Protect the king." His eyes closed.

Lucan bent and put his hand on her shoulder. "Can you fight?"

"Yes." She didn't know if she could or not. She had little feeling in her hands. She didn't care. She would use her teeth and her feet if she must.

"Ula and your sisters will care for Bedivere," Lucan said. He was shouting to be heard. "You and Newlyn report to your commanders. I will command the Corneus contingent. Go!"

There was no time to argue. Cara knew what Lucan had not said, that the Saxons surrounded the city. They must fight through the Saxon line to find a way out for the people trapped behind the burning walls.

Cara lurched to her feet and ran.

Chapter Thirteen

o one in the city slept that night.

It was not just the old houses closest to the wall which the Saxons put to flame. Because the houses were so close together, jostling for space in a city which had none to spare, the flames easily leapt from house to house, from wall to wall, and roof to roof.

Even the keep itself burned. When Cara reached the gates, she saw the astonishing sight of flames leaping *inside* the stone walls, painting the walls with red and orange.

People poured from the gates, staggering, coughing, helping each other along.

Cara saw Bevan helping Lowri walk. He was doing most of the walking for her, for her head lolled on his shoulder. Cara raced up to him. "The Cohort!" she cried.

Bevan shook his head. "No time. Report to my second. Owen. You know him?"

"Yes."

"You can fight with my house, as you have no standing army," Bevan said. He lifted Lowri up and resettled her on his shoulder.

"Any fighters you see, tell them to report to their house commanders."

"Where?"

"Behind the keep, the old orchard, where the rubbish heaps are. Go."

Cara knew the place. She had dug for meat scraps there many times. She spared a thought for Cailleach and the eagle. They were in the heart of the city. Someone would make sure Cailleach was released from the stable. For now, the more pressing need was to broach the walls and clear a path for people to escape the city.

She ran for the back of the keep, moving right around the perimeter of the solid stone structure, which took long minutes. In the old orchard, on the other side of the smelly heaps, a dozen men chopped at the thick palisades with axes, while dozens more stood with their weapons drawn.

Because the stone keep made up part of the wall and surrounded the old orchard, no flames could reach here.

Cara saw Branwen and Eira holding each other. Beside them stood the short man, Owen, who served as Bevan's second in command. Cara moved up to him. "King Bevan asked that I serve your house. How can I do that?"

Owen nodded. "Find a weapon. When the wall is breached, we fight our way to the forest."

They were on the north side of the city here. The forest swung around and came down to the city walls to meet the river, only a dozen or more paces away. Once, the trees had crowded the wall but a generation ago, the trees had been cleared back to a long bowshot from the wall.

"The Saxons will be in the trees," Cara pointed out. Now she understood why Miles had disappeared. He must have caught wind of the Saxon host approaching the city, and they caught him before he could warn them.

"Which is why the armed fighters go first, to clear the way through them," Owen replied. "While you're finding a weapon, tell everyone to come here. Tell them to tell everyone else. Pass the word."

Cara turned and ran.

She found others, many of them dazed and bewildered, and sent them to the wall breach, while she dodged burning and collapsing buildings to find more. The more alert people she instructed to do what she was doing—find others and send them to the orchard behind the keep.

When she found horses tearing through the streets, their eyes rolling, she grabbed their manes and give them to the nearest person, with instructions to take them to the orchard, too.

She was not the only fighter moving through the city. She saw others hauling wagons, six of them on the poles, while children and the weak were loaded onto the back of the wagons.

Five grim-faced and dirty men tossed barrels from one of the grain warehouses, loading another wagon, while the roof of the warehouse burned and crackled.

Even though Cara saw fear in everyone's eyes, there were few people gripped by panic. Instead, everyone salvaged what they could from the flames before evacuating or helped others to leave.

When the flames grew too great to pass through, Cara returned to the orchard. There were hundreds of people there, now. Beyond the broken-down section of wall, she heard the clash of swords and the ringing of blades. The army was clearing a way through the Saxons.

Even more fighters with shields and swords guarded the breach itself.

As Cara had not found a single weapon in her sweep through the city, she remained with the others. She would be of no help at the front lines.

More and more people gathered behind her, waiting. From beyond the walls of the keep and the old orchard, she could hear the fire take the city. It roared and bellowed, punctuated by the crash of collapsing buildings.

Everyone waiting in the orchard and along the street which led to it stood quietly between the flames and the fighting Saxons.

Then, the warriors guarding the breach surged forward.

Owen, standing upon the wall of the orchard, pointed toward the breach. "Run!" he shouted. "Run for the trees and do not stop!"

The people in front of Cara lurched forward and she ran with them.

Beyond the wall laid slain Saxons. She stopped to snatch up the sword from one, plus another's axe, then ran.

Now she could fight.

BEDIVERE GREW AWARE OF THE jolting before anything else made sense to him. Then, the glimmer of sun against his closed eyes.

Sound came to him. The creak of wagon wheels. That explained the jolting. A snort from a horse, the jingle of harnessing. A cough. The shuffle of feet. Far away, the low bellow of a command.

And everywhere, the smell of smoke.

Then he remembered.

He opened his eyes, his heart hurrying, ready to lurch to his feet if necessary, as he scanned his immediate surroundings.

There were no helmets with horse tails. No filthy blonde braids.

The wagon had no walls and he laid on the very edge, for the rest of the wagon carried others, also lying still. All of them were

British.

Bedivere let his muscles sag.

Now he could feel the pain in his right arm and hand.

"Oh, you're awake!" a woman exclaimed, beside him, which didn't make sense. "Merlin!" she called softly.

Bedivere rolled his head and opened his eyes carefully once more.

Cara walked alongside the wagon. She was not the only one crowded up alongside it. For each person lying on the wagon, someone else walked beside them.

Cara was peering ahead, looking for someone. Merlin, he realized.

She waved vigorously and beckoned.

Bedivere couldn't see ahead. He didn't have the energy to lift his head. His body felt as though it has been cast from metal and he could sink through the floor of the wagon from the weight of him.

Cara turned to him. "Merlin will speak to you." Her face was filthy with ash and dirt. Blood, too. Her glorious red hair hung in limp tails over her shoulders. "You may feel drunk," she added. "You've been breathing poppy smoke for most of the night."

He blinked. "Lucan…?" It hurt to talk.

"That is why I am here, instead," Cara told him. She gave him a grim smile. "Lucan is leading the Corneus people." She lifted her chin, gesturing farther ahead. "A half mile up from here." Her smile was warm. "Everyone who made it out is with him. You can sleep, Bedivere."

How many had escaped?

The question went unanswered because he really did want to sink back down into sleep. He struggled against it.

Merlin appeared in front of him. Where had he come from?

Merlin patted Bedivere's shoulder. "Your people are being taken care of, Bedivere. Mark of Kernow is war duke for now. You must sleep. When you next wake, things will make more sense." His hand rested on Bedivere's brow. It felt cool. Then it lifted away again.

Merlin gave him a grim smile. His black eyes were sober. "Arthur is safe. Guenivere, Cai, most of the senior officers. We are heading for a hill…for a safe place. When you next awake, you won't be rattled about as you are. Sleep, Bedivere."

Bedivere frowned. Beyond Merlin's black robe, he could see a long line of people and horses and wagons, stretched out for more than a mile, following the curve of a street he did not know. Everyone walked with their heads down. Armed men rode alongside, shielding their flanks. Their horses clopped through inches of snow, churning it.

Bedivere wanted to ask a question. Something about…his hand? What was the question, though?

Then the need to ask it faded, too.

MERLIN WALKED ALONGSIDE THE CART, studying Bedivere's still form, then moved to walk beside Cara. His face was smeared with ash and blood. There were lines of weariness on his forehead and around his mouth.

"He will live?" Cara asked, her throat tight.

"Oh yes," Merlin said, his tone light. "He likely won't appreciate that fact, when he wakes properly, though. You must remind him of it."

"Me?" She gripped the hilt of her borrowed sword, which she had thrust through the belt she had taken from another dead man. The axe, which had proved useful during the early hours of the morning, hung from the back of the belt.

Merlin shook his head. "There are few lines of command left. I appreciate you lingering here for this long. Lucan is busy and someone must watch Bedivere. I cannot—the valley where we will camp for the night is difficult to find if one does not know the way, so I must lead Arthur to it. Will you stay?"

Cara glanced at Bedivere once more, remembering the long night she had passed through.

Just on sunrise, she had found her mother and sisters clinging to Newlyn, deep inside the trees beyond Venta Belgarum. Officers moved among the trees bawling at the top of their lungs for everyone to fall into line and follow along. Newlyn would protect them…and she suspected her mother would also fight, if it came to it.

"You must find Bedivere and help him," her mother told her. "He saved us. All of us. It is a family obligation only you can fulfill. Newlyn must stay with us." The brisk note in her voice told Cara she could not argue.

The Saxons had been driven far away by those fighters who had found mounts and weapons. Word had come down the file that the Saxons had been driven like sheep, across the river and far away. There had been only fifty or so. Just enough to encircle the city walls, fire arrows and burning pitch balls inside the walls. They had never intended to stand and fight. They melted away into the countryside like mangy wolves.

As the long line of people, wagons and horses moved slowly across the land, Cara had worked her way down the length of it, asking for news of Bedivere. She had not seen him or Lucan since he had fallen.

She came across the wagons hauling the wounded and burned. The wagons were a mobile surgery, for Merlin and the Lady Morgan, Gander, and their assistants were crouched upon the rolling vehicles, working upon injuries.

On the third wagon, Cara found Bedivere. His hand and arm were wrapped in cloth which looked as though it had been torn from someone's hem. It was tied in an efficient way that told Cara a physician had tended to the wounds already.

She looked around for someone to ask about Bedivere's hand, but no physician was balanced upon this particular wagon. Each of the wounded had people walking alongside them. As she looked, a woman reached up to brush snowflakes off the man lying closest to her.

Bedivere had snowflakes on his armor, too. Cara brushed them away and found herself anchored there by the lack of anyone to relieve her or answer her questions.

Now Merlin was asking her to stay.

"I had intended to stay, Prince Merlin," she told him. "Only, I have little knowledge of medicine. I don't know how to help him."

"You can do what we all do," Merlin told her, with an approving nod.

"What is that?"

"The best we can." He patted her shoulder and strode away.

Cara glanced at Bedivere once more. Then she reached and brushed a few more snowflakes from his chest.

MERLIN STRODE UP TO THE clump of men surrounding Arthur at the head of the column. "The pass into the valley is a mile from here and well off the road," he told Arthur.

Arthur's roan stallion, Cynbel, nuzzled his shoulder. Arthur was not leading him. Cynbel simply walked behind his master. A small boy sat in the saddle and an even smaller little girl was propped in front of him, both of them filthy. The girl was deeply asleep, her head on the boy's chest. The boy looked half asleep, too.

Guenivere walked beside Arthur. She carried another small

child on her hip and held the hand of a fourth.

Behind her, Lynette of Calleva carried another child. So did her partner, Eogan. It was a common sight along the file, which Merlin had walked a dozen times already today. With luck, the children would find their parents by nightfall. Some would not be that lucky, though.

Mark of Kernow had taken the place where Merlin had been, before. He grimaced as Merlin stepped alongside him. He was also leading a horse, this one without a saddle and no children on it because of the lack.

Merlin tallied the people at the head of the column. "Where is Cai?"

"Gone ahead with a dozen or more, for firewood and to see what they can hunt," Arthur said. "Mark was just speaking of leaving, Merlin."

Merlin lifted his brow.

Mark's scored face wrinkled into a grimace. "The less people you have to feed, the better. Tonight will be the death of some of them. You're leading them south, Merlin. I can take my people and ride faster than you and spread word."

Merlin tilted his head. "Spread word?"

Mark looked uncomfortable. "Arthur has been feeding and sheltering every man, woman and child who comes a-knocking upon the gates of the city. Now it is time for those of us who still have roofs over our heads to do the same. I will rouse the lands ahead of me as I go. Those of you who last the night won't have to face another one like it, not if I can help it."

Merlin nodded. "You know where we will camp, tonight?"

Mark brought the horse forward, to mount it. "Even if I did not, I would still find you." He hauled himself up onto the horses' back and gripped its mane with strong fingers. "You are leaving a trail a crawling babe could follow."

He put his tongue to his teeth and gave out a shrill, sharp

159

series of whistles.

Cries went up along the file. Dozens of men fell out of the file and hurried ahead, jogging to where Mark sat on the horse. Among them was Dinadan, whose constantly amused expression had been barely dented by the night's disaster. Tristan and Sagramore were there, too, both carrying shields and spears. Tristan's wild locks and fierce black beard were unmistakable.

"Forward! Double time!" Mark shouted.

He kicked the horse into a slow trot with his heels, while the men surged ahead with him. Swiftly the horse climbed the slight rise and disappeared beyond. Then, Kernow's men were gone, too.

Merlin stepped into the space beside Arthur which Mark had left. "Bedivere sleeps, still," he murmured.

"Where is Lancelot? He can serve until Bedivere is on his feet once more."

Merlin had passed Lancelot as he made his way forward. Lancelot had been crouched upon one of the wagons, beside the wounded. "I will speak to him," Merlin said.

Arthur hesitated. "Will Bedivere regain his feet?"

"Oh, he will recover," Merlin said easily. "The hand, though..." He shrugged. "We must wait upon that answer."

"His right hand," Arthur murmured. He sighed. "We have been injured and insulted by the score this day, yet *that* injury seems far more personal to me than any other disaster I've become acquainted with so far."

"Because it *is* personal," Merlin said heavily. "You have never once been without Bedivere's support. Now you taste his absence and it is a measure of what you have taken for granted until now."

"Yes," Arthur said heavily.

Chapter Fourteen

he valley Merlin led the survivors to was small and enclosed on all sides by steep hills. It was reached only via a deep, narrow pass which was all but invisible unless one knew it was there.

A stream crossed one end of the valley. The water had only a thin layer of ice. Everywhere, there were trees with long, crooked branches which reached for a sun which would only show in the middle of the day. They fought each other for light and as a consequence, the gnarled and crooked branches of each tree were interlocked with its neighbors. The up-thrusting branches held a thick mat of fallen leaves, which had captured the snow and kept it from falling upon the earth beneath.

"We will be cold, but we will not be wet, thank the gods," someone near to Cara muttered as everyone wove between the trees.

"We may not even be cold," said another. "Have you heard what they plan to do?"

"A ring of fire, I believe."

"A ring. Right around all of us. We'll be jammed against each other inside the fire ring."

Cara turned to locate the wagon where Bedivere laid. If there was to be a fire—a ring or not—she would ensure Bedivere was as close to it as she could manage. Already, stacks of wood were being laid in a long, curving line through the trees.

She felt a tap on her shoulder and turned.

The man pointed to her belt. "You've got an axe. Can I use it? We can get more wood right here."

She pulled out the axe. "I wish I had thought of it myself," she said ruefully. "To me, it is a weapon. Have it and be welcome."

He hefted it. "Never thought a Saxon weapon might be useful." He hurried away.

Everyone still able to walk and move freely was collecting or distributing firewood or taking care of others. No one sat and relaxed.

Cara spotted Bedivere's wagon through the trees. It had made it through the pass. She hurried up to it as it came to a shuddering stop. The other patients were being lifted or helped down.

Bedivere was stirring groggily.

Cara shook his shoulder. "Are you awake enough to sit up? You can't stay here, Bedivere. Just a few steps, then you can lie down again."

"Cara." His voice was foggy. He rolled on to one shoulder and winced. It was his right arm.

"No, sit if you can," she urged him, trying to lift him. "Or, if you insist, I can carry you over my shoulder." She wondered if she could carry his weight and decided that if it was needed, she would.

Bedivere sat with her hand against his shoulder to stop him tilting. He shook his head, then tried to raise his injured hand to it. He hissed and clutched at his arm with his left hand and studied the black bandages hiding the other.

Cara moved to his left side. "What is it to be?" She added a snap to her voice, to pull his attention from his hand. "Over my shoulder, or walk?"

"Walk. Mithras, let me walk..." he muttered and gave a great shudder.

Cara hooked her arm behind his back, beneath the charred remnants of his cloak. The sharp edges of the carved and decorated armor dug into her arm, where her arm guard and mail did not protect it. "One, two..." She heaved him to his feet and held him upright as he found his balance.

She ducked under his arm and held his wrist to keep the arm anchored. "As slowly as you wish," she encouraged him.

Bedivere took a tentative step. Then another. "I'm not iron, anymore."

"You were iron?" She tried not to laugh.

"Felt like." He took another step. "Black through."

"That was the poppy smoke, I suppose. Gander told me you would be drunk."

A few more steps. "Drunk is more fun."

She did laugh, this time. "Sometimes, it is."

His steps came more evenly. Cara led him through the line of firewood which would become their circle of fire, to the soft patch of earth she had marked as a good location. No one had taken it yet. She eased out from under his arm. "Can you sit by yourself?"

Bedivere stared at the ground. "Sit yes. Only way down is to drop, though. Can't get my knees to work."

Cara hid her smile and ducked back under his arm. "Let yourself drop."

As his weight settled onto her shoulders, she sensed he was trying to lower himself down and not lean upon her. Abruptly, his knees gave way and most of his weight landed on her. Cara gritted her teeth and braced her knees. She sank to the ground, bringing him with her.

He settled on his rear with a heavy grunt. Wordlessly, he settled the injured hand on his lap. He didn't look up at her as Cara brushed off her hands.

"If there is any food to be had, I will find some and bring it back," she told him.

"Lucan should—" he began.

"Lucan is managing the Corneus people. You must suffer my help, instead."

He lifted his chin. "Why?" His tawny eyes were pain-filled, although his gaze was direct.

"You saved my family, Bedivere. I will not forget that."

He scowled. "It does not mean—"

"Yes, it does." She turned and stalked away, moving through the settling people toward where she could see Cai's tall head. If there was food to be had, he would see to the dispensing of it. She would start there. If necessary, she would head into the land beyond the valley and find food of her own. There would be a rabbit or hawk she might find, even in this snow and cold.

There were others drifting out of the valley, carrying bows and knives, clearly intending to do the same as she planned.

Cara found Cai and snagged his attention for a precious moment. She put her request to him.

"For Bedivere?" Cai rubbed the back of his neck. "We have a deer and some rabbits, although they need roasting, first. Come back when the sun is gone and I can spare you a slice or two."

Pleased, Cara returned to where Bedivere sat. He had propped himself up on one arm, his head hanging. The effects of the poppy smoke tended to linger, Gander explained.

"Which is just as well. It helps with the discomfort, afterwards," the old physician had said in his quavering voice.

"Lie down, if you need to," Cara told Bedivere.

"I should speak to Lucan, first. And Cai and Arthur…"

"They know where you care," Cara assured him. She looked

up as a man carrying a flaming branch moved along the line of firewood. He thrust the end into the kindling at the bottom for a few moments, then moving a pace or two farther, and repeated it.

They watched the flames build.

Bedivere said, his voice rough. "Perhaps, just for a moment or two..." and he stretched out upon the earth.

While the flames grew higher, Cara moved over to the nearest tree. The rough bark looked as though it was flaking away from the main trunk. Pleased, she used her knife to wrench a good-sized piece of it free and turned it over. The curved bark would serve was a bowl or plate. She found a stout twig on the edge of the fire which was not yet burning and used it to scrape the roughest parts of the interior bark away, leaving a smooth and gleaming surface. It would do to carry hot slices of meat, at least.

She glanced over to check on Bedivere. He was shivering.

Cara moved around him, lifted his shoulders and removed the remnants of his cloak. She folded it and put it beneath his head. She took off her own cloak and laid it over him.

Imitating what she had seen both Gandar and Merlin do, she rested her palm upon Bedivere's forehead. It was clammy, and far warmer than her own palm. She knew little about medicine, enough to know that was not good.

The circle of fire was burning strongly, now. Beyond it, dark had fully formed. Plus, she could smell the mouth-watering scent of roasting meat. Cara picked up the bark platter and moved carefully through the people sitting and lying inside the circle, over to where Cai had last been.

He nodded when he saw her and nudged the man supervising the nearest fire and murmured to him. Two rabbit carcasses had been skewered upon greenwood branches. The man turned them over the fire by twisting the end, his hand wrapped in his cloak to prevent it burning. He used his knife to shave off several slices of the cooked meat from the outside of the rabbit and dumped them on the bark platter.

Pleased, Cara returned to Bedivere. He had not moved. She shook him. "Bedivere, I have meat." She shook him again.

"Not hungry," he muttered.

"Eat, anyway," she told him. She tore off a morsel of the steaming meat, her mouth watering and her belly cramping. "Here. Open your mouth."

He didn't move.

"Bedivere, do as I say. Eat this."

When he didn't answer and did not move, Cara sat back, perplexed. Illness and fevers were supposed to be the province of women—mothers knew what to do in cases like this. Women of any ability did, too. Cara had spent all her time learning the ways of war and fighting, considering that to be of greater importance.

For a brief, aching moment, she wished she had been more like the soft women in the halls. Then she would know what to do now.

"Bedivere." She shook him again.

His face was damp and his brow dotted with sweat. He gave a soft sound, a barely heard groan, which was more alarming than any cry of pain might be. He could not hear her at all, she realized.

She looked down at the hot meat and the morsel in her fingers. Clearly, he would not eat it. Quickly, almost inhaling the scalding flesh, she gobbled the meal down. If her belly was not aching so much, perhaps she would be able to think of what to do.

Heat from the meal slid down her throat and chest and settled in her middle. She put the bark platter aside, then made her way around the ring of fire until she found Gander and asked him what to do.

"Fever..." Gander nodded. "Not unexpected. Burns are nasty that way. If this were spring, I'd tell you make him a tea of elderflowers." He ruminated.

Merlin straightened up from a patient he was tending, who was too ill to be moved off the wagon. "White willow bark, ground up in water, will work, too."

"White willow…" Cara looked around the valley. "These are not willow trees."

"There should be some outside the valley," Merlin said. "Do you remember the way?"

She gripped her knife hilt. "I…yes." A little. Her heart thudded.

"Look for where this stream runs. Willows like water," Merlin added. He turned back to his work. Someone tugged on Gander's arm, leading him away, and leaving Cara standing alone.

She glanced at the deep night beyond the fire ring. With a deep breath, she leapt over the fire and moved away from the camp.

SHE FOUND A SINGLE WHITE willow, far away from the hidden valley. The last few leaves hung from the thin branches, showing their pale undersides. The early winter had caught even the trees unprepared.

The trunk of the tree was rough with gnarled, furrowed bark. Cara stripped away as much as she could, favoring the inner layer rather than the dried out and crumbling outer layer. She tucked it inside her tunic, for she had no pouch or sack to carry it with and no cloak to wrap it in. The bark scratched at her chest and belly as she also hacked off the slender hanging ends of the branches. They were tough, long and supple and could serve as rope, if she needed it.

By the time she was done, it was late. She heard nothing but a high wind, far overhead, which made her feel alone. It was not a good feeling. There was no moon to light her way. Her eyes had adjusted to the dark and she followed her own trail through the snow to the valley pass, where the tramping steps of many made finding her way back through the pass easy.

On the way, she tripped over a ram's horn, stubbing her foot upon the point. She picked it up and shook the snow off it. It was a find which would serve her, now.

She hurried back to the valley and the fires.

Bedivere was possibly asleep...or maybe not. He still shivered, and he sweated freely, now. She stripped off her cloak. Surely, a man so hot should not be made hotter.

She used the fat stick to grind the willow bark into a fine powder upon the platter. If Bedivere was to swallow this, it must have no lumps. She shuddered to think what it would taste like, even watered down.

She carried the horn over to the trickling stream and filled the hollow end with water, then carried it back to the fire and warmed it. When it was warmer than ice-cold, she took it back to Bedivere and sprinkled the powdered bark in the water and stirred it with the stick.

The most difficult part of the task was rousing Bedivere. She only had one hand and was afraid that if she moved to quickly, she would spill the contents of the horn. It could not be propped upon the ground.

Vexed, she shook and cajoled him, in a voice low enough not to disturb those lying nearby.

"Here, let me help."

Cara looked up, startled, as her mother settled on the ground on the other side of Bedivere. Cara's throat closed over tightly, as relief touched her. "He won't drink!"

Ula nodded. "There is a trick to it, when the patient is fevered. Here." She slid her hands beneath Bedivere's shoulders and raised him off the ground.

His arms flopped lifelessly. His eyes remained closed. Cara might have thought him dead, except for his white face and wet brow.

"Touch the liquid to his lips," her mother directed. "Remind him of his thirst."

Cara dipped her finger in the warm water and dabbed it against his lips. They were hot and dry. As she dabbed, his mouth opened a little.

"Now, trickle it into his mouth," her mother added.

Cara put the thin edge of the horn against his lips and tipped carefully. She poured only a little of the dark liquid, to avoid choking him, then waited. After a moment, he swallowed.

Pleased, she raised the horn to his mouth once more. This time, she did not have to coax him to open his mouth. He drank, even though he did not open his eyes.

When the horn was empty, her mother lowered Bedivere down and resettled his cloak beneath his head. "Put your cloak back over him," she instructed. "The hotter his fever burns, the quicker he will recover." She got to her feet. "I must return to the girls and watch over them. Newlyn is on duty."

Cara wanted to protest and demand her mother stay with her and banish all her uncertainty. That would not be fair to her sisters, though. They were likely as bewildered and cold as she.

Ula touched her cheek. "Do what you must to see he makes it through to the morning. Tomorrow, things will be better."

"Will they?" Cara doubted that. The people in this valley were homeless, without a single possession to their name, including the High King himself. How could it possibly be better?

Chapter Fifteen

It was the longest night of Cara's life.

She could not tell if the willow bark had any effect upon Bedivere, although his shivering diminished. She put her cloak back over him, too, even though her mother's advice seemed to run against all good sense.

Long after her mother had gone, when staring at the dancing flames of the fires made her sleepy even though she shivered with cold, Cara stretched out upon the earth and closed her eyes. Perhaps, if she could sleep a little, it would make the night pass quickly.

She doubted anyone would sleep deeply this night. She could hear no snoring, no soft sounds of slumber.

Men dumped more firewood upon the fires, keeping them burning well, and their movements kept her awake. So did the low murmur of people on the far side of the ring—over by the wagon where Arthur and his senior officers were sitting in a tight circle, their cloaks around them.

She woke with a start when Bedivere spoke and laid blinking. "What did you say?" she whispered, for his eyes were still closed.

His mouth moved, as if he spoke to himself.

"…all…all dead…" he croaked.

Fright crawled up her spine and made the flesh on the back of her neck ripple with coldness. Cara sat up and looked around the camp. Her first instinct was to find her mother, or Merlin, or Gander…someone who would know what to do.

No one stood or sat anywhere within the circle of fire, although she could see the silhouette of guards pacing around the ring, moving to fight off the cold.

She studied Bedivere, wondering what to do. Even though Bedivere shuddered and his face was still white, he was no longer sweating. Was that good or bad? Her lack of knowledge frightened her and made her feel useless.

The hotter his fever burns, the quicker he will recover.

If he was no longer sweating, did it mean he was not hot enough, now? Certainly, she was cold. Her feet were icy. Bedivere had been so hot before it had seemed as though she sat beside another fire.

Perhaps he had sweated out all the water…

Shocked at the simple idea, she bounced to her feet and reached for the horn and hurried over to the stream and filled it and took it back. She wetted his lips. He swallowed. Encouraged, she lifted his head and trickled the water into his mouth. He drank the entire horn's worth of water.

She rolled him onto his left side. Then she laid in front of him and lifted the edge of her cloak. Warmth enveloped her as she shuffled herself beneath it, until her back touched Bedivere. Carefully, she lifted his injured hand and dropped the arm over her middle, so the hand rested on the ground.

"…all gone…" Bedivere muttered.

Cara resettled the cloak. "Not everyone," she murmured, even though he wouldn't hear her. "I'm right here."

His heat was wonderful against her, thawing her flesh. Gradually, her shivers tapered off and sleep—real sleep—stole over her. It was a shallow sleep, for she woke every time Bedivere stirred, or someone nearby spoke or shifted, or the fires crackled too loudly.

Dawn was too far away.

BEDIVERE WOKE WITH A JOLT, when his arm was moved. Daylight, low and filtered by tree canopy, made him blink.

Merlin sat on the ground in front of Bedivere, unwrapping the black bandages around his hand. "I'm pleased to see you survived the night," the wizard said. His face was deeply drawn with weariness and strain. His robe was filthy. His voice was strong, though.

Bedivere oriented himself. He barely remembered this place. There were brief moments which made sense and more sensations which did not, including the impossible impression of deep contentedness while holding a woman in his arms.

"Cara…" he said, remembering. He was shocked by the weakness of his voice.

Merlin nodded, his gaze on Bedivere's hand. "She's gone to find you breakfast. You owe the lady your thanks, by the way. She walked miles in the dead of the night to find willow bark to break your fever. Now, let me see…" He bent over Bedivere's hand, frowning. "Morgan and I, between us, managed to save your fingers. The two smallest were broken…can you feel this?" He prodded.

Bedivere frowned. "It's numb."

"Hmm." Merlin pressed and prodded carefully. "Curl your fingers, please."

Bedivere curled them. He couldn't see if they curled or not, for Merlin's hand was in the way.

Merlin did not nod, or smile.

Bedivere's heart gave another hard knock.

Merlin looked up as a shadow fell over them.

Cara crouched beside them, her gaze on Bedivere's hand. He fought the instinct to snatch his hand away from Merlin, to hide it from her. His heart would not stop thudding.

Cara's face was as neutral as Merlin's. "Cai gave me some salt they found. He said you would want it." She had a flat piece of bark in one hand and a twist of cloth in the other, which she held out to Merlin.

Merlin nodded and unfolded his legs. "Bathe Bedivere's hand in a solution of warm water and salt. Wash the bandages, too, and let them dry before putting them back on the hand." He got to his feet.

Cara's face showed dismay and puzzlement, before it returned to the same stoic expression.

Merlin glanced at the bark in her hand. "Now, if we only had some honey." He walked a few steps on, then bent to speak to the next group.

Cara sat where Merlin had been sitting, balancing the piece of bark. "Someone found some wild oats, under the snow. There are no spoons. You will have to use your fingers, although the meal is cool enough now. Are you hungry?" She looked at him quickly, as if she was dismayed to not have asked this first.

"Starving," Bedivere admitted, his gaze on his hand. He still could not see it, not from his prone position. Deep reluctance stopped him from lifting it so he could survey the damage.

His heart would not quit its heavy beating.

Slowly, he lifted the hand.

Cara reached out with her spare hand and held his wrist. "No, don't look at it yet. Eat, first. Then let me bathe it as Merlin said. Then you can look."

He swallowed and nodded. He didn't have the courage to

look right now, anyway.

He tried to push himself up but didn't have the strength to complete a simple movement he repeated every morning.

Cara put down the slab of bark and raised him into a sitting position. Then she slid a corner of her cloak over his right hand. She settled the platter of oatmeal on his thigh. "Eat that." She got to her feet. "And don't look. I will be back as soon as I can."

She picked up a ram's horn which had been lying nearby and went away.

He was light and weak and starving. Bedivere ate the oatmeal in small handfuls with his left hand. It was thick and almost taste-less, yet it was warm and filling. While he ate, he watched the people around him brushing off the damp of the night and dry themselves before the fires burning in a big ring around the edge of the camp. They were eating small handfuls of gathered food, too. Nuts and berries, the same wild oatmeal as he. Three people were sharing late season, shriveled apricots they'd found still hanging on the tree.

A ring of fire. It sounded faintly familiar, too.

Cara returned with the ram's horn and also a war helmet, which sloshed. Steam rose from it.

She settled back on the ground beside him, with the helmet between her knees. She unwrapped the scrap of cloth to reveal a small salt rock. She crumbled the salt into the water and stirred with a blunt stick, then picked up the black bandages and pushed them to the bottom of the helmet.

"Eat," she told Bedivere shortly, then raised the edge of her cloak, gripped his wrist and slid his hand into the water.

The water was alarmingly hot. He jerked away from it. She gripped his wrist even harder. "It only *feels* too hot," she assured him.

"It burns."

"That will pass," she assured him. "Wriggle your fingers."

He tried and hissed. His hand throbbed.

"Eat," she said again.

He had lost his appetite. The gnawing ache in his hand and the throbbing had stolen it. He heard her lift water and let it trickle over the inside of his wrist. Her fingers rubbed. *That*, he could feel. He tried wriggling his hands again. This time, he could feel them moving, except the two smallest, again.

"Does this hurt?" she asked, glancing at him.

"What?"

"I'm cleaning away the...well, everything that is not your hand," she said carefully.

Bedivere drew in a breath. "I can do that," he said roughly.

"Next time," she assured him. "Wriggle your fingers again."

Bedivere shifted them, noticing the same numbness as before. Only on half his hand could he sense the touch of warm water.

He hung his head, letting the awful truth settle in his chest. His hand was without feeling. Would he ever be able to hold a sword again?

He pushed the platter aside. "Let me see," he growled, the fear thick in his chest.

Cara glanced at him. She lifted his hand from the helmet. "Let it drain," she said quietly. Then she pulled the cloak aside.

Bedivere turned his hand over and back, absorbing the appearance. He had seen burned flesh before—everyone was familiar with the sight of raw, unhealed burns after the last two years of Saxon fireballs and arrows. The sight of the burns on the back and side of his hand did not move him. Burns could heal, treated properly. What really concerned him were the two long lines of stitches on his palm, running almost in tandem from the heel to just above the two smaller fingers.

His hand was swollen and the skin around the stitches bright red and angry.

His throat painfully tight, he tried opening and closing his fingers once more. The larger two and his thumb obeyed. The smaller two didn't move. Instead, pain shot up his arm.

He let the hand drop to his knee, sick anger stirring in his belly.

Cara squeezed out the wet bandages, got to her feet and hung them over a branch of the nearest tree. "The king wants to leave before the sun shows over the hills," she told him. "Do you think you could walk, today? Or shall I show you where the wagon waits?"

She bent again, picked up her cloak and shook it out. Around them, others were also stirring, dusting themselves off. Not every-one moved.

That was what Merlin had been doing, Bedivere realized, with another sick lurch of his belly. He had been checking upon those who he had not expected to last the night.

Including Bedivere.

His breath shallowed as he stared at the ruin of his hand. "Why bother?" he whispered. "I am as those who do not rise—a burden. Leave me here."

"No, that is not what happens now," Cara said. She crouched down in front of him, so her gaze speared his. She looked angry. "You do not *dare* sit there and give up. Do you understand me?"

Bedivere blinked. "You…are giving *me* orders?"

Her black eyes would not let him go. The perfect curve of her mouth flattened. It was only now, when she drew her lips into a harsh line, that Bedivere realized how often he had traced that graceful curve with his gaze, finding it pleasing in its symmetry.

"I will give you orders and I will beat them into you, if you refuse them," she said, her tone flat. "Get up on your feet. Now."

He shook his head. "You don't understand." He raised his use-less hand. "I cannot hold my sword."

"Not until the wounds heal, no." She gripped the sides of his armor, up by his arms. She hauled. "Get up. Up. Now."

"Cara—"

"No!" She shook him. "*No!*" She hauled once more, with such strength he had no choice but to get his feet under him and stand. When he was standing, she turned him and pointed. "There. There is the wagon. Go sit on it and stew in your self-pity alone. Go." And she actually pushed him.

He staggered a pace or two, his legs moving stiffly.

Angry, he whirled to face her. The movement, though, was too fast and too violent. He thrust out a foot, dizzy.

Instantly, she was by his side. "Fool," she muttered, sliding under his arm. "Come along. You are not walking today, that is clear."

His chest hitched at the gentle empathy in her voice. He realized he was embarrassingly close to weeping.

Perhaps she sensed that, because she said nothing more. She helped him settle upon the hard floor of the cart and pulled her cloak around him. Then she turned to leave.

"Where are you going?" he asked, alarmed. Everyone was falling into the same long line as yesterday. The nag which hauled this wagon was being hitched to it once more. The wounded whom he had shared the wagon with were settled back upon it, just as he was.

"I have things to collect." She did not smile. "I will be back."

She whirled and moved through the people streaming back through the trees to the line, preparing to leave. There were shouts from the front, including Cai's deep voice roaring orders.

Bedivere should be there with them, giving orders of his own. Only, he could barely walk.

Instead, he watched Cara weave between the people, until he lost sight of her, his heart thudding heavily. He didn't like that she had not smiled and with a jolt, he realized he had grown used to her smiling—at him, at least. For she did not smile at others.

She hid away and turned her face so they would not see the left side of it.

For him, though, she had begun to smile.

And now she did not.

Had he ruined the tenuous link between them, too?

TRUE TO HER PROMISE, CARA did return to the wagon in time to fall in beside it as it jolted into motion at the far end of the long file of people trailing out of the valley. She had folded the remains of his cloak into a bundle and tied the bundle with what looked to be the narrow branches of a willow tree. She had fashioned a loop from them. The bundle hung over her shoulder, bouncing against the back of her hip and tangling with the ends of her hair.

She carried the ram's horn, too, and it was full of a dark liquid. "Drink it," she told him. "It will help with the pain."

"What is it?" he asked, taking the horn and sniffing it.

"Willow bark. I have more of it for later, too." She patted the bundle against her back. "I must find my mother and my family and see how they fared through the night."

Guilt stirred. He had kept her from them.

"Drink," she told him and strode forward, moving up the line.

He sipped the dusty liquid and grimaced with distaste yet finished all that was in the horn.

A while later, Cara returned. She shuffled alongside the wagon while she placed the pack on the floor beside him and untied it. She removed the black bandages, which were dry now. "They will keep dirt from the wound," she said and reached for his hand.

"At least sit on the wagon while you do that," Bedivere complained. "You'll trip and break your ankle and then where will I be?"

"Right where you are," she said, her tone short. "With me beside you, most likely," she added, with a grimace. She hopped onto the wagon and sat with her legs dangling over the edge. As he was sitting, not lying down, there was room for her.

Quickly, she wrapped the bandages around his hand. It was a relief not to have to look at the jagged wounds in his palm.

Then she repacked the bundle and retied it.

"Leave it here," he told her. "I can keep it for you."

"I must speak to Bevan and Lowri," she said, pushing the bundle toward him. "She is my commander and now I know where they are in the file."

He suppressed his protest. He was pathetic enough, sitting here on the wagon of wounded. Instead, he cleared his throat. "If you see Lucan, ask him if he can spare a moment to speak with me?"

She nodded and moved ahead once more.

They were out of the valley now, and full daylight touched them, although it was weak, wintery gray light. Bedivere shivered and pulled the cloak in close.

Only a little while later, the file passed the first group of people. They were not from the city, for they were clean and dressed properly against the cold. A dozen of them stood upon the side of the road, holding buckets and pails, bags and packs. There were more items and packs sitting upon the frosty ground behind them.

As the file of survivors passed them, they turned and walked along with them, handing out...

Bedivere frowned and leaned to one side to see farther down the file, to determine what they were doing, exactly.

Then a young girl carrying a basket ran up to him. She thrust a small loaf of bread into his hands and smiled at him before she moved on to someone else.

"Thank you," Bedivere managed to say without stuttering. He

raised the bread to his face and inhaled. It was still warm. His mouth watered and his belly squeezed. He tore into the loaf and ate half of it so fast his chest ached as the lump eased into his belly.

He made himself stop and put the other half of the loaf upon the bundle of his cloak. That was for Cara.

A tall man with a bucket and a ladle came up to him and held out the ladle. It steamed.

"Drink," he said, with a nod and smile.

Awkwardly, his cheeks heating, Bedivere fumbled to take the ladle with his left hand. The man saw his difficulty and reversed the handle.

His face burning and his heart beating hard, Bedivere took the ladle and gulped down the mulled wine. It was ambrosial. He murmured his thanks and handed the ladle back.

The man moved on.

A matron with an enormous basket gave Bedivere two rolled oatcakes, both dripping in honey. He balanced one upon the half-loaf of bread and ate the other.

Along the file of travelers, as far as he could see, more people were appearing upon the side of the road, carrying food and drink and all manner of items. As he finished the oat cake, Bedivere saw a man drape a fur around the shoulders of a cloakless woman.

Blankets and furs, cloaks and unadorned lengths of raw wool cloth were handed out.

A gray-haired old man pulling a handcart with contents which rattled and clanged pulled up alongside Bedivere's wagon. "Room there for a pot or two?"

"Pots?" Bedivere said blankly.

"For cooking, fetching water, bathing. A good pot is a god-send. Although these are not as good as they once were but have them and be welcome. Here." He tossed a fat, round-bottomed kettle up onto the wagon. Bedivere steadied it. It was dented and burned and deeply scratched, yet it would hold both food and liquid.

He stared at the kettle, amazed.

Sometime later, an old, rusty axe with a newly honed edge to the blade was added to the pile, and two folded and tied leather sheets.

The same thing was happening all along the long line of travelers. Bedivere watched a woman weep as she wrapped her daughter in a cloak. The murmurs of thank you and gratitude rose into the morning air.

When Cara returned to the wagon, she wore an undyed wool mantle around her shoulders. "There are even more people gathering where Arthur intends to stop tonight, they say."

Bedivere handed her the oatcake and bread. She ate hungrily, swallowed and added, "There is a basket of sliced mutton, farther along. Would you like some?"

"Leave it for those who must walk," Bedivere said.

She glanced at him sharply, measuring him.

He grimaced. "Later, I will try to walk, myself."

Cara relaxed. "Not today," she said. "Tonight, when we stop, you can try, then. This pace is too fast for you, right now."

He held his teeth together, frustration flaring.

She rested her hand on the wagon, close by his knee. "Even a perfect warrior must rest." Then she licked her fingers of honey and said, "I saw Lucan, up with the senior officers. I will fetch him for you."

And she was gone again.

Bedivere stared at the black bandages about his hand, his heart working too hard for a man lolling about while everyone else walked.

A perfect warrior? He was no longer that.

And if he was not, then what was he?

MERLIN SLID ALONGSIDE ARTHUR, MATCHING their pace, a cup of mead in one hand and a hunk of barley bread in the other. He nodded at Arthur as he chewed.

"King Mark has done more than spread word," Arthur said. "This generosity will be the saving of us, Merlin."

"They are building pavilions for us, Cai says," Guenivere added, beside him.

Merlin swallowed and sipped and cleared his throat. "Such a miracle deserves to be marked in a way which lingers in the memory, Arthur. People should not forget how the land and her people rose up to support you."

"You mean *I* should not forget," Arthur corrected him. He held up his hand. "Do not protest. I know how your mind works, Merlin, and for once, I am ahead of you." He turned and picked up Guenivere's hand.

Her eyes widened in shock.

"I cannot give you a wedding worthy of a queen, Guenivere," he told her. "Although, if you will consent to marrying me tonight, you and I will, between us, give back to the people of this land what they have given us, today."

"Hope," Guenivere said, her mouth curving up into a lovely smile which made her eyes seem even brighter.

Pleased, he nodded.

"And a reminder of happier times," Merlin added. "Here, Arthur, take this." He thrust the mead toward him. "I suddenly have much to do!" He spun and strode back along the line.

Chapter Sixteen

he survivors of Venta Belgarum were not forced to walk much farther that day. As the city was in the south of Britain, by traveling only twenty miles east, they reached the very heart of the kingdoms and lands, with the strongest of them, including Corneus, Kernow and Camelard, standing between them and the Saxon shores.

Cai and King Mark found a fallow field, with a narrow river to one side and thin forest to the other. It was there where Arthur and his people arrived a few hours before sunset, to find the generosity of Britain's people they had enjoyed upon the road was but the beginning.

While the survivors marched, word passed from village to cottage to farm, to fort and town and kingdom. Wagons and carts, horses and mules converged upon the field. By the time Arthur's people appeared at the crest of the gently sloping dale, the field had sprouted hundreds of tents, pavilions and makeshift shelters. Between them roared a hundred fires, each with a cooking pot over it and food bubbling within.

At the center of them all, a large white pavilion had been

raised. Cai stood before it, his legs spread and his arms crossed and a large smile on his face.

For Cara, as it was for every soldier in Arthur's retinue, the matter of what tent should be used by whom went without discussion. She oriented herself by the King's white tent and turned to the south, where the northern kingdoms always camped.

She found her mother and sisters and Newlyn beside a small tent of leather and hide and reassured herself they were well-settled. Her three sisters could talk of nothing but the wedding to take place that night, while they fussed and pouted about the lack of a new gown.

"Guenivere will wear what she has worn for two days," Ula said. "If rags are good enough for her, they are good enough for you. A washed face and combed hair will show your respect." And she rolled her eyes as Brigid sighed.

Cara could stand the fuss for only a few minutes. "I must speak to Lucan and the Corneus people, and make sure Bedivere reaches his pavilion safely." And she fled.

When she was within hearing distance of the Corneous tent, Cara could see Bedivere was already settled upon a bedroll before the fire which blazed in front of it. Lucan stood with their senior officers to one side, their heads together. A woman— someone from a nearby farm or village, Cara presumed— stirred the cooking pot over the flames.

Bedivere looked tired, as he stared moodily into the flames, although his face shifted and fell into an attentive expression as the woman spoke to him and filled a bowl with the stew in the pot.

Cara retreated. Bedivere was being cared for. Her obligation was at an end.

Instead, she made her way to the river and washed away as much of the dirt as she could, straightened her clothes and finger -combed her hair and refastened the rings.

Dozens of people were doing the same as her—tidying themselves up for the wedding to come. They chatted together, sounding light and carefree, even happy, despite their soiled, burned clothes.

Cara realized she was the only one who was alone. She fastened her arm guards in place with a heavy sigh.

Overhead, she heard the long, drawn-out cry of a bird and raised her head, startled, for it had sounded like an eagle...

She searched the sky and saw the golden body and wings and caught her breath. The eagle was soaring on the wind, circling lower and lower.

Everyone else looked up, too. Mutters and exclamations sounded.

"Is it going to land among us?" someone asked, alarmed.

Cara drew in a sharp breath, hope flaring, as the eagle back-raked his wings, his big talons thrust forward, keening with a high squeal, plummeting toward her. She got her arm up just in time.

The eagle gripped her wrist, the talons knocking against the arm guard. He tucked his wings neatly against his sides and cocked his head, looking at her.

Cara felt the weight of him on her arm and smiled, delight bubbling in her chest. She lifted her hand and stroked his head with no fear.

The eagle merely blinked at her.

"Oh, you darling thing!" Cara breathed, as her eyes stung with hot, sharp tears. "You can have *all* my supper!"

THAT DAY AT SUNSET, ARTHUR, High King of Britain, married Guenivere of Camelard, before the assembled people of every clan and kingdom and house of Britain. Not a single person wore a garment which was not stained or burned, except the bride. A white cloak with a hood had been found for her, which she donned over her ripped and scorched blue gown. As she had once before, Guenivere wore a simple garland of winter flowers upon her black hair.

With an enormous fire as their backdrop, Arthur and Guenivere stood together, while Merlin spoke simple words of union which satisfied every religion and god known to man. When he was done, a Christian priest blessed them.

There was no feast, but there was music and dancing and a great deal of wine, most of it mulled, or warmed with hot pokers. Very few people went to bed early that night. Most agreed the wedding was the most moving they had attended in many years, despite the lack of pomp and finery.

Life in the meadow fell into familiar patterns for Cara. The next day, Arthur's senior officers and companions met in front of the white tent, just as they had done long before Arthur had taken the keep at Venta Belgarum for himself.

Queen Lowri reported back to the Cohort around the fire in front of the Calleva tent, shortly afterwards.

"There are two things which must be done straight away," she told the women of the Cohort as they sat around the crackling fire. "First, somewhere suitable for winter quarters must be found, plus shelter for everyone else who is not part of the army. There were many people living in Venta Belgarum before Uther took the town as his headquarters. They must be found other homes. The second order of business is to learn what the Saxons are planning next. For now..." Lowri looked around the circle of women. "For now, our priorities must be our houses and families. The Cohort will not ride again this year."

Cara bit back her cry of protest, for every other woman nodded in agreement.

"The burden of clothing and feeding our families falls to us," Lowri added. "We must put aside our shields for now and concentrate on the simple act of thriving. A roof, walls, warm beds and full bellies will occupy our thoughts and time."

"The Saxons are still out there," Cara ground out, her heart running hard. "We cannot leave them to crow over us."

"That will be up to the main army and Arthur's officers," Lowri replied.

Cara could not argue when every other woman appeared to feel the same as Lowri.

Instead, she trained with Lancelot and Pellinore every single day, as she always had, for training had begun again in the thin woods at the side of the meadow. There was no clearing, although once a few trees had been felled, they trained among the stumps which remained. The stumps became natural hazards they were forced to work amongst— or use to their advantage when they could.

Among a long rope line of horses which had been recovered from the city, Cara was delighted to find Cailleach. She took Cailleach back to the hide tent and hitched him to the high perch she had made for the eagle.

Around the edges of the fire and under Cailleach, she spread hay.

The eagle showed no signs of leaving. He would depart each morning to hunt and would return by mid-afternoon or early evening to the perch, to preen and warm himself before the fire. After the first startled oaths from her mother and Newlyn and the nervous giggles of her sisters, her family left the eagle alone.

Cara often fed him with scraps from her meal, even though he was now able to hunt for himself. He accepted the morsels with grave delicacy, although he would not take food from anyone else. They would leave the meat on a stone by the fire for him, which he would hop down to eat once they had left.

Bedivere, Cara learned, was back upon his feet and had returned to his duties as war duke, although he did not wear his sword or armor. He wore heavy winter gauntlets, which disguised his injured hand.

Cara heard gossip among the fighters she trained with that Bedivere's temper was chancy, these days. He had been a hard taskmaster before the routing of Venta Belgarum. Now his discipline and demands verged on the tyrannical.

"It's as if he's trying to make amends or something," Lamorak said, tousling his wild dark blond locks to rid them of snowflakes, during training. His hair was as uncontained as his father, Pellinore's. He was as good a fighter, too. Cara thought he could be even better if only he took training and fighting a bit more seriously. "The gods know what he has to make up for," Lamorak added. "The man is a fighting machine."

Cara said nothing. Her heart sank. She thought she knew why Bedivere was over-compensating, yet it was clear he had told no one about his hand.

Only two days after the wedding, Arthur's page, Linus, fell ill. The boy was only ten. Childhood illness could be frequent and inexplicable, so no one thought anything of the boy's fever.

Cara gave Gander all the white willow bark she still had, to treat the boy's fever.

The next morning at dawn, the news spread like fire around the camp; Linus was dead...and there were another two fighters ill with the same symptoms.

By that afternoon, another five people had sought their bedrolls, too ill and dizzy to stand.

Cara learned of the newly sick when she returned from training that afternoon. Brigid sat shivering in front of the fire, her dress spread as prettily about her feet as she could manage.

"You're not attending Guenivere today?" Cara asked, when Brigid had finished telling her the news of the five fighters who were now sick, too. Guenivere had a court, of sorts— a small circle about the fire, just as Arthur had his circle of officers around a bigger fire.

Brigid shivered again. "I dare not. They say..." She looked around. "They say it is Guenivere's fault, that she brought this upon Linus, that she and the marriage are cursed."

Cara laughed at the notion. When Brigid merely wrung her hands, looking frightened, Cara sobered. "You truly believe that?" she asked, astonished.

"Well, it *might* be true." Brigid looked around for observers. "Her bleeding set in yesterday. They're saying it proves the marriage was not lucky."

Cara rolled her eyes. "Naturally her courses arrived. The wedding was only two days ago." Everyone knew that the best chance a wedding had to bless the marriage was if it was set for the middle of a woman's courses. As Arthur had announced the wedding with only hours to spare, no one had thought to point out that the timing was not fortuitous. "Really, Brigid, I did not think you were so susceptible to gossip."

Brigid shivered again. "I don't want to be sick and die like them."

"Them?"

Brigid's chin quivered. "The other two died, an hour ago. They died screaming and writhing."

Cara soothed the eagle's head and held out a piece of the dried meat she kept nearby for such moments, thinking deeply.

The fever spread across the camp in the next few days. There was no more room in the surgery and the ill were forced to lie upon their own bedrolls, while the physicians and medics traveled from tent to tent.

More than half the camp was confined and laid moaning.

Cara moved through the eerie, empty camp, swirling morning mist around her knees, to collect fresh hay for the fire and for

Cailleach. When she reached the hay cart, she saw that half the horses were uncovered and their oat bags empty. Their owners must be ill, and no one had spared a thought for their horses.

She put down the pitchfork and turned to brushing and drying the horses. She fed them and rubbed their foreheads, to assure them they had not been deserted. The work took time, but no horse stood neglected when she was done.

Then she took hay back to Cailleach and gave him an extra-long brushing for being forced to wait.

That day, she skipped training and left off her armor. She put on the other tunic she had acquired, which was patched and darned and stained, plus the length of undyed wool instead of her cloak. She tied her hair back firmly at the back of her neck and went to the surgery and waited for Gander to return from his rounds of the camp.

"Tell me what you need done," she told him. "I will do anything which does not require a knowledge of medicine."

"It is the basic tasks we need done the most," Gander told her, relief writing itself on his worn face. "Fresh water, fresh cloths to wipe faces with, fires built up. If you can find another six like you, you will be the saving of many. That's all most of these people need now— fresh water and a kind word to keep their spirits up."

"I will find six more," Cara told him. She made her way to Lowri's tent and found, as she suspected she would, most of the Cohort women gathered on the benches around the fire there, except Lowri.

Cara glanced at the closed flaps of the tent. "Lowri, too?" she asked.

Tegan nodded, her face grim.

Cara told the women what Gander needed.

"That is simple enough," Tegan said, getting to her feet. "And it is better than sitting here and waiting for news."

The others rose, too.

"Tell anyone else you come across that they can help this way, too," Cara said. "If they dislike waiting for news as much as you, they will be glad of the work."

She returned to her own tent to retrieve the bucket and tore her other tunic into small squares. She took the bucket to the river to fill it with water, using the hole which had been chopped in the ice. She could see the other women spreading out across the camp, doing the same as her.

Cara took the bucket and rags back to the surgery and got to work. She had experience feeding ill people water they did not know they need. Wiping faces and brows was easy enough. It pleased her that they seemed refreshed by the simple ministrations. As they did not open their eyes to look at her, she did not have to worry about keeping her scars hidden.

Some hours later, when it was fully light, Cara got to her feet and stretched her back. She had remained bent over for too long. She picked up her empty bucket and turned to contemplate the almost silent camp.

The few people who remained on their feet all seemed to be doing the same as her— carrying buckets and tending the sick. Even Gaheris and Gawain moved together from tent to tent.

Cara moved through the camp, heading for the river. The mist which had smothered the land when she rose had lifted, although the day was still a dim, dank one. Low clouds hung overhead, and the land was still and cold.

There were usually one or two others at the hole in the river where people filled their buckets. This time there was only one.

Cara recognized the blue gown beneath the furled white cloak and slowed her steps. Guenivere was on her knees, bending to dip the bucket in the water, before hauling it back to the bank, her back to Cara.

Cara's heart gave a little lurch. The last time she had spoken to the new queen, she had offended her. It would be best to avoid her now.

Then Guenivere's back gave a little hitch and lift. She paused from hauling in the bucket to bring the sleeve of her gown up to her face.

Understanding flared in Cara. So did irritation. "Gods in their heavens...you *believe* what they say about a curse?"

Guenivere scrambled to her feet, a little shriek of shock escaping her, and spun to confront Cara.

"The bucket! The bucket!" Cara said urgently, as the bucket the Queen had left in the water floated to the lower edge of the hole and threatened to slide beneath the ice.

Guenivere whirled again, her hand to her mouth, then leapt, her shoes splashing in the water. The bottom of her dress was submerged, too, as she lunged to grab the rope and pull the bucket out. She looked down at her dripping dress with dismay, her damp face working.

Cara sighed. Even when she sniveled and wept, Guenivere looked beautiful. Cara moved over to her side. "Just ring the water out. It will dry. And put your shoes by the fire...you have a second pair?"

Guenivere wiped hastily at her cheeks. "Lady Cara. I...are you tending the sick, too?"

"Of course. Everyone who isn't sick is doing it. Haven't you noticed?"

"I..." Guenivere swallowed. "I hadn't noticed," she admitted, her voice small.

"Too busy with your own guilt, perhaps?" Cara asked, her tone dry.

Guenivere's mouth parted in surprise. Then she straightened and dropped her hem. "Yes, I suppose I am," she admitted softly. "I had forgotten that about you. You do not shy from the truth."

Cara shrugged and bent to fill her bucket. "As most people

shy from me, there is no need to avoid upsetting them with the truth. I speak as I see things."

Guenivere gave a soft, pretty laugh. "I know what that is like— having people shy from you."

Cara sent her a sharp look, then lifted the full bucket and put it on the ground beside Guenivere's. "Why do you care if they do or not? You are Arthur's queen."

Guenivere smoothed out her dress. "I cannot help Arthur's people, if they cannot stand to be in the same room as me."

Cara tilted her head. "You didn't mind Queen Morgan running away from you."

Guenivere's crystalline gaze met hers. The corner of her mouth lifted. "No, I did not mind that at all."

Cara laughed. "I do wish I had seen that."

Guenivere's smile was glowing. Then she sobered. "Not that it did a bit of good. Morgan returned to her ways almost instantly. It is as if my speaking to her made her double her efforts."

"It most likely did," Cara said soberly. "You can't attack one like her head on. She is too strong. You must attack her flank. If you can divert her attention in the other direction while you do it, you'll have a better chance of landing your blow."

Guenivere's lips pursed in a bow. "Fighting tactics. Are you a very good fighter?"

"Good enough. I am still alive."

Guenivere nodded. Her smile returned. "I actually thought it might have been Morgan who brought this disease upon us, then spread the rumor that it was my fault."

Cara whistled. "That is an unworthy thought for a queen... and I wouldn't put it past Morgan at all. But really, my lady, I do not believe this is anyone's fault. I heard Gander say it was the shock of the fire, the escape and traveling on foot in winter and most especially that first night under the trees, that is to blame for this fever which sickens everyone. Not enough food, no shelter and snow, too. If you really want to help Arthur's people, that is how you could do it."

Guenivere's eyes narrowed. "Build them a city?"

"Yes, with your own two hands, and you have only a day to do it," Cara said flatly.

Guenivere giggled. She pressed her fingers to her mouth to hold the sound in and looked around with a guilty expression.

"You should stop doing that," Cara added.

"Giggling? Oh, I know. A queen doesn't giggle."

"I mean, worrying about what everyone thinks."

"That is rather harder to do," Guenivere admitted. "I know what they say about me." She paused. "Life here is not at all what I thought it would be like."

Cara could feel her mouth turn down.

"Oh, I do not mean the lack of food and...and, well, everything," Guenivere said quickly. "We had very little in Camelard, too. I don't believe anyone in Britain is living off the fat of the land this year. The Saxons have made sure of that. I meant only that...well..." Her cheeks tinged pink. "I thought married life would be different."

Cara raised her brow. "As I am not married, I can offer not a whisper of wisdom in that regard."

Guenivere shook her head. "You don't mind bald truth."

"I prefer it," Cara replied.

"Do you seek it out? Is that why you know of the source of this illness and that Arthur's greatest need is for shelter?"

Cara felt a genuine puzzlement. "That is merely the information passed down to his officers..." she began. "Are you not involved in his council, my lady?"

Guenivere grimaced. "Not at all. If I were at Camelard, I would be relegated to the spinning room to weave his war cloaks."

Cara drew in a great breath of astonishment. "It is of little wonder you have absorbed the gossip and believe it. You hear nothing else."

"Then Arthur's needs— shelter and...and so forth...these are spoken of openly among the commanders?"

"Yes, and they in turn tell their fighters. Queen Lowri tells the Cohort...which I suppose is your Cohort, now." She drew in a quick breath. "That is what you should do, my lady. You should command your Cohort!"

"I am not a fighter," Guenivere said, her tone rueful. "Arthur would forbid it, especially and until, well, you know." Her face flushed again as she put her hand against her flat belly.

"You are the nominal head of the Cohort and you could attend the meetings. Lowri would be your war duke. Then you would learn what we learn and would know better how to help Arthur."

Guenivere's smile was small. "I will talk to Queen Lowri about it...and Arthur, of course."

"He is not ill?"

"No, but Merlin will not let him move out of the tent. He insists Arthur avoids the air which the ill breath out, as if it will stop him from falling ill."

"As he has not yet fallen ill, perhaps Merlin is right," Cara pointed out. She bent and picked up her bucket. "I must continue. There are too many sick."

"Yes, there are," Guenivere said with a sigh and picked up her own bucket. "Will you...would you...I mean, as your Queen, I would like you to attend me...from time to time, when you are not...when you care to."

"You could simply order me to attend you, my lady," Cara pointed out.

"I don't want to do that," Guenivere said quickly. "I don't want to...to change you. I feel that if I insist, you will not come to me as you have here today."

"Truth, at all costs?" Cara hefted the bucket. "Then, I will attend...from time to time."

Guenivere's smile was small and warm. "That would please me very much. Thank you, Cara of Brynaich."

Chapter Seventeen

uenivere moved along the other path which had formed in the flattened snow. Cara used the first path to climb up to the end of the camp where the surgery was located, her thoughts whirling.

The route through the camp took her past the Corneus tent and the ring of smaller shelters which housed the Corneus contingent. She couldn't help but glance through the chinks in the tent flaps to check who laid ill on their bedrolls, even though she could not bring herself to tend anyone from that house.

Movement in the big tent snagged her attention. Cara stopped where she could peer almost directly through the not-quite-together flaps. Her heart squeezed and hurried on.

Bedivere stood with his hand to his face. She could not see what he was doing, for the tent flap was in the way. As usual, he seemed to be angry. Even when he was alone, he was angry.

He was growing a beard. His chin and cheeks were dark with growth.

As she watched he spun, cursing, and threw something hard enough to make the side of the tent bow out with a soft puffing sound.

He brought his hand—his left hand—to his jaw, his head down.

Understanding came to Cara in a rush. Before she could think better of it, she put the bucket down and moved around the big fire and pushed the tent flap aside.

Bedivere whirled, tensed as if he intended to leap to the attack.

Cara brought up her hand. "It is only me."

"What are *you* doing here?" He breathed heavily.

"I saw you through the opening." She moved around him, toward the back of the tent. There were two bedrolls and a soft pack at the back of the tent, plus a pile of Bedivere's armor on top of it. There was little else in the tent, not even a rug for their feet. A small brazier in the corner would keep the tent warm at night while they slept.

"It does not explain why you are here," Bedivere said. His tone was harsh. She knew why. She edged farther around, toward the side of the tent where she had seen it bow out under the impact of the object he had thrown.

"I thought only to see for myself..." she began, playing for time. Then she spotted the object and bent and picked it up.

The metal shaving blade was an old one, with an obsidian glass edge, which was newer. She turned the blade over and over. Her father had used one similar to this.

Bedivere's anger bubbled over. He snatched at the blade, his face red. "Get out! Now, before I carry you out and dump you in the mud!"

Cara evaded his hand, holding the blade out of his reach. She put her finger to her lips. "Shh. Do you want everyone in the camp to know I am here?"

Bedivere's mouth parted. His gaze slid to one side, as if he was checking the camp for eavesdroppers, even though they were standing inside the tent.

Cara held the blade by her side. "I know why you are here by yourself, in the middle of the day," she murmured. "I can help."

Bedivere's jaw tightened. "You have no idea—"

"You cannot shave with your left hand and your right won't hold the blade," she said softly and braced herself. She was ready for Bedivere's anger to scald her, because he found the brazen truth as uncomfortable as most other people did.

Yet his anger subsided. He stared at her, a deep furrow between his brow and pain in his eyes.

Cara nodded. "I also know you have not told anyone of the stiffness in your right hand. That is why you where those large gauntlets, so no one guesses."

The pain seemed to build in his face. "How dare you..." he whispered, yet there was no threat, no heat in his voice. It was a token process. She had stolen all his heat and anger.

Cara stepped closer. "Sit down."

"Give me the blade."

"Sit, Bedivere. You are too tall for me to do this standing... unless you would prefer I slash your throat instead?"

His gaze met hers. He searched her face, trying to measure if she jested.

The bald statement, though, completed the work of reassuring him that her intentions were good. Yet he still could not bring himself to acknowledge it. He settled on the bedroll with bad humor. "If you slice my cheek open I will—"

She jerked his chin up with her other hand, as she fitted the blade in her fingers as she had seen her father do. "If I do, you will have a scar like mine. Perhaps I *should* slice your cheek open."

He opened his mouth to protest.

"Shut up," she growled and brought the blade up against his cheek, just above the first of the dark whiskers. He had already applied a thin layer of oil. There was no need to add more.

Carefully, she scraped a long line from his upper cheek to his jaw. The whiskers cut cleanly, leaving smooth flesh.

Cara looked around for a cloth.

Silently, Bedivere picked up a rag from the bedroll beside him and handed it to her. His gaze, though, did not meet hers.

Cara wiped the blade and scraped once more. The soft scratching was the only sound in the tent, except for Bedivere's heavy breath.

"Do you think this un-mans you, having someone else do for you what you cannot do yourself?" she asked, her tone light.

"I have shaved myself since I was thirteen," Bedivere said heavily.

"It is just as well I am a no-account half-breed Saxon, whom no one cares to speak to, then, hmm?" She deliberately avoided his gaze, concentrating on the slide of the blade and wiping it clean with each pass. "I have no one to tell your secret to."

He didn't speak.

"Oil?" she enquired.

Bedivere reached for the small, unstopped bottle sitting be-tween two yellowed clumps of wild grass and handed it to her.

Cara applied more oil to the other side of his face and contin-ued, letting the silence grow, which it did for many heartbeats.

When she was on the verge of speaking, Bedivere spoke in-stead. His voice was low, filled with dread and another quality she did not at first recognize. "I cannot hold my sword."

The two small fingers, the ones which had been injured... clearly, no feeling had returned to them.

Cara took a last swipe along the sharp edge of his jaw then wiped the blade with slow movements. "You have two fingers and a thumb. Of course, you can hold your sword."

"But not with any *strength!*" he ground out. The pain in his voice made her chest ache. "I am Arthur's war duke...how can I lead men into battle, if I will drop my sword at the first clash with a Saxon?" His anger was as strong as the pain. There was frustration there and embarrassment, too.

For a man like Bedivere, who had spent his life striving to be the perfect warrior, who had given up his lands and his title in order to serve Arthur, this was a deep, agonizing blow.

Cara let herself look at him. Her heart lurched again, for his eyes glittered. He was not openly weeping—Bedivere would rather die than do that, she knew. Yet he was as close to it as he would ever come.

She picked up his hand—the one with the two vivid red slashes on his palm—and held it. "There is a way through this, Bedivere."

His fingers shifted against hers. "I cannot see it."

"I will help you…if you will let me." She met his eyes again.

He searched her face, her eyes, looking for a sign that he could trust her.

Cara did not have to lean far to press her lips against his. She felt him stiffen in surprise, although the moment of tension evaporated almost instantly. His arm slid behind her and pulled her even more tightly between them. It seemed right that his injured hand was between them.

She had thought she was kissing him, yet it changed swiftly. In this, Bedivere was still a man, whole and infinitely experienced. He pulled her down onto the bedroll with him, his long body heavy and hard against hers, which felt just as right.

He traced the two lines on her face, then kissed her again, his freshly shaved cheek smooth against hers. The pain in his eyes was gone. Only heat remained.

AFTERWARDS, CARA LAID UPON HIS chest, as he lifted and let her hair fall so the rings clattered with soft knocks against each other.

"Your hand works well enough for that," she observed, catching a glimpse of the red lines on his palm as his hand rose and fell.

He paused. She felt his heart thud heavily.

"Well enough for other things, too." She lifted her chin to meet his gaze.

The pain didn't return to his eyes. She was satisfied.

Then he raised his hand, showing her the palm and the red scores. His larger fingers were straight, while the smaller remained in a soft curl. "The lines," he said. "Do they look familiar to you?"

Cara considered them. The line arrowing up to the ring finger was longer than the other. If the other had continued, they would have come to a point together. "No."

He turned his hand around, so his fingers hung downward. It was an awkward position. He ran the finger of his other hand along the red lines, which now arrowed downward. "I see these marks every time I look at you." Then he reached up and traced the scars on her face.

Cara caught her breath. Her heart beat hard.

Bedivere slid his hand into her hair. The curled fingers tangled and brushed her ear. He brought her mouth to his once more.

GUENIVERE PUSHED THE HEAVY TENT flap aside and ducked under it, her heart hammering.

Arthur, who was still a stranger to her despite nightly intimacies, looked up from the scroll he was peering at, while Merlin stood politely to one side of the chair. It was not the great chair which had adorned the dais at Venta Belgarum, but a simple bench—which was still more than most people had to sit upon these days.

Merlin saw it was her and relaxed. She had seen the druid toss men from the tent. He would let no one come too near the King lest they give him the fever which plagued the camp.

"Is that...water?" Merlin asked. "Have you been helping with the sick?" He looked faintly alarmed.

"Is your dress wet?" Arthur added, looking amused, although the lightness did not reach his eyes. The cares and concern in his eyes never fully went away even when they were alone.

"I know where to find shelter for the winter," Guenivere said.

Arthur lowered the scroll. "Excuse me?"

Merlin, though, turned to face her properly. "Where?" was all he said.

"There is a hill—a big fort, it used to be—a day from Camelard. It lies across the way from Ynnis Witrin. There are old stone buildings on it and a spring which never fails, and it is *huge*, Merlin." Guenivere came forward, her wet hems slapping softly. "I don't know whose kingdom it lies within, but I do know no one wanted to use the hill *because* it is so large. The palisades would take enormous numbers of people to repair and maintain them, and we have a whole city of people!"

Arthur frowned. "It is big enough for a city?"

She nodded. "It has never been breached—just like Camelard. No one can steal upon us there—I doubt even a single arrow would reach across the causeway."

"Does this miraculous place have a name, Guenivere?" Arthur asked softly.

Elated, Guenivere replied, "Why yes. The locals call it Camelot."

Chapter Eighteen

ara slipped out of the Corneus tent before the day waned, and before Lucan and the Corneus men returned to their campfires in front of it.

Bedivere seemed to understand her reticence. He did not argue when she sat and dressed in her old tunic and trews and hastily donned her boots once more. Instead, he stroked her hair and let her go.

When Cara returned to her mother's tent, though, she could not slide into it without remark, for everyone stood in front of the tent, talking over the top of one another, their arms crossed and their shoulders stiff.

"What has happened?" Cara asked, coming up to the tight group.

"We have to leave! Again!" Brigid protested.

Cara looked to her mother for a better explanation.

"They've found winter quarters," Ula said. She grimaced. "We are to leave tomorrow at dawn. I imagine they want to move away from this place and leave the fever behind."

"Or find shelter…" Cara murmured. Had Guenivere something to do with this sudden change of circumstance? "How are we to carry the sick? Most people cannot stand by themselves, yet." She thought of the ill she had tended that morning.

"By whatever means we can arrange, Cai said," Newlyn replied. He sounded unhappy. "We don't have a horse to our name except Cailleach," and he glanced at Cara's stallion.

"Cailleach will be happy to carry as many as he can," Cara replied.

"Will he pull a wagon, though?" Newlyn said. "I know where there is an old abandoned one, with the wheel off. It only needs an iron pin…"

"Of which there is none to spare, or it would have been recovered by now," Ula said, her tone firm.

"We don't need wagons, or wheels," Cara said. "All we need is rope and sheeting and tall, thin trees. The thinner and stouter the better…and there is a forest of them right there." She pointed.

Brigid wrinkled her nose. "You are making no sense at all, Cara."

Cara impatiently kicked aside the layer of hay until the damp earth beneath was revealed. She crouched and drew in the soil. Two lines which almost met at the top, while they grew slowly apart farther down.

With a jolt, she realized she was looking at the markings on her face, once more, only both sides were the same length.

She brushed off the cold invisible fingers which touched the back of her neck and drew two lines across the first two. "A horse, or even a man, or a strong woman can drag this easily. A person can sit upon the platform in the middle, or children, or anything you want to carry with you."

Everyone peered down at the markings on the earth.

"Where did you learn of this, Cara?" her mother asked softly.

"I just thought of it," Cara said. "Lancelot said that once, before chariots, the tribes used to drag everything along with them. He remembers everything about war, going back into times everyone else has forgotten. And there is snow, now, so pulling will be easier."

"There are more wagons than the four we had after the fire, too," Newlyn said, his tone thoughtful.

"I'll get my axe," Cara said, heading for the tent.

WHEN THE PEOPLE AT NEIGHBORING tents saw the sled device Cara and Newlyn made, they raced for the trees to chop down their own carriers.

The business of packing the few possessions they had and preparing to pack the remainder first thing in the morning took up the rest of the day. It was long past sunset when Ula called them to the fire and handed out cups of the stew she had put together and by then, Cara was exhausted. It had been a long and unexpected day.

The next day, the camp was disassembled by the light of a dozen campfires and hundreds of torches. Those who were still too ill to move were placed upon the wagons. The ill who could stagger by themselves and sit by themselves were placed upon the sled carriers. By that time, there were hundreds of the sleds, for they were very simple to make.

The company set out as the very first rays of sunlight peeped over the top of the trees, leaving behind smoking fires and little else. Far overhead, Cara's eagle circled, hunting for his breakfast. He had followed the company as they moved farther west, deeper into the summer country and the kingdoms still untouched by the Saxons.

The day favored them with a cloudless sky, no wind to speak

of and a weak sunlight which still warmed their faces.

People nodded approvingly as they turned their faces up to the light. "It is a good sign," they declared.

The approval seemed to run up and down the length of the company. Even the ill managed to smile.

The day was short. They were still traveling when the sun lowered and was gone. Torches were lit, and they continued on. Food and drink were passed down the line. They ate as they walked, for there would be no stopping until they reached their destination.

Now and then, an officer or one of Arthur's companions would range back along the length of the company, assessing and answering questions. It was how they learned about the name of the place where they were heading.

"It is a curious name, 'Camelot'," Ula said, huffing a bit as she pulled her sled over a bump in the road. "It is almost the same as Camelard."

"Perhaps because they lie close to each other, they share names which are close," Brigid said.

"It is because they both lie on the River Camel, I suspect," Cara said.

Everyone glanced at her, even the people ahead of them, and the guards striding alongside them with their spears and shields.

After a moment Newlyn, who was behind her, said, "Well, that makes sense."

A little while later, another officer trotted back along the line. He did not carry a torch as the others had. Cara did not realize who it was until he drew up alongside her family, who each hauled a sled. The horse stepped slowly beside them.

It was Bedivere.

He nodded at Cara. "I understand it is you we must thank for these…things."

"They work well enough," Cara said defensively. "We would be in the same meadow until next summer if we waited until there were wheels and carts enough to carry us all."

"We would," Bedivere said, his tone grave. "You removed Merlin's greatest headache last night. He actually laughed when he saw the contraptions."

"They are only what the tribes used before they built chariots."

"Yes, that is what he said." Bedivere touched his hand to his forehead. "Queen Ula, do you want for anything?"

Cara realized then why he did not carry a torch. His left hand held the reins. He did not want to test his right hand with the weight of a torch, not in front of others.

"To stop and sleep would be most welcome," Ula replied.

"That will not happen for some time yet. Perhaps you should recline upon your own sled for a while?"

Ula rolled her eyes.

Bedivere laughed and nudged his horse forward.

Cara stared after him, hiding her smile.

He had *laughed.*

A short while later, one of the youngest of the Corneus soldiers walked back to their position. "I am to pull your sled for you, my lady," he told Cara's mother.

Even by the light of the torches, Cara spotted the pink in her mother's cheeks. "I am not feeble."

"Rest, mother," Cara told her. "In a while, when you are recovered, you can pull it yourself once more."

So Ula settled upon the platform of her sled, with a soft sigh of relief which only Cara heard.

Along the length of the company, others were being relieved of their burdens, or their sleds were taken from them. The swapping of burdens and loads continued for the rest of the night. Sometimes, those who were ill also got to their feet to attempt to walk and relieve the one who carried them of their weight for a while.

There was much good-natured banter and jokes passing up and down the line, along with the food and the wine. The burden of walking and pulling a heavy load seemed lighter than it should be, even though their breath fogged the air and Cara's cheeks and nose burned with the cold. It was as if they had left behind not only the fever which had plagued them, but all ill-humor, too.

It helped that the way ahead became smooth and even. They had left the dales behind and the trees, too. The ground on either side of the road glistened in the moonlight and glittered when the torches shone upon it. It was ice. The ground, she realized, was not ground at all, but deceptive bog, dotted with clumps of weeds and grasses which gave it the appearance of solid earth. They were in the summer country.

The road wound in meandering curves and bends.

Another officer trotted down the line. "Not long now," Lancelot told them, his horse prancing with excess energy, as if it had not been working all night. Lancelot sat upon the restless beast as if he sat upon a cushioned chair. "Although it will be a race as to who gets there first, the sun or us," he added.

Cara said, "Lancelot, may I have a word?"

He tilted his head. "Of course."

"I cannot move over to you," she added, patting the sled she pulled.

Lancelot swung down off the horse with the same energy his stallion displayed. He came over to her and held out the reins. "Hold these for a moment."

She took them from him.

"Now, let me pull that for you," he said, ducking under the branch and coming up behind her. "Rest for a moment while you speak."

"No, I—"

"Haven't rested all night," Newlyn said, his voice sharp.

Lancelot pushed on her shoulder, so that Cara was forced to duck down and under the sled rail. She straightened and marveled for a moment at the sight of Lancelot pulling a sled like any other man. His elegant tunic and dark clothes and the gold pin holding his cloak closed make a mockery of the drudgery. So did the twinkle in his eyes.

"You wished to speak to me?" he said to her. Unlike her, he was not blowing and gusting over the work of hauling the sled.

"Yes." Cara moved closer, holding the reins out to her right so Lancelot's horse would not trip over the splayed ends of her sled. She lowered her voice. "It is about Bedivere."

The good humor faded from Lancelot's eyes. He sobered. "What of him?" he asked, just as softly.

Cara explained.

THE SKY WAS MOST DEFINITELY growing lighter in the east when an excited whisper ran along the company. "Camelot! Camelot! It is just ahead!"

Slowly, while the sky grew from black to indigo to a blue tinged with pink, the bulk of a great hill fort rose above them.

They were farther away from the fort than Cara realized, for they continued walking while the hill grew even larger.

The growing light picked out concentric rings of earthworks circling the top. Three of them, all great ditches.

As she climbed the causeway through the watery land and up the side of the hill, she saw that the ditches were very deep indeed. They must have been dug deeper with each succeeding generation of people who occupied the hill. There were old spikes driven into the ground at the bottom, crossing each other like prickly barbs, although many of them were missing and some were burned to black stumps.

She dug her feet in as the road steepened and the sled seemed to grow even heavier, until suddenly, the road leveled. Then she saw what remained of the palisades which must have once circled the top of the hill. They ran for what seemed to be miles, before they curved out of sight around the hill. There were many gaps and sagging sections which would have to be repaired. She wondered where the mighty trees would come from to repair the walls, for as she passed through the gate, she saw the palisades stood three times taller than she did.

The ground inside the wall was even and smooth, covered in snow which had seen no boots, except those of the company which now spread across the land. At the far end of the hill, which was roughly oval, was the shadowy bulk of stone buildings which Cara could immediately tell were Roman in design, even though she could see no details yet.

Beneath the snow under her feet, laid stones gave firmer footing. Almost in the exact center of the hill was a square stone wall, knee high, and covered over with timbers. She heard faint bubbling. A stone-lined ditch ran from the low wall, down either side of the hill toward the walls. In the center of the ditch, water sparkled and jumped.

The spring, which welled even now in the depth of winter.

Cara lowered the sled with deep thankfulness and stretched her back. Everyone was doing the same around her and she realized dawn was nearly upon them. She could see everyone without benefit of a torch.

"Look, look!" someone cried.

Cara turned to see what they exclaimed about. People pointed. She turned again, and caught her breath, astonished.

The sun lifted over the horizon as they stood marveling at the view. From the foot of the hill, the land laid flat and still, a mist hovered over it like a blanket. It made it seem as though the hill was floating upon the white sea.

The flat land spread for miles and miles, out toward the night sky which still lingered in the west.

As the sun painted a golden line across the mist from the east to the west, Cara saw, near to the other horizon, another hill almost identical to this one. Lights showed at the top of it and a single square tower thrust up into the dawn sky, at the very top of the conical hill. Between that hill and this was nothing but the misty sea.

"Avalon!" someone whispered and made a powerful sign which was not the Christian cross.

"Ynnis Witrin!" cried another. "We are blessed to have found this place!"

Chapter Nineteen

amelot was not there simply for the taking. The first business of the new court was to establish precedence over the hill and the land.

Everyone slept for the balance of that first day in the dusty rooms which were still whole inside the old Roman palace at the end of the tor. They built fires upon the floors and laid beside them and slept. They were too tired to care that they slept upon raw stone.

Then the work of rebuilding Camelot began.

Arthur sent out officers and Merlin to meet with the king upon whose lands Camelot was located. Even more men were sent to find stands of trees which could rebuild the palisades.

More people were tasked with gathering food and hunting, while anyone with any building experience or knowledge in engineering were assigned to build swift, temporary houses which only needed to last for the balance of winter.

The king whose land Camelot was upon was a man called Melwaes. Merlin and the other officers escorted him to Camelot to deal with Arthur over the use of the hill.

Cara was a witness to the early parts of that negotiation, for she happened to be with Guenivere when the royal party arrived.

The party which included Merlin and the officers who had been sent to escort Melwaes also included two people whom Cara remembered only a little. They were richly dressed, the pair of them, and the woman had completely white hair, even though her face was unlined and youthful.

"The Lady of Corneus," Guenivere murmured. "I remember her, even though she has not returned to Arthur's court since she was made duchess of Corneus. Mair and her husband, Prince Arawn Uther of Brocéliande."

Cara raised her brow, impressed by Guenivere's knowledge.

Guenivere smiled. "As a political asset, I have learned it is best to know who the other political parties are and where their loyalties lie. In this case, Mair is ferociously loyal to Arthur, while Rawn is loyal to Mair, which ties Brocéliande to Arthur in two ways, for his brother, the King of Brocéliande, is also loyal. Corneus lies only a little farther to the south, you know."

"I did not," Cara said stiffly. "I am from the north."

"Aye, ye are," Guenivere said, copying her accent.

They both laughed.

Then Guenivere nodded. "The man with the golden torc must be Melwaes. I have yet to learn where his true loyalties lie. He has only just become king. His father was quite mad, I'm told."

Cara considered the short man who climbed down from his horse. He had a cast to his eyes which gave him an unfortunate appearance, although the eyes themselves seemed intelligent enough.

"Arthur is waiting. I must greet his guests," Guenivere murmured. She brushed off her gown. They had been sweeping the chamber she had been given as her own. The two of them stepped out upon the open verandah at the sound of the horses and shouts of greeting.

Arthur stood with Bedivere and Cai in the big courtyard in the middle of the house, watching the riders dismount.

Mair, the Lady of Corneus, picked up her gown and hurried to where Bedivere stood and threw her arm around him and held him tightly. Her husband, the Prince, who Guenivere had called "Rawn", stood back, smiling.

Lucan rushed into the courtyard through the archway and over to the pair of them and pulled Mair away from Bedivere and hugged her himself.

Bedivere moved around them and slapped Rawn on the shoulder. They gripped each other's arms, laughing.

Merlin and Melwaes wove around the family and over to where Arthur, and now Guenivere, waited.

Cara moved around the verandah, creeping closer so she could hear what they said. If she stayed on the verandah, she would not be including herself in the official royal party, which would be unforgiveable.

"…King Melwaes, my lord Arthur. He is the son of the late Maleagant, may the gods speed his passing," Merlin added. "Melwaes' lands encompass this hill, my lord."

Melwaes's jaw was tight and hard as he gazed at Arthur. "King Arthur," he acknowledged. "It was a surprise to me to see the light of your fires upon my hill this morning."

"I'm sure. We were forced to move in the middle of the night to the first safe haven we could find. You may thank the Saxons for your shock," Arthur replied. "I am sure we can come to terms which will admirably suit you, Melwaes. The hill is clearly un-used—you would derive income from a place which has produced none for some time."

Melwaes looked as though he was about to argue. Cara recognized the look in his eyes. Even though this hill had been abandoned and considered unusable, he would protest over the loss of it and try to drive the terms as high as possible. It was a grasping, greedy strategy…but then, these were hard times. Perhaps he had many people looking to him for shelter and protection. Most kings were beset these days.

Guenivere lifted her voice in the pleasant musical way she had when she wanted to sooth ruffled feathers. "Perhaps this conversation would go more smoothly inside, over a cup of mulled wine?"

Melwaes glanced at her, irritated by the interruption. Then his gaze swung back again and stayed upon her face.

Arthur said, "My Queen, Melwaes. The Lady Guenivere."

Guenivere held out her hand. "King Melwaes. Your hill has the most stupendous outlook. I keep finding myself coming to a halt and marveling at the view. What *is* that big hill in the far distance? Is that yours, too?"

Melwaes' hand, as he took her fingers, trembled.

Cara crossed her arms, suddenly cold, as she watched him bow over Guenivere's hand.

"That place is the unholy Ynnis Witrin," Melwaes told her. "The Apple Isle, they call it, those who dare step upon its cursed shores."

"It is an island?" Guenivere said, her tone polite. She gave no reaction to his harsh tone and words.

"In all but fact, for there is only one way to reach it, which only the people who are permitted to live upon it know." He gave her a reassuring smile. "There are fourteen miles between you and those pagans. You are quite safe here, my Lady."

Cara held herself still. She knew very well Guenivere was not a Christian.

Guenivere gave Melwaes one of her warmest smiles, the kind which tended to leave men blinking and wordless. "Oh, I'm so glad you are here to explain this to me, my lord! I was under the impression Ynnis Witrin had a monastery and a chapel which is open to everyone. How fortunate to have you tell me now, before I visited to pay my respects."

Melwaes visibly preened. Cara saw Arthur and Merlin exchange silent glances.

"I believe there is a tiny chapel at one end," Melwaes said, his tone off hand. "I have not been there myself, of course."

Guenivere half-turned toward the house. "Do come in, my lord. The wine is freshly made and hot. Tell me about the spring here. Is it true it has never failed? Not even in the driest of seasons? That is most extraordinary for a spring which climbs so high…"

Their voices faded as they moved deeper into the building.

Arthur cleared his throat and stirred. He crooked his fingers at Merlin and Cai. "Let's not hurry in," he murmured. "With luck, Guenivere will save us having to negotiate terms at all."

They headed for the house, their steps slow, their voices soft.

Cara shivered again and went to find mulled wine of her own.

The next day, Lancelot and Pellinore marked out a flat area at the far east end of the hill, near the gates. They hammered pegs into the ground around the perimeter. An old stone floor made up part of the area. Turf and rocks were the rest—all natural hazards and uneven footing to keep the fighter wary and alert. It was to be the training area.

By the time Cara arrived after breakfast, the engineers and smithies were already marking out a street where they would build their shops and forges. The street would lie between the training arena and the gates.

Fighters found their way to the arena over the next hour, even though there would be no formal training that day. Instead, Lancelot and Pellinore spoke with each fighter, establishing their health and strength and determining what weapons they had. A great many weapons, shields and armor had been lost in the razing of Venta Belgarum.

Cara settled on one of the bigger rocks to wait, with one eye on the narrow street forming between the skeletal frames of what would be shops.

Bedivere appeared not long after she arrived. He stood at the edge of the marked out arena, his gauntlets hanging at his sides. His jaw flexed as he took in the warriors in the arena, with Lancelot and Pellinore in the middle of them.

Cara hurried up to Bedivere.

"*This* is your solution?" he said, his tone harsh. "I trusted you." The condemnation in his voice was rich.

"And you must trust me a little longer. Please, Bedivere. Wait and hear him out."

"Him?" Bedivere looked over her shoulder and rolled his eyes when he saw Lancelot approaching. "I will spend no time discussing this. You know how I feel about it, Lancelot."

Lancelot lifted his hand, a gesture for calm. "I know how you feel," he said, his voice low. "But I can help you, Bedivere."

Bedivere's face darkened. "She told you." Fury tinged his voice.

"Yes, and Cara was right to," Lancelot replied. He gripped Bedivere's cloak. "Step over here, well out of the way. Hear me out, Bedivere. Will you do that?"

Bedivere's gaze swung to Cara. His fury leapt. His face worked.

Cara felt a little ill. She had expected him to be angry, yet this palpable rage was frightening. This would ensure that Bedivere never looked favorably upon her again.

She made herself speak the truth as she knew it, anyway. "Lancelot can show you how to fight again, Bedivere—even better than before. Stronger, even."

"Yes, listen to her," Lancelot urged him, while trying to pull Bedivere out of the way of the fighters squeezing past them. Bedivere remained as solidly planted as the rock Cara had been sitting upon.

Bedivere shook his head. "Your way is not honorable."

"But it *is* effective. You have seen the results for yourself upon every battlefield in the last ten years." Lancelot gave up trying to shift Bedivere anywhere. He dropped his hands and said simply, "Do you want to be able to fight for Arthur once more, Bedivere? Or do you want to return to Corneus and live upon your sister's lands, a useless, *wasted* warrior?"

Cara winced.

Bedivere drew in a breath which shuddered. "Where is the honor in either choice?"

Lancelot threw out his hand. "The gods take *honor!* I fight to kill Saxons, to see their heads roll upon the ground, for daring to take our lands away from us, and from our families and our children! That is *my* honor!"

Bedivere shuddered.

Lancelot pushed his hand through his black curls. "Arthur cannot win this fight without you, Bedivere. Do you want to see the Saxons roll across Britain? Do you want to see everything burn the way Venta Belgarum did?" He lowered his voice. "You *know* how desperate we are! How can you *not* consider this?"

Bedivere swallowed. The furrow between his eyes was deep. He was torn. Cara could see it in his eyes and the hard line of his shoulders.

Lancelot sensed it, too, for he said in a milder tone. "Would you come with me for a moment? I have something to show you."

Bedivere blew out his breath and nodded.

Lancelot walked up the street, then through an intersection, heading for the gates. Already, Cara could see how a village was forming around them. There were no walls, yet, but there were plans and outlines and a humming sense of industry.

One of the smiths, the big man they called John Welland, was building his forge out of rocks, with clay slathered onto them to hold them together. He nodded at Lancelot and got to his feet as they approached.

"John," Lancelot said. "Would you show Bedivere?"

John moved silently over to a bucket and washed the mud off his hands. Then he stepped over to a roughly nailed-together barrow of raw tree trunks, which held a few of the tools of his trade. He would make what else he needed, Cara guessed.

He unwrapped a rag from something and brought it over and held it out to Bedivere. "It was found in the fens near here. It's a very old design, but it is worth studying."

Bedivere took the old sword hilt, with deep reluctance slowing his movements. It was rusty and the leather around the hilt had been eaten away. Even so, Cara could see the hilt was longer than any hilt she had ever seen on a sword. The blade, beyond the out-thrust wrist guards, was wider than any sword she had ever seen before, too. She didn't know how long the sword would be, for the blade was snapped off, a foot from the hilt.

"The hilt is too long," Bedivere said. His voice was strained.

"That be a two-handed sword," John Welland said. "You don't see many of them. Takes a strong man to wield them, on account of the blade."

Bedivere looked up at the giant man. "The blade?" he repeated. The strain showed around his eyes, too. He was still fighting himself and everyone around him. As usual, he held it all inside him.

"Four, five-foot blade at least," John said, in his slow, placid voice. "That's why it's so wide at the base. The man who can use it could reach farther and cut wider than any man with a normal sword." He paused. "Just so happens, I know where there is a big lump of star metal. The kind that drops from the sky. To make a sword like that—" and he nodded at the old, rusty relic in Bedivere's hands, "—would take a special kind of iron. Star metal is very strong. It's a big enough piece to make a sword like that, too."

Bedivere looked back down at the rusty, ancient weapon in his hands. Slowly, he turned the iron around, and gripped the base of the hilt. Then, even more slowly, he took the hilt with his left hand, curling his fingers around the metal. He looked up at Lancelot. "How do I use it?"

Cara pressed her fingers to her mouth to stop herself from crying out her relief and her joy.

Chapter Twenty

The next morning, before breakfast, Cara saw to Cailleach's needs and to the raising of a perch for the eagle, which had returned to guard Cailleach's side. When she was finished, instead of hurrying to her meal, she moved across the hill to the old Roman house and the room she knew Bedivere was now using. Lucan still had the use of the Corneus tent, farther afield, where the rest of the Corneus men camped while waiting for more permanent quarters to be raised for them.

She tapped on Bedivere's door. When he opened it and glared at her, she slipped inside. She reached for the oil and the shaving blade, which sat on the chest beside the bedroll on the floor.

She patted the chest.

"If I am to learn to fight with this hand, I should learn to shave with it, too," Bedivere growled.

"One thing at a time. You will test your hand enough for the next while."

He closed the door. "You tricked me."

She didn't bother asking what he was referring to. "I failed to tell you what I had in mind. There was no trick."

"You knew I would hate it."

She met his gaze. "I knew."

"Yet you did it anyway."

"Arthur needs you. That was my only concern." *That* was the lie, although she would never tell him so.

He growled, a touch of his fury from yesterday coloring the sound.

"Sit. I am hungry and you are forcing me to wait for my breakfast," she said.

Bedivere remained where he was.

"Did you know that when you are in a quandary, your face turns red?" she asked sweetly.

He swore under his breath and threw himself upon the chest. "Cut me, and I will take the same from your flesh."

She pulled his chin around so she could reach the cheek. "The Saxons beat you to it by six years. Now stop talking, so I can do this properly."

He stopped talking. Cara oiled and shaved him quickly, because she really *was* hungry. She wiped the blade, stoppered the oil and tossed the rag upon the chest as he rose to his feet, smoothing his fingers over his jaw.

"I will see you in the arena, after breakfast," she said curtly.

"You are not breaking your fast in the main hall?"

The main hall, now, was the open section of the house. Rough tables—some of them only tree trunks shaved down and pegged together—had been placed around the impluvium in the middle, beneath the rectangular hole in the roof.

"I have never broken my fast in the main hall," Cara said.

His gaze moved to her face. She realized she was pulling her hair over it. She dropped her hand but couldn't stop it from curling into a fist by her thigh.

"Your family's pavilion is at the far end of the tor." Bedivere's tone was reasonable. "The hall is ten steps away. You would eat faster if you go there. As I am already heading there, you may as well come with me."

Her breath came faster. "I thought...you were angry with me."

"I am," he returned in the same flat tone. "I extend the courtesy of an officer to a warrior who has proved their use."

"Ah..." She grimaced. "Then I decline your invitation." She opened the door.

"I would *like* you to accompany me," Bedivere said, his tone even harsher.

Cara didn't look back at him. "You should not be seen with me, war duke." She slipped out and shut the door, then hurried across the yard to the archway and out of the house, almost running.

When she reached her mother's tent, she had no appetite for the gruel which was cooking in the pot over the fire, either.

BEDIVERE STOOD IN THE SAME place as he had yesterday, watching the fighters going through their basic drills, all their swords up in the air over their heads.

Cara lowered hers, her heart hammering.

Bedivere looked almost sick with uneasiness, as he hovered at the end of the lane, yet she could not bring herself to go over to him.

Lancelot patted Pellinore on the arm, where the two of them stood in front of the lines of fighters. Pellinore nodded and took over the calling of the positions, both feet and arms, sword point, and hands.

Lancelot threaded his way around the edge of the arena and spoke to Bedivere.

Cara moved her sword slowly through the positions as Pelenor called them out, her gaze upon the two of them, until her sword point knocked aside her neighbors' because she was moving too slowly. She apologized and lowered the point to the ground and leaned upon her sword, frankly watching.

"Bedivere the Perfect is here to learn? The gods move in mysterious ways!" Bryn muttered, on her other side.

"Is that why John Welland has been sitting there looking half asleep since we arrived?" Druston asked, on Bryn's far side. He was breathless.

Welland rose to his feet as Lancelot drew Bedivere over to where the big smith had been sitting upon an upturned bucket, which put his long legs up near his shoulders. Welland picked up another rag-swaddled bundle, this one much longer than yesterday's.

Cara's mouth opened in surprise. Welland had made a sword...already? She did not think it was possible. Her curiosity outweighed her hurt feelings. She moved along the space between the drill lines, ducking swinging blades as they whistled past.

Pellinore and Lancelot discouraged fighters from moving through the lines when the drills were in progress. It was too dangerous. Fighters were supposed to move out to the edge and go around. Only Cara didn't have the patience for it. She knew the drills well enough to anticipate the movement of the swords.

She stepped out at the top of the line and moved over to where Welland and Bedivere and Lancelot were examining the sword Welland had uncovered.

Cara looked at the skeletal, flat, unadorned metal, disappointment touching her. It wasn't a sword at all. The hilt was raw iron, flat and far too slender and long. There was no blade. Where the blade should be was a lump of iron, slightly flattened and without an edge.

Yet Bedivere and Lancelot were smiling in appreciation as they studied it.

"It's so long!" Lancelot said, his hand on Welland's shoulder.

"Bedivere is a tall man," Welland said. "Not tall like me, although this length of sword should suit his height." He turned the sword around and presented the hilt to Bedivere. "Try it. I would like to see how the length suits you."

Bedivere hesitated only for a fraction of a heartbeat. He curled his right hand over the raw, unpadded hilt. He wore the heavy gauntlets, which no one would find odd, because the day was crisply cold. As his fingers closed around the hilt, he quickly raised his left hand and gripped the bottom half of the long hilt.

Welland stepped out of the way as Bedivere raised the sword, point upward, testing the balance.

"Heavy," Bedivere breathed.

"Some weight will be lost in the forging," Welland said. "It won't affect the balance though. Swing it, please. I would like to see the natural plane."

Cara raised her brows. She was not entirely sure what that meant. There was clearly far more to the making of a sword than the hammering of hot metal until a thin edge was formed.

Everyone stepped back, while Bedivere swung the blocky, unformed blade. It whistled, anyway. After a few swings, he shook his head—not in dismissal, but in amazement. He let the tip swing upward and held it so the blade was horizontal. Then he rested his finger beneath the blade, just behind the hilt. "There is the balance point, even with the blade unformed. You are a master craftsman, John. Even with the long hilt, it has not overbalanced."

"Will the forming of the blade and the loss of weight affect that?" Lancelot asked.

Welland shook his head. "The wrapping and grips on the hilt will counter the loss. I am pleased. The length is just right. See— he swings it, yet it does not scrape the ground. It is a good length for him—it gives him the greatest reach yet will not trip him up."

"Thank you, John," Bedivere said. He swung the sword once more, then held the hilt out to Welland.

Welland wrapped it carefully. "I will continue to work on it today, now my forge is firing. Lancelot says you are without a sword at all, my lord?"

Bedivere looked surprised. Then he wiped his surprise from his face. "Yes, I have no weapon I can use," he replied carefully.

Lancelot's expression didn't change at all.

The drills, Cara realized, had ground to a halt. Too many people watched the exchange.

Welland hefted the sword, which did not seem large in his arms. "The day after tomorrow...perhaps tomorrow, if the metal is as good as I think it is and can hold the temper." He nodded and walked away.

The fighters had clumped together and were murmuring to each other.

Lancelot scowled. "Back to work!" he shouted. "Barnard, bring the bag of practice swords."

"Yes, my lord!" Barnard said. He dropped his sword and ran over to pick up the heavy sack in which the rusted and neglected practice swords were kept. The swords squealed and knocked together as he brought the bag over to Lancelot.

Everyone returned to their drill positions, including Cara.

She moved through the drills, more than half her attention upon Bedivere and Lancelot as they picked through the swords. They were examining the hilts. She knew they were looking for one with a longer hilt, which Bedivere could use two handed. There were several in the bag with decorative, extended pommels. If Bedivere kept his gauntlets on, the decorative elements and the rough edges where thieves had levered out the jewels which had once sat in them would not scrape his hand. It would let him keep his left hand on the hilt, to compensate for only having two good fingers of the right hand to grip with.

As Cara had guessed, Bedivere settled upon one of the swords with the longer pommel.

Lancelot pointed at Cara and spoke to Bedivere.

"Guess you're training the newcomer," Bryn murmured.

Cara rolled her eyes and tried to appear upset. Everyone disliked having to teach newcomers the basic drills and principals. Fighters experienced in the field yet new to Lancelot's way of fighting tended to resist every single instruction. They argued with every principal.

Bedivere, who had been pulled into this training against his will, would be twice as bad. He was a senior officer and Arthur's war duke. Of *course*, he would insist upon understanding every single nuance of the training.

She wasn't upset about having to train him, but she *was* wary. Would Bedivere find the reasoning nonsense? Would he belittle everyone in the arena and call attention to the lack of honor in the way they fought? Would he resist the underhanded tactics Lancelot taught?

Dropping a sword to one's left hand, using both hands for leverage, hiding extra blades under one's armor…even the women in the Queen's Cohort had learned to sharpen their hair combs and as a last resort, slash at their enemy's face. Preferably the eyes.

Bedivere's ancestors were likely among those who had presented themselves upon the field outside Rome and honored the outcome of a man-to-man test of strength and walked away. Bedivere would hate the no-quarters-given way of thinking Lancelot tried to instill in everyone who trained with him.

"The Saxons give no quarter and don't give a damn about your honor or the rules," Lancelot would often say as he strolled around the edge of the training area, watching everyone move through the drills. "If you are to remain the man still standing, you must discard such thoughts yourself. They did not serve us in Rome. They will not serve us against this enemy, either."

The last two years of Saxon incursions, when the Saxons had fired their flaming arrows upon innocent villages and towns from their hidden places, burning out homes, families and entire kingdoms...these last two years had done more to prove Lancelot right than any other year before them.

Eleven battles had been fought against the Saxons. Eleven brutal battles, including this summer, plus a hundred undeclared battles like the one at Venta Belgarum.

Surely Bedivere would understand why so many fighters turned to Lancelot and his way of fighting? Now Bedivere was forced to it, would he accede to the sense of it?

As the line beside Cara shuffled down to give Bedivere a position next to her, Cara brought her sword up over her head, in the general ready position. "Like this," she said.

"You have both hands on your sword," Bedivere pointed out.

"Because I need the strength. That is why you train with me. This way. No, keep the end of the sword up, don't let it drop behind you. Up, with your wrists strong."

Bedivere copied her.

"Then down, this way..." She brought her sword down slowly, so he could see the arch and the movement of the point.

"The tip is up. It is a hacking motion," Bedivere said, copying her.

"If you want to stab, you can. This way." She brought the sword up once more. This time, she brought her wrists up, so the sword point dropped down in front of her. She brought it down toward the ground, the iron whistling. "That one is only good from the back of a horse."

"Yes, I can see that." Bedivere repeated the first movement, then nodded. "Next," he said, his voice flat.

Just like that, he had accepted the positioning and movement.

Feeling slightly dazed, Cara took him through the set of eight basic movements and then the position of his feet...then, just as quickly, the changes of hand grip. She was tentative about explaining them, knowing that some of the shifts and grips would not work for him...although she could not say so in the middle of the training field.

"Just tell me what they are. Show me," Bedivere said, with a shake of his head. "I will work it out, later."

Cara showed him the positions, including the complete reversal of hands involved in the stabbing motion she had used at the very beginning.

Bedivere argued over none of it. He merely listened, tried out the positions, nodded, then demanded the next one.

Then the next...until she had covered everything.

She was winded. Bedivere had absorbed what took most beginners three or four days. By the time she was finished, the drills were done and the fighters broke up into their smaller groups for mock fights. Everyone liked the mock fights. They learned a great deal from participating or observation. Each movement of a fight was broken down and the choices each fighter had made examined closely.

"You will need to practice the drills before you participate in a fight," Cara told Bedivere as they moved into one of the circles.

Bedivere glanced at her. "I will, hmm?"

When Lamorak, who was directing the group, called for the next pair of fighters, Bedivere raised his hand. "I will." He stepped into the ring, the sword on his shoulder, before Lamorak could protest.

"And who will fight Bedivere?" Lamorak said.

No one put up their hand.

"He is your student, Cara," Lamorak said. "Step in, please."

Cara gritted her teeth, holding back her protest, for Lamorak was correct. It *was* her place to put Bedivere through his paces.

She stepped in and the ring closed around her.

Hector, Lancelot's half-brother, winked at her as he leaned on his sword. He was enjoying this.

Bedivere brought his sword up to the ready position. His sword was perfectly placed. He moved around the ring, watching her. She had never seen that look in his eyes, before. It was unwavering, implacable. The stare of a deadly enemy. It was what the Saxons saw when they confronted him, she realized.

Cara shivered and raised her sword. Before her blade came to the horizontal, she leapt, bringing the sword down. It was the unexpected.

Bedivere's sword whistled as it swung and blocked her, jarring her sword up into the air, and numbing her arm, too. He had executed the perfect defense.

Everyone in the circle muttered.

"Again," Bedivere said, beckoning her. He put his hand back on the hilt and lifted the sword. "As hard as you can."

Just like that, Bedivere took control of the bout. He directed her, forcing Cara to test him with every conceivable form of attack, including the underhanded ones such as switching her sword to the other hand and feinting to make him think she would switch, and then not.

She did not get passed his guard a single time.

Cara put her sword point on the ground and leaned on it, her breath bellowing.

Bedivere straightened and dropped the flat of the blade on his shoulder. "I see the potential," he said, more to himself than anyone in the ring. He looked around the ring. "Next!" he called and stepped through the perimeter. He kept walking, right up to where Lancelot and Pellinore were talking. He tossed the sword to Lancelot, nodded at him, then moved out of the arena.

Cara was not the only one to watch him go.

Lamorak cleared his throat. "That, everyone, is why he is war duke."

The next morning, Bedivere arrived at the training arena at the same time as everyone else. He had not been in his room when Cara went there before breakfast and his cheeks were not shaved.

He carried the new, double-handed sword on his hip, in a temporary scabbard.

That was why he had not been in his room, Cara realized.

Bedivere was not alone. Lucan, Gawain *and* Gaheris were with him.

"Bedivere says we must try this newfangled style of yours, Lancelot," Gawain said, not sounding at all upset. "I can't see the point myself. If Bedivere says it's worth it, then I'm willing to give it a try. So…what do we do?" He put his hand on his sword and looked around the arena.

Cara was relieved when Pellinore did not assign her to teach the three newcomers.

Bedivere took up a position beside her as the drill lines formed. When he withdrew his sword, though, everyone around him turned to watch. The sound the sword made as it sliced through the air was flat and heavy, unlike any other sword Cara had ever heard swung.

The sword was magnificent. The blade had been honed to perfection and shone in the early morning light. The long double-length hilt was wrapped in leather and silver wire, giving Bedivere a better grip. A heavy red jewel glistened in the pommel.

"Gods and gossamer, the thing is a *monster*," Druston exclaimed, which made even more heads turn.

The fighters gathered in around Bedivere, trying to examine the sword for themselves.

"A *double* hilt? It'll get in the way!" someone protested.

"No, it's offset. See the balance? Bedivere…my lord, would you hold it so…see?"

"The blade would chop a tree trunk! The *width* of it!"

"Heavy bastard," someone muttered.

"The weight gives extra power, so long as the balance is good," came the reply.

Cara realized Bryn had moved over to stand beside her. She glanced at him. His gaze met hers and he leaned close. "Are you and Bedivere...together?"

Cara recoiled, horrified. "Why would you ask that?"

Bryn shrugged. "You're the only one standing back." His smile was good natured. "Not that you have anything in common with the man, although I've seen stranger couples."

Cara's throat tightened. "No, there is nothing. Nothing at all. He is the *war duke*, Bryn!"

"So?"

Cara stared at him, nonplussed. She could find nothing to say to that at all.

"Bedivere!" someone called from within the group huddled around him. "What will you name her?"

"Yes, sword needs a name," came a growl of agreement.

"It's name is Rúad," Bedivere replied.

Bryn smothered a laugh and looked at Cara. "Nothing at all, then?" he asked. He walked away, still chuckling.

Cara stalked from the arena, her temper driving her every step. She knew why Bryn had laughed. Her gut burned with the knowledge.

Rúad was the goddess queen of Ireland.

The red-headed goddess.

Chapter Twenty-One

ara's mornings were usually full. Now she had no training, she had nothing to do. Cara brushed Cailleach until he protested at the touch of the bristles. The eagle accepted a morsel or two, then refused more food. She shook out her bedroll, stoked the fire, laid fresh hay on the snow. After that, there was little to do but fume. Occupying her hands did not occupy her mind. Her temper simmered, each time she recalled what had happened in the arena.

Her mother's pavilion was on the east side of the hill. Most of the pavilions and tents had been set up as they were in a war camp. The location of her mother's pavilion meant Cara could see everyone who walked along the central street which had formed.

When she had run out of things to do, Cara sat on one of the tree stumps which had collected around the campfire. She put her hands toward the flames and watched everyone as they walked by. Many men walked past with dressed trees over their shoulders. They headed to the section of palisades being rebuilt.

Her attention was drawn to each tall man who passed by. Each time she would relax when she saw who it was. It surprised her how many people she recognized. Cara had thought she knew few people in Arthur's court. She did not mix with them. She knew more army men than she did the women and children of the court. Yet everyone who went by had a familiar face. She may not be able to place the name, although she recognized them.

Toward noon, when Bedivere strode past, Cara straightened, her heart thundering.

Before she could reconsider the wisdom of what she was doing, she lurched to her feet and hurried after him. Bedivere was not walking fast yet his long legs swallowed the ground. Cara had trouble keeping up with him. She did not want to catch up with him altogether, not out here in the open where everyone could see them. She hung back, keeping his broad shoulders in sight, as he moved across the length of the tor toward the old palace where his room was located.

As he moved through the tiled archway into the main courtyard, Cara quickened her pace to close the distance between them. She entered the courtyard in time to see him go into his room.

She hurried onto the verandah, looking around for observers. It was a cold day, and everyone was inside.

When she reached Bedivere's door, she paused, her heart leaping even harder, for Bedivere stood there with one hand on the door, holding it open. Clearly, he had been waiting for her. He was not smiling.

He stood aside, waiting for her to come into the room and shut the door behind her.

Cara whirled to confront him. Her temper, which had been simmering all morning, spilled over. "How dare you call your sword after me!"

"You think I called the sword after you?" He seemed amused. "What gave you that idea?"

"The redheaded goddess!"

235

"Perhaps the goddess is mine." He unbuckled his sword belt and laid the great sword over the chest.

Cara's temper would not let her think properly. She squeezed her fingers into her temples. No words availed themselves.

Bedivere didn't seem to mind her silence. He turned away from the chest and came over to where she stood quivering by the door. Her breath was snatched away as he bent and pressed his lips to hers.

For an astonished moment she stood still. She could feel her body responding to his touch, yet her heart and her mind were still too angry.

Cara got her hands up between them, rested them against his chest and shoved.

Bedivere didn't step back, although he did sway. It was enough. Cara slid out from between him and the door, to the middle of the room.

"That does not fix anything," she snapped.

Bedivere crossed his arms. "It was not meant to fix anything."

Heat rushed through her. She trembled with it. "Then perhaps you should fix things before you try kissing me again." She moved toward him, her temper compensating for the impact of being this close to him. "Get out of my way."

Bedivere stepped out of the way. She opened the door.

"I *will* kiss you again," he said, his voice low.

Cara stepped through the door and just barely resisted the need to slam it shut. It would draw far too much attention. Then, still steaming, she stalked away from the verandah, wishing she had not gone there in the first place.

"Cara!"

The hail came from behind Cara as she reached the tiled archway. Cara recognized the voice. It was Guenivere. Reluctantly, she turned back toward the courtyard.

Guenivere stood at the edge of the veranda where Arthur's

bedchamber was located. She waved Cara over to her.

Cara sighed and obeyed. When she stepped on the veranda, Guenivere smiled at her. "I am so pleased to see you are here. I just learned that Arthur has invited Morgan to dine with him for the midday meal. Please come with me and attend the meal. I would feel far more comfortable with someone like you beside me."

Cara wanted to protest that she was far too busy. In fact, she was not busy at all. Everything she might do in an afternoon she had already done this morning. Yet the idea of dining with kings and queens filled her with dread. She tugged at her old training tunics. "I am not dressed nearly well enough to dine with the King."

Guenivere grasped her hand. "What you are wearing is perfectly adequate. No one has nice clothes except Morgan. If we appear at the table in rags, perhaps she may notice how much she stands out among us." She pulled Cara along the veranda.

Cara let herself be led into the main hall, where the best of the tables had been set up in a small group on the other side of the pool. Servants had finished laying the table. Arthur sat in the chair at the head of it.

He lifted his brow when he saw Cara. Cara trembled. She had only ever spoken to Arthur directly once or twice. As much as possible, she stayed out of the King's way. He and his company were not for the likes of her.

"Princess Cara," Arthur said. "I understand we have you to thank for the saving of Bedivere after the burning of Venta Belgarum."

"You may also thank me for Bedivere's injuries in the first place," Cara said, without thinking.

Both Arthur and Guenivere glanced at her with startled expressions.

"He saved me and my family," Cara added hastily. "If not for him, we would have burned inside our house."

"Bedivere is a champion of women and children," Arthur said. "If it had not been your family, then it was likely he would have injured himself saving another family. I would not feel guilty for his injuries. Things happen in war."

"Please sit, Cara," Guenivere said. Guenivere settled on the other chair.

As there were only benches available on the other side of the table, Cara took one of the short benches at the far end.

"The Lady Morgan is not joining us today, after all?" Guenivere asked.

"Oh, she will be late as usual," Arthur said.

"Then, as the Lady Morgan is not here right now," Guenivere said, with a glance at Cara, "I wonder if I may speak to you about her, Arthur?"

Arthur's glance flickered toward Cara. "Now?"

"There is little opportunity to speak to you about small domestic matters," Guenivere said. "I do not mind speaking in front of Cara, if you do not. She has my complete confidence."

Cara stared at the queen, astonished.

Before Cara could regather her composure, Guenivere went on. "I would like you to consider sending your sister away from court, Arthur."

Arthur did not react. Cara grew wary. The king's temper was legendary. The smallest things could upset him, while wholesale acts of war did little more than make him shake his head. Everyone said he was just like his father, Uther, in that regard.

This time, Arthur merely shook his head.

Cara relaxed.

"I realize that, as a husband, I should try to indulge your wishes," Arthur told Guenivere. "In this, you are asking too much of me. She is my sister, and she is a valuable physician. Too many soldiers would be dead, if not for her. For that alone, I do not see the wisdom of putting her aside."

"Yes, she is a gifted physician," Guenivere said. "I am not asking simply because of my personal dislike for her, which I am sure you have heard about."

Arthur's jaw shifted. Cara could tell by the expression in his eyes that he had heard the story of Morgan and Guenivere's confrontation. He rubbed his jaw.

"The fact is, Arthur," Guenivere continued, "Morgan has taken yet another lover. Have you heard about this? Poor King Mark looks more haggard every day. Now she has taken up with Guinguemar, the Lord of the Isle of Avalon."

Cara had seen Guinguemar arriving at Camelot to pay his respects to the High King, who now occupied the tor within sight of Ynnis Witrin. Guinguemar was a somewhat shorter man with a great bushy beard and a halo of hair which seemed to have a life of its own. He appeared to be laughing at everything. In a way, Guinguemar reminded Cara of Accolon of Gaul, who had been obsessed with Morgan. Morgan had killed Accolon when he tried to rape her, she claimed. However, it was common knowledge that she and Accolon had been lovers for months.

And now she had taken up with Guinguemar.

Arthur rubbed his jaw once more. "I see Morgan is reaching for power once more. Guinguemar controls an island of secrets. That would appeal to her."

Guenivere showed no frustration. "Do you see what I mean about her ways upsetting everyone else?" Her tone was patient.

Arthur shook his head. "Mark is an old campaigner. He has lived through far worse than a woman too easy with her favors. It has always surprised me he became involved with her in the first place."

"That is because she is your sister and you do not understand the power she has over men. Morgan uses that power," Guenivere said. "And I am quite sure, husband, that she does not use that power for the good of the High King."

"Morgan has always worked toward the good of Morgan," Arthur said in agreement. "She is only a woman. She can plot feminine conspiracies with complete freedom, for all I care. Mark and the others must guard their own hearts. I will not deprive Merlin of a good surgeon—not when we are fighting the Saxons nearly every day."

The note in his voice told Cara he would not be moved on this. Guenivere must have sensed it, too, for she held still, then relaxed and reached for the wine flask. "Wine, Arthur?"

They continued to wait for Morgan. Before the woman arrived, another man appeared at the entrance to the hall, which was really the steps up from the veranda. There was no doorway. There were only two columns at the edges of the wide-open space.

Arthur looked up. "Speaking of Mark…"

Cara turned around. King Mark stood waiting for Arthur to beckon him forward.

Arthur waved.

Mark came up to the table, his hand gripping his sword. "I apologize for the intrusion at this time, King Arthur."

"You are always welcome to speak to me. You and yours have saved the people of Venta Belgarum. I would be an ungrateful cur if I resented your intrusion at any time. Well, perhaps not *any* time." He gave a small smile.

Guenivere blushed.

Mark did not respond to the jest. His expression remained grave. "I fear, Arthur, that my time here is done. I can no longer remain at court."

Arthur glanced at Guenivere. "Cannot? Or do not wish to?" he asked Mark.

Mark rubbed the back of his neck. "For more than a year I have lingered at your side, because it is the only place a fighting man should be. Tristan has argued all that time that we should be protecting your southern borders. From my palace I can see the Saxons cooking fires at night and their smoke during the day. I would serve you better if I were to guard those borders. Yet you need every man beside you, including me." He shifted awkwardly. "Good sense dictates I return, although we both know there is more to it than that."

His gaze dropped to his feet. "I have been a fool, Arthur. They say there is no greater fool than an old fool. Now I understand the depth of my idiocy."

For a moment silence gripped the little table. Arthur didn't move.

Guenivere slid her gaze to Cara. The Queen's expression was neutral.

Cara could understand what Guenivere was not saying. The woman was not gloating because she was right. She was *distressed* because she was right.

"Morgan is your sister," Mark added. "I can do nothing about the position I find myself in except to withdraw. If I linger here..." He shrugged.

Arthur's throat worked. Even though he said nothing, Cara could feel his temper building. He was frustrated. It was possible he was also embarrassed, having been proved wrong so shortly after maintaining he was right—and in front of his wife and her guest, too.

He thrust himself to his feet and held out his arm. "Under the circumstances, I cannot argue that you stay, either. I know you will serve me just as well guarding the borders. Your good health, Mark."

The two men gripped each other's arms.

Then Arthur pulled Mark against him and held him briefly.

Mark could not meet anyone's gaze. His eyes shifted as he looked at the floor, at the walls and cleared his throat noisily.

241

"Thank you, my lord. I do not intend to linger here. We will be gone before sunset."

"Do you have enough men to travel safely to Kernow?"

"I have Tristan, Sagamore and Dinadan. With those three and a dozen men, I believe we might hold off the bulk of the Saxon army, should they try for us." Mark rolled his eyes. "I would wonder where Tristan got his drive and determination upon the battlefield, except I know a young war duke once told him to learn his trade first, before aspiring to be king."

Arthur laughed. "I had almost forgotten about that." He kept his arm around Mark's shoulder and walked him toward the steps onto the veranda. "I wish you well. Travel safely."

Mark hurried away.

Arthur returned to the table.

Cara held herself still. Even though Arthur had laughed and had been gentle with Mark, she knew he was angry. Perhaps the familiarity she had with her own reckless anger and how it could burn suddenly and hot allowed her to sense Arthur's. She glanced at his deep red hair. They had that in common.

Arthur lowered himself to his chair and drummed his fingers upon the table.

Guenivere did not speak.

"This changes nothing," Arthur said, his voice low and hard. "She is still needed in the surgery, no matter who she shares her bed with."

"Yes, my lord," Guenivere said softly.

Soft high notes of a woman's voice sounded from a long veranda. It was Morgan's voice, although she was not yet in sight. Then she glided up the stairs, an elegant figure in dark green and gold, with a green veil over her hair and a gold torc about her neck. Her appointments were queenly. Cara wondered how she acquired the baubles and finery everyone had been deprived of for well over a year.

242

Even though Cara did not care for the vagaries of fashion, she found her gaze lingering upon the details of Morgan's gown, jewelry and appointments. It had been so long since Cara had worn something pretty. Her one gown was worn, the hem stained, and she had no jewelry to her name at all.

Was this part of Morgan's charm? Did men gravitate to her because she wore beautiful things?

Morgan smiled as she approached the table. "Oh dear, am I late?"

Arthur thrust himself to his feet once more. His face was touched with red and a deep furrow creased his brow. Even Cara recognized the unfortunate timing of Morgan's arrival. Cara understood exactly how he was feeling. The sight of her had triggered Arthur into roiled frustration. If Arthur's temper ran as Cara's did, then he would do something rash, now.

Arthur rested his tightly fisted hand upon the corner of the table. "Yes, you are late." His voice was strangled with fury. "You are late, slovenly and your lax ways are an embarrassment to me."

Morgan laughed, a light, high trill. "Arthur! Did you suddenly become Christian while my back was turned?" She brushed at the rich fabric of her gown. "You have never given a damn who I mingle with. Nothing I do is a reflection upon you. The court well knows the distance which lies between us, even though we are siblings." Her voice grew firmer, as she grew more sure of herself. "Since you invited me to remain with the court, I have contented myself with working in the surgery. I am sure Merlin would speak for me in that regard."

Cara recognized the implied threat. She was reminding Arthur of her use at court, trying to offset whatever Arthur was about to say.

Arthur shook his head. "I find any benefit you bring to the surgery is negated by the upheaval you deliver elsewhere. I warned you when I first allowed you to stay at court that I would not abide your manipulations."

"What manipulations?" Morgan put her hand to her chest, as if she was stressed.

"Do not try that upon me," Arthur said. "You have forced me to send away one of my most senior officers, a man who is virtually a right arm to me. You have used Mark dishonorably."

Morgan sobered. It was as if she had discarded with pretense. Her eyes narrowed. "Mark is returning to Kernow?"

"This very night."

Morgan smoothed down the fabric over her hips once more. This time the gesture was unconscious. A nervous mannerism. "I should say goodbye to him…"

"You should see to the packing of your own belongings," Arthur said. "You will not be spending tonight here in Camelot, either."

Morgan grew still. "You are sending me away?" Her voice lifted, with a strange note. Cara realized that the uneasy note was genuine. Morgan, for all her excesses, thought she had understood exactly how far she could stretch Arthur's tolerance.

Now she has learned she was mistaken.

"I am sending you away." Arthur repeated flatly. "Return to Tintagel, if they will have you. Or, if you wish, I will provide you with an armed escort and you can return to Rheged."

"Rheged!" Morgan spat the word. "That is not my home. It has never been my home."

Arthur shrugged. "Tintagel, then. I care not."

"Cador's wife would never accept me!"

"Then find another place. You no longer have one here. I have spoken." Arthur's voice rang like the tolling of the bell. "Now, leave me."

Morgan stood still and silent. Her throat worked. Cara tried to feel pity for her, but could not.

Then Morgan's gaze fell to Guenivere. "This is your fault. I will remember that."

Guenivere shrank back.

Arthur's hand settled on her shoulder. "For that, Morgan, I remove my generosity. You no longer have until sunset. You will leave now." His voice was dangerously quiet. His blue eyes glittered. "Go to your room and take whatever small belongings you can carry. Your horse will be saddled and waiting for you at the gate."

"Without an escort?"

"If you can find a man willing to escort you, you must do with that."

Morgan's gaze moved over Arthur's face and his still figure. She measured him, trying to discern if any leverage remained which she could use to change his mind.

Her face worked. "You think the success you have found is all your own work? You are *nothing*. Without me, everything you have turned your hand to will wither and rot. Alliances will crumble, your friends will die and everything you love will turn to ash."

Arthur's face turned red. "If you respect the gods at all, Morgan, then do not say another word. Turn and leave. *Now.*"

Morgan picked up her hem, turned and silently glided away.

Cara let out a soft sigh, as Morgan stepped down onto the veranda and moved out of sight.

Guenivere drew in a breath which shuddered. Cara heard it clearly across the table.

Arthur patted her shoulder and picked up his wine cup. "I am suddenly without appetite." He drank deeply.

Guenivere wisely said nothing.

Arthur crooked his fingers. The servants came with the tray of food. They placed it between the three of them and added dishes of water to clean their fingers. It was very Roman.

"There is no need for you to go hungry because of my bad mood," Arthur told Guenivere. His gaze shifted to Cara. "Please keep my wife company while she eats."

"Of course," Cara told him.

He looked at Guenivere once more. "In a few days' time, you may remind me of how wrong I was in this. I am sure I will need the reminder in the future."

"Thank you, Arthur," Guenivere said softly.

He nodded and strode away, took the steps two at a time and hurried across the courtyard to the archway which led out onto the new main street. He disappeared.

Guenivere let out a shuddering breath and rested her head on her hand.

Cara pushed the queen's wine cup closer to her other hand.

Guenivere's gaze met hers. "I had not suspected the depth of hatred in her."

"That is because she hides it well." Cara reached for her own wine cup and drank.

And so, King Mark of Kernow left Camelot as the sun was lowering. Nearly everyone upon the tor lined the street to watch Mark leave with his retinue of people and Tristan, Sagamore and Dinadan. Cara stood with Guenivere at the top of the street. They watched the file of armed men on their horses pass through the newly repaired gates, down the sloping causeway through the fens, until they disappeared into the late evening mist.

Close to the front gates, down by the smiths and their forges, Cara saw the small figure which was Bedivere. He and the senior officers formed the last guard as King Mark passed through.

With King Mark gone, Arthur would be depending upon Bedivere more than ever.

If the Saxons attacked now, with Bedivere still recovering from his injuries and learning how to use his new weapons, with Mark departed and all the Kernow people with him, would Arthur's army have the strength to withstand a Saxon assault?

No one saw Morgan leave.

Between noon of that day and noon of the next day, her quarters were emptied. No one saw her again that year. Yet only four days later, rumor came that Morgan was now living among the priestesses on Ynnis Witrin.

"A fitting place for her," Pellinore growled, when the news passed through the training arena.

Pellinore was the only one to comment openly about her fate. Camelot moved on as if Morgan had never been there.

Cara, though, could not forget Morgan's parting words to Guenivere and Arthur. Just like Merlin, Morgan had the Sight. What had she glimpsed in the future?

Everything you turn your hand to will wither and rot. Alliances will crumble, your friends will die and everything you love will turn to ash.

In the deep of the night, as she laid staring at the stars through the chink in the flats of the tent, Cara recognized that Morgan had cursed Arthur. She did not for a moment think, however, that the curse had been aimed at her, not until she rose the next morning.

Chapter Twenty-Two

ara liked the quiet hours shortly before and after dawn, when she cared for her horse and took care of her weapons and armor, maintaining them and making sure they were kept in peak condition, ready for war at any time.

When she had first joined the Queen's cohort, inspections of her equipment and weapons had been constant. These days, no one bothered to check on the sharpness of her blade, or her well-oiled horse harness.

Because of the routine, she had grown to enjoy the silence of early morning, when the only people up and about were fellow soldiers like her. It was a measure of how busy and crowded with other people the rest of her day was, that she could find these painfully cold moments in the depths of winter a solace.

When the predawn chorus began, the sounds roused her. Cara pushed aside the furs which had been given to her. They kept her warm despite the bitter cold of winter, which not even the small stove in the middle of the tent dispelled.

Shivering, she put on her boots and cloak and slipped out of the tent, seeking the bucket she used to fetch water for her horse. She was still not properly awake and would not be for a few moments, yet.

The bucket generally sat on the other side of the tent, close to the horse. She rounded the tent and reached for the bucket, before she noticed the empty perch.

Cara straightened, the bucket still on the ground. Her heart thudded heavily.

She turned on her heel, quartering the area around the tent. Her family's tent was surrounded by other pavilions, temporary shelters and men sleeping out in the open, around campfires.

No one stirred. It was still dark.

Cara turned back to the perch. Her throat was dry. The eagle was always on the perch when she got up in the morning. *Always.* Since the eagle had found her in the meadow, there had not been a single morning when he had not waited for her to provide his breakfast. She even had meat on a platter waiting beside the bucket, covered over so he would not steal it during the night.

What had happened?

In her heart, she already knew. She was just not ready to accept it yet.

Cara moved through her day, feeling numb. She cared for her horse, tended to her weapons, and attended training. She moved through the drills as if someone else shifted her arms and legs. She did not volunteer to fight during the bout but stood around the ring, barely hearing and seeing anything which took place.

If Bedivere was at the training, she did not notice. She realized she had failed to see him or even look for him until she returned to the tent around noon.

She did not care.

The eagle did not return that day. Nor was he on the perch the next day. Or the day after that.

Cara did not go to training that day. She could barely rouse herself to feed her horse before returning to the furs and pulling them over the top of her head. She slept, because it was easier than thinking.

It was nearly solstice. The days were short. The light beyond the tent did not grow much brighter than the dawn. She suspected it was snowing again and did not care. She did not bother looking through the tent flaps to check the sky. None of it interested her.

Her family all had duties and obligations elsewhere in the camp during the day. They left her alone. It was likely they did not know she had not stirred beyond caring for her horse. Later in the evening she would be forced to deal with them. For now, she was left alone.

Even though she had slept enough, Cara kept her eyes closed. She let her thoughts drift.

When the tent flap was pulled back with a sharp snapping sound, her irritation rose. It was probably her mother. Cara prepared herself for her mother's tirade about people who lingered in bed for too long. She would be lectured about laziness and responsibilities.

Her mother did not speak.

Cara sighed and pulled the furs higher.

"Then you are not ill," Bedivere said.

Cara pushed the furs aside, her heart racing. "What are you doing here?"

He stood with his hands on his hips, filling the tent with his presence. "You were not at training."

"It is not the first time I have foregone training." She pulled furs up again. "Leave me. I wish to sleep."

"What has happened?"

"Nothing. Go away."

The furs were torn away from her. Cara cursed and sat up, clutching her arms around her. It was cold in the tent.

Bedivere stood with the furs in his hand.

"Give them back to me."

Little light remained in the tent. There was no lamp and the day was dull. In what light there was, Cara could not see his face clearly. Was he angry? Or was Bedivere acting as the war duke and had come to see why a soldier had not reported for duty? If that was the case, then he should have sent Queen Lowry, or her wing commanders, not come himself. Either way, Cara did not welcome his presence right now.

He dropped the furs to the floor, which was nothing more than old oat sacks torn open on one side and spread flat. "I have seen your face every day of training. Something happened, three days ago. I don't think you saw or heard anyone while you were training. You are usually one of the first to step into the ring for a practice bout, yet you have not done so for three days. And now, you have failed to attend training. Tell me what it is. Tell me what has happened."

"Nothing which needs concerned you, war duke."

He swore softly. "Everything in Arthur's army concerns me. If you will not tell me what happened, I will start asking questions of everyone who sleeps near this tent and everyone to whom you speak during the day. Guenivere likes you. Shall I ask the Queen what bothers you? Shall I ask Arthur?"

Cara flinched. "You would not dare bother them with such a triviality…" She bit her lip.

Bedivere shook his head. "It is not trivial, if it keeps you away from that which you love. Tell me what happened."

Cara beat at the floor with her fist. "Did you not see it for yourself? Did you not see the empty perch? The eagle has left. He *left* me." Her throat closed over, her eyes ached with tears and the sobs rose within her. Humiliated, she covered her face with her hands and turned away from him. It was too late, her weeping shook her, straining at her throat and stealing her breath.

When Bedivere's hands rested on her shoulders and he tried

to turn her toward him, Cara fought his control.

"And now you feel there is no one for you," he said softly.

It unraveled the last of her restraint. This time, when Bedivere pulled her against him, she sagged against his shoulder and put her arms around his neck. His heat and his strength drew all her sorrow from her in deep paroxysms. While she wept, he soothed her, not with words but with his hands, which tangled in her hair and stroked gently.

As her tears tapered off, shame burned in her cheeks. She did not have the courage to look him in the eyes.

Bedivere lifted her chin, making her meet his gaze. There was no amusement in his, no disgust. "He might return, yet."

Cara shook her head. "Eagles mate for life. Either something befell him or he found his mate. He will not be back."

Bedivere's gaze roamed over her face. Cara tried to turn her face away, embarrassed by her wet cheeks and her stormy outburst over the loss of a bird.

He shook his head as she shifted her chin, caught it and held her face still. "You do that—hide your face. You should not. Not with me."

The look in his eyes made her shiver. Warmth ran through her. "How can I do anything *but* look away from you? I do not understand you. I do not understand why you are here. You are the perfect warrior. And I am...not."

Bedivere raised his right hand. He wore no glove. He showed her the two deep red slashes on the palm. "Both of us are scarred, now." And he kissed her.

Despite her wet cheeks, her tantrums and her churlishness, he pulled her into his arms and held her there. The kiss lengthened and deepened and Cara at last understood that this was why he had come. He spoke of soldiers and duty and being concerned, yet this was why he was here.

They twined together. He lowered her to the furs and demonstrated the truth of her suspicions.

AFTERWARDS THEY LAID TOGETHER BENEATH the furs, their breath slowing. Beyond the tent, hammers upon iron rang in musical notes. The day moved on around them, leaving them alone in the tent.

"You do not say what you are really thinking," Cara said.

Bedivere kissed her temple. "Kings speak. Their subjects listen. I am not a king."

Cara cradled a small, warm thought in her heart, wondering if she had the courage to share it. She raised herself enough to meet his gaze. In the late afternoon sun, his eyes were golden as they settled on her face.

"You rule *my* heart," she whispered. "Whatever you say, I will hear it."

His eyes widened a fraction. He turned his head away.

Cara was too afraid to move. She thought that if she did, she would break this moment and it would be lost forever. She trembled, wondering if her daring had already broken it.

"After all you have done for me..." His voice was low and rumbled against her. "After everything you have done for Arthur. You pulled me from a black cloud I did not know how to escape. You are ferocious in your defense of Arthur. You befriended his queen when no one else would. You think you are unworthy because in your blood runs a little of that which flows in the veins of our enemies. Yet you have taught me that if anyone is unworthy, it is I. Men call me war duke and seek my wisdom, when I have none to give. A woman with red hair made me question everything. And in groping through my humility, I have found a strength I did not know existed." His gaze met hers. "Of course, I could not stay away. Of course, I had to find you. You are the source of my strength. Only, I am afraid that if I seek you out, you will fly from me like your eagle did to you." He rolled his head to one side again. "I do not have the courage to face that. It is why I do not say what I am thinking."

Cara's heart raced as if she was upon the battlefield, fighting for her life. In a way, that was exactly how she felt. In addition, she was giddy. Bedivere wanted her! He wanted to be with her.

"And now," Bedivere said, worry threading his voice, "the lady does not say what she is thinking."

A great shout went up from outside the tent, from a distance which sounded as if the shouter was close to the gates. Then came the deep thud and distinctive sound of the gate bars being raised and dropped to one side, as someone opened the gates. The shouting increased and was picked up by others.

Bedivere sat up, his head tilted as he listened. "Someone was just let in the front gate. One set of hooves." His gaze slid to her. "A messenger." He reached for his clothing.

The shouting was picked up by even more people. The message was passed from mouth to mouth, winding its way up the hill to the top of the tor where most of the tents were located, including this one.

Now they could hear the words in the shouted messages.

"Tristan! He's half dead."

"He must have ridden without cease all the way from Kernow."

"Tristan! He rode by himself. What would bring him back here?"

Bedivere shook his head. He thrust his boots on, moving faster than before. "If Tristan himself brings the message, then it is a critical one which must make its way to the King. Mark sent his best fighter to ensure it was delivered." He stood and whipped his cloak around him. "It will be bad news."

Cara finished dressing in silence. She could not protest that he stay here with her. Of course, he must go to Arthur and learn what the message was.

They both stepped out of the tent together. One of the boys whose task it was to send messages back and forth across the tor, from the palace to the front gate, to the smith shops and engineering shops, or to the tent of anyone whom the King wished speak to, led a weary horse past them.

A cluster of worried soldiers and people followed the horse. The horse had foam at its mouth and hung its head as if it could barely manage the next few paces. Upon its back lolled Tristan, as exhausted as his horse and barely staying upon its back. His head hung and blood daubed his tunic.

Cara's chest tightened when she saw the blood.

Bedivere glanced at her. "I must go."

"Arthur will need you," she said in agreement.

Bedivere hurried ahead of the horse, so he would reach the palace and King Arthur's side before Tristan and his message arrived.

Cara could not linger by her tent and wonder what the news might be. Like the others, she fell in behind the horse and followed it and its weary rider along the street, through the arch and into the palace courtyard.

Many hands reached up to help Tristan to the ground. He staggered yet managed to stay on his feet.

Arthur and Guenivere, Cai and Merlin, along with many other senior officers and companions, stood upon the veranda before the main hall. Tristan straightened and shuffled to where Arthur stood. He swallowed heavily before speaking.

The courtyard was hushed as Tristan said, his voice croaking, "Saxons, my Lord. Thousands of them. They have trapped Mark upon Badon Hill with the bulk of his army. All their leaders are among them. Aesc is there." He cleared his throat.

"Someone get the man some wine," Arthur said.

A ripple of movement, then a boy ran over to Tristan and held up a cup of wine in both hands. Tristan took the wine and gulped it. He dashed his sleeve across his mouth and shook his head. "Cerdic and his son Cynric have crossed over, too. They landed on the south coast not far from Badon. The scouts say there were three hundred ships—and they lost hundreds in the storm which pushed them here. They have joined Aesc and yesterday, they marched and came upon us at Badon Hill."

Mutters sounded. Those around the courtyard who listened shifted uneasily on their feet as they absorbed the implications of what Tristan was saying.

"They crossed in winter," someone hissed. "The gods save us!"

Tristan drained the cup and handed it back to the boy. He straightened his shoulders and looked at Arthur. "It is a war host, my Lord. It is bigger than anything I have seen before—anything my uncle has seen before. Even though it is only three days until the solstice, the Saxons intend to march upon you. They intend to win. They are razing..." Tristan wavered. "They are reducing everything they come across to scorched earth."

With a sigh, Tristan sagged. The boy caught him and collapsed himself, before a dozen hands reached to prop both of them up once more.

Cara could not help but look toward Bedivere, where he stood near Arthur. Bedivere's face was still. He showed nothing of his thoughts, as usual.

Corneus was close to Kernow's borders. If the Saxons moved beyond Kernow, if Mark did not hold them where they were, then they would march through Corneus and raze Bedivere's lands to the ground, too.

Arthur raised his voice, so his words rang across the courtyard. "Prepare for war! We take every man and woman capable of holding a sword. We ride at dawn and we will not stop riding until we meet the Saxons and defeat them where they stand. Go. Go and prepare."

Arthur whirled and strode into the hall. Bedivere took his place and raised his voice, too. "Senior officers! Companions! Report to the main hall with your tallies by sunset."

Bedivere turned as if he meant to follow Arthur. His gaze caught Cara's across the courtyard. He held still.

"Bedivere!" Arthur shouted.

Bedivere turned and went into the hall.

Chapter Twenty-Three

ven before Cara made it back to her tent, word had passed through Camelot. Messengers streamed through the gates, on foot and on horseback, to slide across the deep winter landscape. They were to call for men and arms, for a great rousing of effort, to confront the Saxon host gathering in the south.

Cara found Queen Lowri outside her family's test. Lowri was barely recovered from the fever which had gripped her. She told Cara to prepare to fall in at dawn with her horse and weapons and little else. There would be no stopping on the road and no rest. Arthur intended to meet the Saxons as soon as possible, to halt their spread across the vulnerable and venerable kingdoms in the south and into the heart of Britain.

Cara begged a handful of meat and a hunk of bread from the palace kitchen and ate as she packed and fussed over her sword and gear. However, her equipment was at battle readiness and had been so since the last battle. It left her little to do.

The smiths' hammers clanged late into the night as last-minute work was completed upon blades, arrowheads, wheel rims and more. People moved back and forth along the street, carrying supplies and food.

Cara sat upon the rock before the fire, watching them. Nothing remained for her to do. Newlyn was off preparing with his troop of sentries and guards, for he would ride to war tomorrow, too. For that reason, her mother rested in the tent behind Cara, weeping silently.

Brigid attended the Queen, as one of Guenivere's official companions and ladies. Cara knew Arthur would forbid Guenivere from riding with the army. She must remain safely at Camelot, for which Cara pitied her. To stay behind and wait for news would be intolerable to her.

The twins were both beside their mother and possibly asleep, for it was very late, and still Camelot burned with energy as the preparations went on.

Cara watched Druston and Bryn pass by. They had their arms around each other and were sharing a flask of wine. Their pavilion was down near the arena...were they returning to it now? Were the deliberations of Arthur's council over?

Through the space between the two nearest tents a shadow slipped. The light of the many torches did not reach that far corner. Bedivere moved over to where Cara sat. He bent and picked up her hand. His was warm. It was his right hand.

He tugged her to her feet and pulled her back into the shadows. He led her through the tents and shelters, around to the palace gate then through it. By then, Cara knew what he intended and welcomed it.

The palace was dark, with few lamps burning. He slid along the verandah and opened the door to his room and stood aside.

Cara stepped in and halted, astonished. "It is *warm* in here!"

"Hypocaust," Bedivere said. He pointed to the grill set in the floor. "They finally finished cleaning it and set the furnace this afternoon. Just in time for us to leave a warm bed..." His gaze met hers and she could see him clearly, for a lamp burned upon the chest. "…and warm arms," he added softly.

Cara flowed up against him, more than willing to be warm arms or anything which he required of her. He gathered her up against him, as if she was small and light, and kissed her.

This kiss was different. Cara knew why. She had seen it this afternoon, when his gaze met hers across the courtyard, for her thoughts had turned the same way as his. For now, she ignored the bleak, cold future and delighted in his kiss.

"I knew you would not come to me," he breathed, his mouth trailing over her cheek, his lips teasing her jaw and throat. "But I am out of time and cannot wait— "

"Shh…" She kissed him to halt the words. "Tell me later."

IT WAS *MUCH* LATER BEFORE either of them had breath speak of anything but desire. It was the stillness before dawn, which Cara could sense even though she was inside. She had spent too many nights sleeping with the sound of the night around her.

"You should sleep," she chided Bedivere, as he trailed his fingers over her, making her heart skip and her body to stir.

"I will sleep later." His voice was hoarse.

She knew he meant much later— after the battle ahead of them.

"Cara…" Then he grew silent.

Cara rolled onto her side and put her head on her hand. Bedivere was already on his side. It let her meet his gaze. "What are you thinking?"

He drew in a breath and let it out. "That my thoughts would frighten you."

Cara shrugged. "I am already afraid," she said softly. She

rested her hand on his chest. "Tell me."

He caught her hand in his and she felt the rough scars on his palm brush her fingertips. "Tristan says it is a war host larger than any ever before seen. The Saxons mean to win this, now. They mean to wipe us from Britain and take it for themselves. It has driven them for a generation, and now they know they can reach out and take it." He looked away.

Cara's heart beat heavily. "Two years of raids and fire storms has weakened us."

Bedivere's gaze came back to hers. "More years than that, although these last years have sucked the strength from us. Now they strike in the heart of winter, when they know Arthur's forces are scattered across the land, while his commanders tend to their home hearths. Aesc and Cerdic between them must have planned this years ago." He closed his eyes. "In council, I say nothing. Show nothing. In here, though..." His fingers touched his chest. "In here, I know we are out of time. This is the end, Cara. The last great battle of Britain."

Cara kissed him. "Look at me."

He did.

She shook her head. "None of that matters."

He gave a soft laugh. "As war duke, it is my responsibility to measure the weakness and strength of the army and give Arthur a realistic assessment, so he can plan the battle and array his men effectively— "

Cara put her finger upon his lips, to halt the flow of words. "No, none of it matters. Not here, not right now. Shhh..."

Bedivere drew in a breath, subsiding.

"Do you remember when you argued that I should not fight out of anger or hatred?"

"I was wrong," Bedivere said quickly. "I see that now."

"No, you were right." She picked up his hand once more and kissed his fingers. "There are far better reasons to go into battle,

261

better reasons to win, no matter what. I was blind to them. You made me see."

Bedivere's gaze was steady. "Do not speak them now," he said softly. "Keep them."

"But— "

It was his turn to shake his head. "If you hold the words to yourself, then I have every reason to fight to come back and hear them. Do you understand?" His voice was low. Urgent.

Cara sighed. "Yes," she breathed. "I do understand."

Bedivere lifted her hair away from her face and traced her scars. Then he lifted her chin, so she was forced to look at him. His gaze, golden and warm, would not let her go. "*You* have the same reasons, Cara."

She nodded, for she could not bring herself to speak. Hope blazed like a new sun in her chest, hot and bright. Now she *did* have reason to return. She would carry it with her into battle.

Bedivere drew her to him one last time. "Because of you, *for* you, I will win through and stand upon Camelot once more."

He kissed her.

ONLY A LITTLE WHILE LATER, shortly after Bedivere finally released her and let her steal back to her tent, Cara settled upon Cailleach's back and hung the food and water sacks over his neck. She settled her sword into the scabbard stitched into his saddle blanket and patted his neck as he pranced nervously, his breath snorting in billowy clouds. Around him, restless, flighty war stallions also sidled and skipped, sensing the tension around them.

Dawn was heralded by pink streaks in the sky to the east, yet torches were the only light for now. They were held by the hundreds of people gathered along the sides of the street, right up to the gate, wrapped in cloaks and shivering, while the army prepared to ride out.

Arthur moved through the rank and file, pausing for a word, here and there. He even stopped and spoke to Newlyn. Her brother sat white-faced upon the stallion which had been found for him. He nodded at Arthur, his eyes wide.

Arthur continued through the lines until he reached the two wings of the Queen's Cohort. He murmured to Lowri and moved on to where Cai held Cynbel for him and climbed upon the stallions back.

Cai swung up on to his horse and signaled.

The clear notes of the horn rang out. *Forward!*

The gates were thrown open with the great, deep double thump and groan of the hinges, and the company moved forward. Farewells were called out, blessings and wishes sent after them.

They were on their way. There would be no stopping now until they met the Saxons.

The day dawned bleak and gray as they wended south-east. As they crossed the land, riders and warriors waiting by the side of the road would raise their hands in greeting. Cai or one of the other senior officers— often, it was Bedivere— would call out a greeting and ask for their strength. They would name their numbers then fall in with the ranks behind them.

Many of them would thank Merlin for passing word along. "A battle to end all battles," one grizzly commander called to Merlin, as he passed by the head of the company to add his troops to the end of the file. "That is hard to resist, especially if it means the end of the bloody Saxons!"

Cara recalled Bedivere's fears, his realistic and private assessment of the army. She said nothing.

The day stretched on, with the horses kept just under a trot to conserve their strength and to allow those on foot to keep pace. The foot solders marched at a pace which would rival,

Lowri said, that of the Roman garrisons, had they still been here.

"The Legions could march twenty-five miles a day," Lowri added, as she let her horse fall back, to share her wine flask and oat cakes. "Of course, they would stop at the end of their day. We will not. It is thirty-five miles to Badon Hill once we have wound through bog and fen and crossed fords which are open to us."

The company did make one unexpected stop, however. Shortly after fording a river which flowed so swiftly no ice gathered except at the edges, a far-off horn sounded, light and clear.

"That is no Saxon horn," Tegid muttered, as everyone raised up to see ahead.

A shout sounded from the head of the company, where Arthur's new banner flew. Merlin kicked his stalwart old horse into a canter and raced ahead.

The road crested a low hill and turned to run south. When the company reached the bend a great shout of joy went up.

Cara glanced at Tegan, who lifted her shoulders. She could not guess either.

Then it was their turn to reach the crest.

The vale ahead was wide and clear of snow— for the snow had petered as they traveled south toward the coast with its warming breezes. The grasses should have shown dry and yellow. Instead, the entire valley floor seethed with—

"British warriors..." Cara breathed. "There must be hundreds of them!"

"Thousands," Tegan said, her tone judicious.

Merlin stood near the thick collection of banners which waved above the commanders of the new forces, who had gathered together at the head of the valley. Arthur and his companions dashed forward to meet them, Bedivere among them.

"I don't recognize the banners at all," someone murmured, behind Cara.

Cara narrowed her eyes, studying them. One banner featured a great tree, which stirred her memory. "Brocéliande!" she said, astonished. "These are Lesser Britain troops!"

Tegan shook her head. "Word was sent only last night. It takes two days to cross from Lesser Britain and another day to come this far inland...it cannot be them."

Yet it was. When Queen Lowri returned to the two wings of the Cohort, she was smiling. "The Lady of the Lake sent them— and came herself." Behind her, the other commanders who had ridden to greet the new arrivals were also returning to the company.

"Vivian spent a month rousing all the kings of Lesser Britain," Lowri added. "She hounded them to make the crossing at once, despite the winter seas. Every house is here. Even Hoel has come." Lowri fell into line with the Cohort.

"Vivian has the Sight, like Merlin," Lynnette muttered.

"She is also a surgeon and healer," Lowri said over her shoulder. "With Morgan gone, her skills will be most welcome."

The now much larger company— more than double the size it had been— moved on. The sun set and torches were lit. Food and wine warmed over the flame of the torches was handed along. Everyone shared what they had, as the march continued.

The pace slowed, for those on foot were weary and the horses, too.

"Conserve your strength," Lowri told her Cohort. "Rest. Sleep if you can— tie yourself to your horse if you must. Trust your mount to follow the others."

The jests and teasing slowed, then stopped, as tiredness gripped the company. Soon, all that could be heard was the clop of the horses and the march of tired foot soldiers.

And sometimes, soft snores.

Cara could not relax enough to let herself sleep, even though she trusted that the women around her would make sure she stayed on course. Tegan was stretched out upon her stallion, her arms around his neck and her cheek pillowed on his mane. Lynnette occasionally reached over and tugged the stallion's cheek strap if he seemed to be veering away from the company.

Long before they reached their stopping point, rumor of the Saxons ahead grew. It began with the faintest whiff of wood-smoke, which grew stronger. Then, on the far horizon, the sub-dued glow of firelight.

As they drew closer, the light climbed higher and shifted and flickered.

Flames.

"How many fires does it take to light a night sky in that way?" Lynnette murmured.

Cara's gut felt cold. "Too many," she breathed.

A fresh alertness passed through the company. People stirred. The foot soldiers marched without misstep or stumble.

The senior officers moved back along the very long line of the company, murmuring their instructions.

"Silence, as much as you can. We give the Saxons no warning."

As they moved back, torches were extinguished. Chatter was hushed.

Cara blinked until her vision adjusted to the moonless, star-bright night. She glanced up at the sky wheeling overhead, the great Sickle clear and glowing.

"We fight them at night?" Lynnette breathed.

"They attacked us at night," Cara whispered.

"Silence!" Lowri murmured.

To the east, a different type of glow painted the sky. Dawn was coming.

The company halted with the light of the Saxons' fires domi-nating the night sky, defeating the pale light of dawn. Cara heard soft voices, far ahead, moving closer.

Then Lowri bent to listen to the officer just ahead of her, Druston.

She nodded and turned back to the riders directly behind her and murmured, too.

They, in turn, swiveled to speak to the riders behind them, which was Lynette and Cara.

"The scouts have reported back. Every war leader and man of strength the Saxons have lies sleeping among the host. If we destroy the host and its leaders, we destroy the Saxons for good. Take that into battle with you. And tell the others."

Cara drew in a sharp breath and stared at Tegan.

Tegan nodded. There was a fierce glow in her face. "Tell them," she repeated.

Cara's heart swelled. Her tiredness vanished. She turned and told the rider behind her what Tegan had told her, and watched the same sharp shift in that rider, as hope flared.

"Prepare yourself," Lowri called softly, as she tossed aside her food sacks, pulled out her sword and picked up her shield.

Everyone, not just the Cohort, reached for their weapons. They fastened buckles and gripped shields, adjusted helmets and hefted swords. Armor was settled into place and tightened.

No horn signaled them to move forward. Instead, the head of the company— the thick group of companions who surrounded Arthur in every battle; Cai and Bedivere, Lancelot, Pellinore, Lionel, Leodegrance and Bricius, Cador, Idris, and now the lords of Lesser Britain— stepped forward. The company lumbered into motion behind them.

Step by step, the pace quickened. Those riders in the rear spread out, coming alongside the main file, so Arthur's host was as wide as it was deep. They spread across the width of the land, so that when they crested the rise ahead and could see the Saxon campfires for themselves, they would be able to sweep across the width of them.

The Cohort, whose responsibility it was to guard the flanks, made their way through the host to the edges, splitting up into two wings, with Lynette leading one, and Lowri the right-hand wing.

Soon, the horses broke into a trot and those on foot into a run. Cara's heart thundered as they crossed the star-lit plain, crested it and saw before them the Saxons.

A sea of firelight spread across another shallow plain, to lap around the base of a high fort upon a steep hill, ringed with fortifications and walls.

Mount Badon.

They had been seen. A great cry lifted up from the Saxons. Iron rang, as the Saxons leapt for their swords and their axes, stirring from sleep, shouting at their companions, warning them of the threat facing them.

Arthur did not wait for the Saxons to properly stir. With a shout and a blast of the horn, the leading ranks of Arthur's army galloped down the short hill to smash upon the Saxon sea.

Lowri swiveled on her horse to shout at her wing. "Stay together! Protect the flank! We will go around!" She pointed with her sword, thrusting it into the air to the right of the Saxon host.

As Lynnette's wing would be doing to the left, Lowri's wing galloped to the right, keeping pace with the front edge of the army. The mass of Arthur's army flowed over the Saxons sea, splitting them and separating them. Even from her position on the ground and to the far right, Cara could tell there were far more Saxons than there were Britons. If not for the whispered hope which she had been given a short while before, she might have quailed at the vast numbers of Saxons rising to fight them. The knowledge burned in her chest and her mind that every Saxon leader was here, and if they could reach them...

The Saxons surrounded Mount Badon. Arthur's army, particularly the Queen's Cohort, surrounded the Saxons. They galloped hard, moving about the far edges of the Saxons, slowly but surely encircling them. As they kept pace with the front line of Arthur's men, it meant that Arthur's men were encircling them to.

For the first time, the Saxons tried to break and escape along the far edges of the big circle. Lowri had been ready for that. She shouted and pointed. They rode toward the stream of Saxons running away from their companions. Swiftly, the Cohort dealt with them.

Fighting and riding had stolen all Cara's fear. As often happened in battles, she lost track of time. Nothing but the moment before her and the enemy in front of her meant anything. She focused fiercely upon the next stroke, the next tactic, the next man to bring down.

Their progress around the outside of the circle slowed, as they stopped to deal with Saxons who tried to edge around and come at Arthur's men from another angle.

As they worked, the sun rose. Full daylight blazed upon them. Unlike the last few days, this day was cloudless. The weak winter sun let them see everything— the blood, the desperation and the implacable faces of the Britons who, despite their fewer numbers, were driven by more than a simple desire to win.

Cara knew what drove them because it was in her, too. The knowledge that one way or another, this war with the Saxons would be decided today. There were no more chances to win. Either they broke upon the rock of Saxon might, or they would win for themselves the peace they had long worked for.

Cara did not know for how long she had been fighting when Queen Lowri raised her voice in a war cry. "Cerdic! Cerdic flees!"

Cara kicked her horse into motion before Lowri gave the order. It was done without thought, without consideration. She was driven to act by the fact that one of the Saxon leaders was within her reach. One of the leaders was trying to leave. He was trying to escape.

He must be stopped.

She galloped forward, a harsh cry tearing from her lips, her sword above her head. She could see Cerdic now. He was tall, with a full beard and the silver war helmet which from beneath sprouted thick, grubby blond hair. His chest plate was British, likely stolen from a fallen warrior. He had a great knife in one hand and a monstrous axe in the other. He carried no shield, for five warriors protected him.

He looked around at Cara's cry. So did his warriors. All of them threw up their arms as she bore down upon them. Cara dropped her horse's reins, jumped upon his back and threw herself upon them. She brought her sword down in the great sweeping and hacking motions she had learned were the most effective at bringing a full-sized man down. She didn't think at all. The motions came to her, ingrained from endless drill and practice.

In her first two strokes, she slew two guards. She could hear Lowri screaming at her from behind. Only now did Cara realize she had dropped to the ground and placed himself among the armies. She was no longer on horseback. She was vulnerable.

She didn't care. As the last two Saxons warriors stepped toward each other, bringing their shoulders together to protect the man behind them, all she could see was Cerdic's blue eyes blazing at her. He thought he was invulnerable. He thought she was a weak woman.

The knowledge sat in her chest, as certain as one day followed the next, that she would win this fight because he thought her to be weak. It made him complacent.

First, she must deal with the two warriors shielding him. They were wary now because they had seen their fellows fall to her sword.

Because they were wary and ready to react at her slightest movement, it was natural to misdirect them. Cara raised her sword as if she was about to drop it down to her right. They both surged in that direction, bringing their shields up. As soon as they jerked their shield arms up with, she threw herself to the left, twisting so she could bring the sword whistling around in a left-handed sweep.

Because the warrior on the left had raised his sword to cover his left flank, it left his right open. Her sword sliced into his middle, under his raised elbow. She felt the blade bury itself deep.

The warrior cried out and dropped, wrenching her sword down.

Alarmed, she yanked. Her blow had been so powerful the blade was buried in his ribs. She tugged desperately, as the final warrior snarled with happiness at her predicament.

He raised his axe high over his head, ready to dash it upon her head and lunged at her.

Cara kept hold of her sword with her left hand. She crouched and snatched the long knife out of her boot. As she rose to her feet, she slammed the knife into the warriors' armpit, up high and level with his heart.

He stared at her for a moment, puzzlement in his eyes. Then his eyes grew blank, and he fell.

Cara stepped on the first warrior and yanked her sword out with a massive heave. She swapped her sword and knife, as she considered Cerdic.

The leader of the Saxons had seen her take on his men and win. Now he knew she was not a weak woman. He had the measure of her. His face was grim.

Cara would not make the mistake of underestimating Cerdic. She had never underestimated any man she met on the battlefield, precisely because she was a weak woman and must compensate for that weakness against every enemy.

This was Cerdic!

She could hear Lancelot's and Pellinore's voices murmuring instructions in her mind, repetitions from countless training sessions. *"Watch the wrist. The wrist will often tell you what a man intends, when nothing else does.… Breathe!… Where is the sword tip? Always watch the sword tip…!"*

Cerdic crouched, preparing himself for the confrontation. In that instant, Cara knew what to do. It was the unexpected thing. She leapt before he had completed his crouch and got himself into position. She brought the sword up, the effort pulling a cry from her lips. The sword, which was heavier than most women could bear, sang as she brought it down with all her might.

She did not aim for his neck. When one aimed for where they wanted the sword to go, it weakened the blow. Instead, as she had been trained, she aimed for the center of his chest. The edge of the blade came down upon the nape of his neck, just above the edge of his armor. She felt the blade bite and snag within his flesh.

It didn't matter that she had not cut deeply. Only a man like Idris or Cai would be able to bury their sword so deep it disappeared. She didn't need to bury it nearly that deep. Cara yanked the sword out and backed away quickly.

Cerdic looked at her with surprise. He thought she was retreating.

Cara waited for the awareness to reach his eyes. Already the blood fountained from his neck. He should feel it draining from him at any moment.

His hand lifted up, the fingers moving weakly. The strength was leaving him already. Awareness came into his eyes. His smile was bitter. He used the last of his strength to raise his finger and point at her.

Cara watched him die calmly.

"Cara! Behind you!" The cry was faint. It was Lowri. The Cohort was far away from Cara now. She was in the very heart of the battle. She spun and saw the thick cluster of companions surrounding the Pendragon banner. The Saxons swarmed at them, as keen to destroy Arthur as Arthur's men were to execute the Saxon leaders.

And now only one Saxon leader remained.

The death of Cerdic had not gone unnoticed. The Saxons screamed and cried out their fury. Faces turned toward her. Axes raised and shields were hefted into place. A wall of Saxons came toward her.

Abruptly, the calm which had held her and contained her thoughts while she dealt with Cerdic broke like a dam. Fear rippled along Cara's spine. Her belly clenched and her heart hammered.

She got her sword up, her arms trembling, as the first of the Saxons reached her. Now she was the one defending herself. Her thoughts froze as she blocked and blocked again the swinging axes and swords and knife edges which came at her. No thought of attack came to her for she was too busy fending off the weapons trying to reach her.

She stepped back a pace, then another pace. She didn't know what was behind her, which was dangerous. Lancelot constantly railed at them to know the land around them, to know who was where. She had lost track of where she was and who was with her. There could be another wall of Saxons right behind her. The first she would know of them was when one of them buried their axe in her back.

Her armpits prickled and her throat closed over. Only training kept her sword up and kept her blocking each attack and thrust.

She couldn't think.

From far away, Cara heard another cry. It was harsh and filled with fury and fear. She knew the voice.

Bedivere.

Don't look up. Cara fought to keep her attention upon the enemy around her. Yet her heart skittered and her chest ached, knowing Bedivere was near.

When the knife slid into her side, the sharp pain tore through her entire body, and made every sinew tighten and freeze.

The Saxons had defeated her.

WHEN BEDIVERE SAW CARA CONFRONT Cerdic, he did something for which he would put any other man in irons and keep him on a diet of bread and water for days to encourage him never to be distracted again: Bedivere looked around. He took his eye off the enemy.

It felt as though an invisible hand had reached into his chest and was now squeezing his heart. Fear was a coppery taste in his mouth. It was a high singing note in his mind.

The whistling of the sword and the smack upon his shield pulled his attention back to the enemy in front of him. Still he could not stop himself from seeking for her with his gaze. What was she doing upon the field itself? Why was she not upon her stallion, where she could fight with the advantage of height in her favor?

When he looked next, Cerdic had fallen, to the consternation of the Saxons, who screamed aloud their fury. They gathered around Cara, a thick wall of them.

Bedivere abandoned his position. There was no thought in it. He dropped his shield and gripped the long hilt of his sword. He felt the weapon come alive in his hand. He brought it up to the high ready position. There was no thought in that, either. The only consideration was to use anything which would give him the strength to push through the Saxons who surrounded her.

He hacked and swung, shoved and punched. He severed limbs. He cut open necks and chest and sliced at legs.

Let her live. Let her laugh another few moments.

The Saxons grew thicker and his desperation greater. He fought using every skill and tactic from the vast array he had learned over the years. All thoughts of honor and the proper way to fight vanished. Cara was just beyond the Saxons, out of his reach. He would win his way to her. In the silvered, calm part of his mind, he knew nothing would stop him from achieving it.

He slashed and chopped, his arms swinging harder and harder.

Then, suddenly, he was through. He shoved aside the last Saxon, in time to see Cara drop to the ground, her hand to her side and blood squeezing between her fingers.

His heart stopped.

Bedivere stepped in front of her and turned. He hefted the big sword. Now all his fear was gone. Instead the calm certainty washed over him. He looked at the Saxons who gathered around them.

He smiled. "Fight me if you dare."

The Saxons laughed because Bedivere was the only Briton standing. They thought they would win because there was more of them.

They were mistaken.

They rushed him and Bedivere went to work. He kept his ground, his feet spread, protecting Cara. He didn't need to shift his feet, for the sword was heavy enough and his strength great enough to defeat anyone who came at him.

Then he heard another shout. It was not Saxons. "Here! Cai! Gawain! Help Bedivere! Hurry!"

Bedivere knew the voice. It was Lancelot.

He smiled once more. Even though the Saxons still stood, even though they thought the battle was not yet over, they had lost. In his heart, in his soul, Bedivere knew he had the strength to take on every last one of them, if he must, because he would not let them win. He refused to.

No one who stood beneath Arthur's banner would let them win.

AESC BROKE WHEN THE SUN was at its highest. Perhaps he became desperate, when the battle continued longer than he thought it should. The loss of Cerdic was a blow and the British refusal to give way ground at the Saxons. They thought they had superior numbers. They thought it was impossible to lose.

When they did not easily win, the heart was plucked from them. Aesc rashly chose to tackle Arthur directly. His British commanders stepped aside and let Arthur decide the matter.

Had Aesc forgotten that Arthur was a great warrior, as well as the king? No one would ever know, for Excalibur took Aesc's head, then Arthur thrust Excalibur through the Saxon's heart, to be sure of the matter.

The remaining Saxons broke and ran.

For the rest of the day, the younger warriors rode across the land, chasing Saxons down, while the senior officers and Arthur climbed to the fort upon Mount Badon, to greet King Mark as the gates were thrown open.

Bedivere only learned of it long afterward. Arthur did not need him, while Cara did. He carried her up to the fort, to where Merlin and Vivian, Lady of the Lake, had set up their surgery in the open field at the end of the tor.

There were many wounded and Bedivere knew Cara would have to wait her turn. Merlin, Gander and Vivian, plus a dozen more people skilled in healing were frantically staunching bleeding wounds and dealing with injuries which were urgent.

Only, as soon as Merlin noticed Bedivere sitting by Cara's

still form, his hand against her side to hold in the blood, Merlin hurried over, with the boy who carried his heavy chest of tools struggling behind him.

Merlin knelt upon the ground beside Cara. "I heard she killed Cerdic." He lifted Bedivere's hand away and looked at the wound. He shook his head. "A knife wound. It might've been worse. They would have torn her limbs from her if they had been able to reach her, for what she did to Cerdic." He put his hand upon Bedivere's shoulder. "She will live and have a scar to remember this by. Let me work. Go and find Arthur. He will need you."

Bedivere shook his head. "I am his war duke. The war is over."

Merlin nodded. "Yes, it is." He got to work.

Bedivere stayed and watched.

Chapter Twenty-Four

It took many days for Arthur's army to finish dealing with the Saxons. They were driven far to the east, to cling to the shoreline or to scramble upon their boat and sail across the sea, away from Britain. Arthur was ruthless in pushing them as far back as possible. "I will not let them linger to form another army and harass us again. They have no leaders left. Now is the time to rid ourselves of them."

Accordingly, everyone who could be spared was sent out in groups and troops to scour the land of remaining Saxons.

Cara was aware of none of it. Five days after the battle of Mount Badon, she returned to Camelot. This time, it was she who laid upon the wagon while Bedivere walked alongside. Cailleach was hitched to the wagon and seemed happy to plod along behind it. Cara was not the only wounded warrior lying upon the wagon, but Bedivere spoke only to her.

She was in pain and unable to think clearly, for Merlin kept her foggy with poppy smoke. She slept a great deal. When she did open her eyes, it was to see Bedivere watching her. She managed a smile before drifting back into sleep.

Finally, she opened her eyes to find herself inside and warm. The stone walls and smaller windows told her where she was. This was Bedivere's room. She was no longer foggy and her thoughts flowed freely. Her side ached only a little.

Cara blinked and turned her head to the side.

It did not surprise her to see Bedivere there. He had a book scroll in front of him, the rolls held open with flat stones.

"Should you not be taking care of matters for Arthur?" Her voice was weak and hoarse.

Bedivere looked up from his book. "Have you not heard? The war is over. The Saxons have gone. Merlin says they will not be back."

"Not ever?"

"He says he cannot see that far into the future although for as far as he can see, they will not be back."

Cara shifted and hissed as her side twinged with pain. She grew still once more.

"You should not move around too much. Merlin has had to re -stitch your side three times. Even while you slept, you were still fighting."

"How long have I been asleep?"

"On and off, for many days."

"And Merlin has been here to see me?"

"You are not aware of how many people have stopped by to see for themselves that you are recovering. Even Arthur has come to see you. Guenivere, too. Pellinore, as well. He was annoyed you were not awake, because he wanted to tell you how proud he was of what you did. He said it was a perfect example for his students and he wants you to demonstrate to them as soon as you are on your feet."

"I'm not sure I remember what I did. I wasn't thinking clearly at the end." She hesitated. "Has Lancelot visited?" Of all the visitors, including Arthur, she wanted to know that Lancelot in particular was pleased with what she had done. He was the man who had given her the skill to match Cerdic and defeat him.

Bedivere's face lost the good humor. "Lancelot has left Camelot."

Cara tried to sit up but could not. She was very weak. She hissed as her side stabbed her and grew still once more. "Gone? Where did he go to?"

"The Lady of the Lake emptied Lesser Britain of all its lords and standing armies. Claudas, their old enemy, took advantage of it. From somewhere he gathered an army, even in the middle of winter, and attacked the easternmost kingdoms, including Brocéliande and the Perilous Forest, where Lancelot was raised. He and Hector have sailed with the Lesser Britain kings, to fight Claudas one last time, so that Lesser Britain may enjoy the same piece which Greater Britain now faces."

"I don't understand. Lancelot swore to serve Arthur."

"And now the Saxons have been defeated, his promise has been fulfilled. Lancelot did assure Arthur he would return once this last task has been completed."

Cara frowned. "There is something about this which troubles you, too."

Bedivere shook his head. "I do not know Lancelot well. I have only got to know him better in the last few weeks, thanks to you," he added. "All the time I have known him, I have always felt that Lancelot was a generally truthful man."

"Lancelot has always said exactly what he thought," Cara said. "Even to Arthur."

"Only…" Bedivere scratched at his jaw. "I cannot put my finger on it precisely. It felt as though, even as he was explaining to Arthur about Claudas and making his perfectly reasonable request, that he was not telling Arthur the real reason why he wanted to leave."

"Perhaps Lancelot already misses war," Cara said. "After all, he has dedicated his life to being the best warrior possible."

"A perfect warrior?" The corner of his mouth turned up in a small smile.

"You have shaved," she whispered, as she watched the small warm expression appear. "Or did you find someone else to do that service for you?"

"I thought it was time for me to learn how to shave with my left hand." He rubbed his jaw. "After all, I have had to learn a great many new things lately and none of them have been the death of me. Shaving seemed simple in comparison."

"Then you no longer have need of me." Disappointment touched her.

Bedivere shoved the book aside, the parchment crackling and the scroll ends knocking together. He did not simply lean closer. He stretched himself out, so he was lying along the edge of her furs. His eyes were golden with heat and with intensity. "That is where you are wrong." He stroked her forehead with his hand and brushed the hair from her temples. "When you are stronger, I will show you exactly how wrong you are."

His lips pressed hers, softly.

Her heart gave a heavy thud, but not with pain, or fear.

Not this time.

KNOWING THAT BEDIVERE WAS THERE waiting for her seemed to give Cara extra strength. In only two days, she was able to rise from the furs, with Bedivere's help. Guenivere sent a gown for Cara to wear. It was a soft green and the sleeves were wide. The fabric was warm. There was a darker green cloak to go with it, and warm soft boots made from deer hide.

As Cara could not raise her left arm above her shoulder, Bedivere brushed her hair and trained it back from her face with the silver rings. His dexterity surprised her.

He lifted his hand with the two score marks on the palm. "I do not need all my fingers for this. Besides, if I can withstand you shaving me, then you must withstand me brushing your hair."

Taking small steps, Cara let Bedivere lead her from the room and across the courtyard. A great many people came up to her as she walked slowly in the cloudless winter sunshine. Cai, Pellinore, Lamorak, Elaine, Cador, Lynette and even Queen Lowri spoke to her and praised her efforts during the battle of Mount Badon. While Cara murmured a confused thank you, her cheeks burning, Bedivere merely held her elbow and smiled.

Cai would have patted her shoulder, only Bedivere got his arm up and fended Cai away from her. Cai shrugged self-consciously and said, "Of course, you must dine with Arthur, tonight. He will be pleased to know you are up and about once more."

Bedivere moved her on before anyone else could rush up to them. He walked her out of the gateway and around the palace.

Cara had never been on this side of the palace before. It was at the very end of the tor where there was nothing but knee-high grass, now yellow and damp, for it had been crushed beneath the blanket of snow for weeks. The snow had gone and the bent grass remained.

"Did you bring me here for the air? There is nothing else to see here." She smiled anyway, because it was good to be outside.

Bedivere raised his face to the sun. He shielded his eyes with his hand. "Remember I told you that you were wrong?"

"Which time was that? I recall several times you have insisted I was wrong."

Bedivere remained still and did not answer. Cara did not rush to coax him to respond. She had grown used to his silences, and it was a nice day.

Then Bedivere made a soft sound and pointed. "Look. There. Do you see them?"

With a jolt, Cara realized Bedivere had been looking for

something, not just letting the sun bathe his face.

She looked in the direction where he pointed.

Far away, made small by the distance, two birds circled in the air, their wings spread.

For a moment, Cara peered at them, puzzled.

"Wait for a moment," Bedivere said softly. "They will come closer and then you will see. They have returned and circled Camelot every day since Mount Badon. I think they are looking for you."

Cara drew in a sharp breath as hope flared. She put her hand up against the sun, and peered at the two birds, waiting for them to come close enough to see them for herself. Gradually, they did. They were low in the air. Low enough that they would skim over Camelot. As they barreled toward them, Cara could hear their wings rustling in the wind—two great, glorious, golden eagles. They rode the air in unison.

The larger one had white feathers in his tail. The smaller one flew close to his wingtips. She had a golden chest.

Cara turned on her heel as the eagles flew overhead, the larger one crying a loud, long note. She laughed, even as her eyes stung, as the pair of eagles circled around Camelot, their wings flapping and tilting as they navigated the sky.

Twice they circled overhead. Each time as they came around the back of the palace, they gave long crying notes.

Then they turned west and headed for the sea.

Cara wiped her eyes. She didn't mind that Bedivere saw her do it.

"Eagles mate for life," he said.

"Yes."

Bedivere drew her close to him. "Before the battle, there were things we left unspoken, for later."

Cara nodded. Her heart ached.

"I presumed I understood the thoughts in my heart, then."

Bedivere's voice was rough. "I thought I saw it clearly, but I was mistaken. I only understood everything clearly when I saw you surrounded by Saxons, with Cerdic at your feet."

Cara drew in an unsteady breath. "I was overcome with madness. Cerdic was there. I knew I could defeat him. Only, it wasn't what made me jump from my horse." She frowned. "I'm not entirely sure…"

"You are not sure, because you have not been sitting beside the one you love, trying to figure it out for days and days. You have been sleeping all that time. Only, I have the answer, now," Bedivere said. "You used to fight in anger. I used to fight without it. I thought I was wrong and that anger would compensate for this." He held out his right hand and flexed it, so the two stronger fingers straightened and left the other two curled. "I was wrong. You were wrong. It was love which drove me onto the battlefield and made me fight. It is love which drove you to leap upon Cerdic and defeat him."

Cara felt the jolt down to her toes. Before she could say anything, Bedivere spoke again. Suddenly, now, he was speaking of everything in his heart, every thought he had. She did not dare disrupt this moment.

"Not just love for me," he said, his voice low. "You fought for Britain and for your king. You fought, because you could not stand the idea of the Saxons taking this land away from those who are most precious to you. You fought for your mother and your sisters. And you fought for me."

Her heart hurt. Her throat was so tight with emotions, it stole her breath and her words. "Yes," she said, her voice is hoarse as his. "That is it exactly. How did you know?"

Bedivere tucked her hair behind her shoulder and touched her face, his fingers tracing the scars. "Because that is what drove me. I have never felt it before, and it is the most powerful thing I have ever experienced. I would have fought the entire Saxon army by myself, if I had to. It was *that* strong. I do need you, Cara. You are what gave me the strength to overcome this." He raised his hand once more, to show her the scars. "You gave me hope, when all was darkest."

Cara put her arm around his neck, as much to hold herself up, as to press herself against him. "If you insist upon saying such things, then you really must kiss me to finish them properly."

He kissed her. It was a gentle touch of his lips. Even so, she could feel the heat and promise in his body and his eyes. "I think I can do better than a simple kiss. Marry me, Cara."

She felt the jolt to her toes. "No, Bedivere, that is not what I meant. You cannot marry me. You are Arthur's war duke, one of his companions. I am..."

"You are Cara of Brynaich, a hero of the battle of Mount Badon, and I love you. Marry me to demonstrate to everyone that we, that Britain, has a future and you want me to be part of it."

Cara drew in a deep breath. "If you put it that way..."

Bedivere shook his head. "I will put it another way, then. Marry me, damn it, because I love you and I cannot think of the future without you in it."

"Yes," Cara breathed.

Then, at last, he kissed her properly.

Did you enjoy this book?

How to make a big difference!

Reviews are *powerful.*

Authors like me, without the financial muscle of a sleek New York publisher backing me, can't take advertisements out in the subways and billboards of the world.

On the other hand, New York publishers would *kill* to get what I have: A committed and loyal group of readers.

Honest reviews of my books help bring them to the attention of other readers. If you enjoyed this book I would be grateful if you could spend just a few minutes leaving a review (it can be as short as you like) on the book's page where you bought it.

Thank you so much!

Tracy

The next book in the Once and Future Hearts series.

The sixth book in the series is *The Abduction of Guenivere,* which will be released in April 2020.

In the meantime, if you enjoy ancient historical romances:

Diana by the Moon

A heart wrenching story of love, loss and triumph.

Diana, an independent Roman woman in a time when women are mere property, is forced to provide food and shelter for an entire northern British estate. She trusts no one.

Alaric, fierce and proud Celtic warrior, and trusted lieutenant to the upstart British leader, Arthur, must have Diana's estate to complete his mission. Failure would doom all of Britain.

Alaric and Diana reluctantly cooperate to ensure survival, but famine, Saxon raids, a harsh winter and the conniving of mutual enemies test their resolve.

A story of sacrifice, courage, loyalty and ultimately, a love that erases the boundaries of culture and upbringing, providing hope for a better future for themselves and those who follow in their footsteps.

—

Top 100 Best Seller
#1 Bestseller, Ancient World Historical Romance
#1 Bestseller, Historical Mystery, Thrillers and Suspense
Reviewer's Top Pick, *Romantic Times Magazine*
Night Owl Reviews Reviewers' Top Pick
All Romance eBooks Bestseller, Historical Romance
Frankfurt E-book Award nominee
Finalist, Emma Darcy Award
"Must Read" 2014 - Cocktails & Books

This novel **drew me in** so completely, so thoroughly, **time just simply faded**. *Diana by the Moon* is **a work of written art**. Tracy Cooper-Posey has penned **a beautiful story**; of one woman's courageous journey of self-discovery amidst turbulent times. *Love Romance Passion*

About the Author

Tracy Cooper-Posey is a #1 Best Selling Author. She writes romantic suspense, historical, paranormal and science fiction romance. She has published over 100 novels since 1999, been nominated for five CAPAs including Favourite Author, and won the Emma Darcy Award.

She turned to indie publishing in 2011. Her indie titles have been nominated four times for Book Of The Year. Tracy won the award in 2012, and a SFR Galaxy Award in 2016 for "Most Intriguing Philosophical/Social Science Questions in Galaxybuilding" She has been a national magazine editor and for a decade she taught romance writing at MacEwan University.

She is addicted to Irish Breakfast tea and chocolate, sometimes taken together. In her spare time she enjoys history, Sherlock Holmes, science fiction and ignoring her treadmill. An Australian Canadian, she lives in Edmonton, Canada with her husband, a former professional wrestler, where she moved in 1996 after meeting him on-line.

Other books by
Tracy Cooper-Posey

For reviews, excerpts, and more about each title, visit Tracy's site and click on the cover you are interested in: http:// tracycooperposey.com/books-by-thumbnail/

Scandalous Scions
(Historical Romance Series – Spin off)
Rose of Ebony
Soul of Sin
Valor of Love
Marriage of Lies
Scandalous Scions One (Boxed Set)
Mask of Nobility
Law of Attraction
Veil of Honor
Scandalous Scions Two (Boxed Set)
Season of Denial
Rules of Engagement
Degree of Solitude
Ashes of Pride
Risk of Ruin
Year of Folly
Queen of Hearts

Scandalous Families – The Victorians
(Historical Romance Series – Spin off)
His Parisian Mistress
Her Rebellious Prince

Once and Future Hearts
(Ancient Historical Romance—Arthurian)
Born of No Man
Dragon Kin
Pendragon Rises
War Duke of Britain
High King of Britain
Battle of Mount Badon
Abduction of Guenivere
Downfall of Cornwall
Vengeance of Arthur
Grace of Lancelot
The Grail and Glory
Camlann

Kiss Across Time Series
(Paranormal Time Travel)
Kiss Across Time
Kiss Across Swords
Time Kissed Moments
Kiss Across Chains
Kiss Across Time Box One (Boxed Set)
Kiss Across Deserts
Kiss Across Kingdoms
Time and Tyra Again
Kiss Across Seas
Kiss Across Time Box Two (Boxed Set)
Kiss Across Worlds
Time and Remembrance
Kiss Across Tomorrow
More Time Kissed Moments
Kiss Across Blades
Kiss Across Chaos
Kiss Across the Universe
Even More Time Kissed Moments*
Kiss Across Forever

Project Kobra
(Romantic Spy Thrillers)
Hunting The Kobra
Inside Man
Heart Strike

Blood Knot Series
(Urban Fantasy Paranormal Series)
Blood Knot
Southampton Swindle
Broken Promise
Vale
Amor Meus
Blood Stone
Blood Unleashed
Blood Drive
Blood Revealed
Blood Ascendant
Flesh + Blood (Boxed Set)

Vistaria Has Fallen
Vistaria Has Fallen
Prisoner of War
Hostage Crisis
Freedom Fighters
Casualties of War
V-Day

Romantic Thrillers Series
Fatal Wild Child
Dead Again
Dead Double
Terror Stash
Thrilling Affair (Boxed Set)

Beloved Bloody Time Series
(Paranormal Futuristic Time Travel)
Bannockburn Binding

Wait
Byzantine Heartbreak
Viennese Agreement
Romani Armada
Spartan Resistance
Celtic Crossing
Beloved Bloody Time Series Boxed Set

Scandalous Sirens
(Historical Romance Series)
Forbidden
Dangerous Beauty
Perilous Princess

Go-get-'em Women
(Short Romantic Suspense Series)
The Royal Talisman
Delly's Last Night
Vivian's Return
Ningaloo Nights

The Sherlock Holmes Series
(Romantic Suspense/Mystery)
Chronicles of the Lost Years
The Case of the Reluctant Agent
Sherlock Boxed In

The Kine Prophecies
(Epic Norse Fantasy Romance)
The Branded Rose Prophecy

The Stonebrood Saga
(Gargoyle Paranormal Series)
Carson's Night
Beauty's Beasts
Harvest of Holidays
Unbearable
Sabrina's Clan

Pay The Ferryman
Hearts of Stone (Boxed Set)

Destiny's Trinities
(Urban Fantasy Romance Series)
Beth's Acceptance
Mia's Return
Sera's Gift
The First Trinity
Cora's Secret
Zoe's Blockade
Octavia's War
The Second Trinity
Terra's Victory
Destiny's Trinities (Boxed Set)

Interspace Origins
(Science Fiction Romance Series)
Faring Soul
Varkan Rise
Cat and Company
Interspace Origins (Boxed Set)

Short Paranormals
Solstice Surrender
Eva's Last Dance
Three Taps, Then....
The Well of Rnomath

Jewells of Tomorrow
(Historical Romantic Suspense)
Diana By The Moon
Heart of Vengeance

The Endurance
(Science Fiction Romance Series)
5,001
Greyson's Doom

Yesterday's Legacy
Promissory Note
Quiver and Crave
Xenogenesis
Junkyard Heroes
Evangeliya
Skinwalker's Bane

Contemporary Romances
Lucifer's Lover
An Inconvenient Lover

Non-Fiction Titles

Reading Order
(Non-Fiction, Reference)
Reading Order Perpetual